I0632140

KANE
MAN OF WAR

KANE
MAN OF WAR

by

JANETTE ANDERSON

BearManor Media

2010

Kane: Man of War
© 2010 Janette Anderson
Janette Anderson Entertainment
WGA West 1374532

All rights reserved.

For information, address:

BearManor Media
P. O. Box 71426
Albany, GA 31708

bearmanormedia.com

Cover design by

Typesetting and layout by John Teehan

Published in the USA by BearManor Media

ISBN—1-59393-357-6

Dedicated
To my father, John Lockley.

Chapter 1

Reaching under the back of the coat, Kane Branson pulled his .38 from the belt of his tight black jeans. He checked it was loaded. Turning very slowly in the parched earth, he aimed, pulled the trigger and shot his screaming wife between the eyes. Not content with one bullet, he fired again and again till the gun was empty and it lay smoking in his hand. He watched her fall to the ground in slow motion, and roll in the decaying dirt. Dead…dead…blood rushing from every gaping wound on her young body.

A dream, it was a dream, the same one he had had for the last week, whenever he fell asleep. Would it ever stop? Yet again he woke hurriedly and tried not to shout out her name. No one must know what he dreamed in his darkest moments of despair.

Kane Branson leaned on the grey leather upholstery of the back seat of the black limo. His trademark snakeskin boots rested on the length of the seat. He was tired, very tired and it showed in the lines of his face. His steely blue eyes lacked the fire and luster they once had. His long blond hair was turning a dramatic shade of silver grey, and his moustache and short beard only complemented this.

Kane peered at the ever increasing amount of raindrops on the now closed tinted windows of the car. Moving his heavy coated arm very slightly, his bare hand wiped the rain induced mist from the window, and he stared out at the lights on the small but efficient runaway. It seemed like an eternity since the chauffeur driven car had pulled up and parked there, and Kane couldn't see anything but rain and blurry lights. He glanced down at his gold Rolex. Ten-fifteen p.m. He watched as the second hand beat time round the clock face. Turning the watch band slightly, the words on the back became clear to Kane.

'Forever yours: Kelly.' Did it mean the watch or her? Kane pondered the point a moment.

The partition between chauffeur and passenger slid down slightly.

"Sir...." No reply and he tried again, "Commander Branson...I think the flight is delayed because of the weather. It's getting worse. Control tower says there is a severe weather watch over most of Sydney. Would you like to..."

Kane interrupted. "We wait. Sam said he would be here and he will." Conversation ended as far as Kane was concerned, his deep voice offering no hesitation. Never-the-less, the flight was nearly an hour late and Kane was a little worried. Leaning back in the comfy seats, the warmth of the car made Branson's eyes close. His thick wool coat enveloped him, and hid his dark blue jeans. His mind succumbed to fitful phases of slumber yet again, and new dreams filled his over crowded mind.

A face loomed in his subconscious. Bright bubbly eyes, long golden hair that danced in the breeze and an impish nose wrinkled in fun when she laughed, taunting him. Kane woke with a start. "Kelly," he yelled so loudly that the glass partition slid down further.

"Commander...Kane..." Hunter leaned over the seats, as Kane shot forward, perspiration running down his face. "It's a dream, sir... Kane...It's okay, sir."

"No...," he screamed. "It is not okay! It's never going to be the same again, you stupid bastard. Fucking hell!" and he slammed his fist against the car's interior. "This is a nightmare, and I wish I was dead." Kane paused...he hadn't meant to say that out loud.

"But you aren't, sir. You are very much alive, and you have a mission to do. Your son will be here soon. You said so yourself. I'll radio base and find out the status of his flight."

Kane's face was unreadable. From the violent outburst of sheer anguish, he had reverted immediately back to the stone cold killer he had become. One difference...he had a license to kill.

Hunter turned away from his boss. At forty, Hunter was also an Australian undercover cop like Kane, only Kane Branson was the commander, and Hunter would never make the level of his boss. None-the-less, Hunter was loyal to the core and his command of languages extensive. His firearm expertise was beyond question, as were his martial art skills. And Hunter was not there by any accident. He was there to watch out for his boss. He turned his dark curly hair, pony-tailed back in place, to look at Kane. Hunter's dark eyes narrowed, as he peered through the driving mirror, and his brow furrowed as he viewed the man in the back seat.

Here sat Commander Kane Branson, almost sixty years old, a man of war, a man who had probably seen too much action in his years with the Australian Federal Police. A man who should be home enjoying the company of his young wife Kelly…and his five children. But, he wasn't. He was seated in a limo, parked on a runway on a private air strip waiting for his oldest son to join him there, and to begin a mission of a lifetime…and one possibly to end it.

"Son-of-a-bitch…that was a bumpy landing! Worse than the ones on Lantau Island. Be glad to get off this puddle jumper. Not like the big jets, no sir," exclaimed Sam Branson. Olive skinned as a Chinaman could be, tall, slim with shoulder length blond hair that hung over his thick black sweater, Sam could see the landing lights clearly through the pouring rain. As he looked harder, he could make out another set of lights, ones that flashed on and off in a distinctive fashion, and ones that generally heralded a limo.

"Kane," breathed Sam. He had never called Kane 'dad' or 'father', not in the five years he had known him. Sam reflected that the last few years had been strange. Finding out at thirty-five you had an AFP agent for a father and a step-mother of twenty-five, and three stepbrothers and sisters, came as quite a shock. Discovering that you had a whole prolific history in the drug world was another. Sam himself wasn't exactly the epitome of an angel: bartering drugs in Hong Kong, working with his step-uncle, the infamous Vau Cheng in Lantau, and then watching his mother, Lilia Cheng, Kane's lover, die.

Sam returned from his memories with an abrupt start as the pilot yelled to him.

"Mr. Branson."

Even after five years the name sounded alien to him. Sam had been called Cheng for so much of his life before he knew he was legally a Branson.

"Your father's limo is waiting for you at the end of the strip," shouted the pilot, as the engines toned down from a roar to a dull humming noise.

"I see it. Travels in style, doesn't he?" stated Sam, as he obtained a better view of the car.

"Always, sir. Your father is, after all, Commander of the AFP, as well as a respected man and one the force would follow to hell and back."

"That's what worries me the most…they would! And maybe they already have!"

"You can disembark, sir. Be careful, the steps maybe slippery with the rain."

"Yeah, sure. I will be fine." Although Chinese, Sam's accent was more English than Asian. His wealthy mother and stepfather had given him the best education money could buy, and it showed.

Sam collected his winter coat and his carryon bag. He hadn't brought much with him as he hadn't had much time to pack. And if he had done, he didn't know where they were going from here. Tossing the coat on, he pulled the collar up against the cold rain. Disembarking the plane flight, he carefully came down the steps to the safety of the tarmac. The headlamps of the car dipped again and guided Sam Branson to meet his father for the first time in three years. The last time they met was in the courtroom, when Sam's uncle had stood trial for atrocities to the Country of Australia. Since then the two had stayed in touch by phone, and Sam was overjoyed when he was appointed godfather to his stepbrother, Kip, Kane's latest son with Kelly, and possibly his last child. This was done by proxy as both Kane and Sam were in different parts of the globe at the time.

As Sam neared the limo's side, Hunter stepped out into the night rain, and gripped the door handle. He nodded to Sam as he climbed inside the waiting car, brushing rain from his coat as he went. Sam was not prepared for Kane's statue-like appearance. Sam sat down with purpose in the back seat next to Kane, and looked into his father's face, the commander, the killer. Kane, the man of war.

"Sir." It was the only word Sam could think of.

"Sam…good to see you, son. I am glad you could come." Kane spoke only with his mouth and not with his eyes, nor his heart. And Kane extended his hand to his son.

Sam reciprocated the gesture and both men's grips were tight. Kane left his hand there far longer than was necessary as if he needed the physical contact with his son. Sam glanced at Kane's hand. It was rock solid steel with a grip of death.

"How are you?" 'God, that sounded pathetic,' thought Sam.

"Doing the best I can."

"And Kelly?" Sam had to ask and now was as good a time as any.

The grip tightened.

"Kelly is…lost to me. She has to be as it's the only way I can function." There was no life in his eyes as he spoke, no fire…no anything.

"You don't know that, Kane. The report said missing…" argued Sam.

"I know what the fucking report said. I wrote half of it!" Kane yelled at Sam. "God damn it. She's been missing for nearly two weeks. Chances of getting her back are slim to none…you know that…" he was interrupted.

"That's in your report, sir. I also read that she left with…." Sam didn't want to say it. Kelly had been seen leaving the base with another man.

"Go on, say it! She didn't leave with me. I was off globe-trotting yet again, because I couldn't delegate anything as usual. Fucking hell, Sam! When will I learn to delegate?" Kane's voice hit a crescendo as he spoke. "She was with another man!" He had said it at long last… another man, and his Kelly!

When Kane received the news that Kelly had not returned home that night, he caught the next flight out of Japan International airport. Arriving in Sydney, Kane was greeted by his son-in-law, Dan Lord, and a party of high-ranking AFP agents. He was whisked through immigration and passport control, and ushered into to a waiting unmarked car in a no-parking zone. Once in the limo, Dan recounted what they thought had happened. The preliminary report read:

"Agent Kelly Branson, aged thirty years, was seen leaving the Sydney headquarters on Friday, October 22nd, at 9p.m., with a man dressed in black. He was mid forties; dark- skinned and appeared to have an accent. Mrs. Branson, wife of Commander Kane Branson, was dressed in black jeans, beige suede boots, with a dark grey jacket. A witness saw the two arguing, but could not hear exactly what they were saying…"

Kane had asked them to stop reading at this point. He couldn't digest the situation. This could not be happening. Not his Kelly. She wouldn't just run off with someone else, would she? And they were arguing? There had been a search right from the first minute. Not a clue had been found as to where she was. Nothing, and Kane had had to explain to his kids what was happening. Would she have left of her own free will? A question of late that Kane could not answer for sure. Kelly had been acting a little strange for a couple of weeks before he left for Japan. He figured that she didn't want him to go. On that account, he was right. She told him that she needed some time for herself, more out of defiance, trying to make him jealous, staying out with the girls. She thought he would miss her. They had argued a couple of times about the subject. But Kane reflected that he was pushing sixty and she was thirty, with three children of their own and maybe it was simply that; a way of teaching him a lesson. Kelly had refused to talk about things of late. So, Kane had gone on the last trip on his own, purposely, to teach her that she couldn't always be on his missions, and now he was living to regret it.

"So you want to go straight to the house? Was a long trip, right?" Kane's questions were more like statements.

"Sure, that's fine." Sam was really trying to find out why he was there. Kane hadn't said anything yet that he couldn't read in the report. He still had no clue where they were going and how they were going to find Kelly. He did know, however, that he was family, and maybe that's why Kane needed him.

The engine purred as Hunter started the limo, driving away from the private airport clearing security as they went, and headed into the rains of the Sydney night.

The occupants of the car were silent, each with their own thoughts. Hunter thought it was strange that father and son, who had not seen each other for so long, had nothing to say to each other. Then again, no words were needed. The car sped through the streets of Sydney to the far side of the city. Pulling into a driveway, they noticed that the rain had finally decided to slow down a little. As they stopped at the door, a little after midnight, Hunter jumped out of the car and let Kane and his son out of the limo. As Sam climbed out, he glanced up at the palatial building that Kane called home. Last time in Australia there had been no time to visit Kane's house. Now, he was about to make up for it. This place was a palace. How Kelly could leave all this, and better still, why would she leave Kane? Last time Sam had seen Kelly she was devoted entirely to Kane, and somehow he didn't think that had changed. Gut instinct told him so.

The large oak front door opened, interrupting Sam's thoughts. Sam recognized Dan Lord from Lantau Island, and behind him stood a young woman about thirty-two years of age with long blond hair, bearing a striking resemblance to Kane. This must be Sage, Kane's daughter by his first wife, and his stepsister.

Kane stepped inside the hallway first, followed by Sam. Hunter shut the car doors and closed in behind Kane. Sam thought this unusual. It was as though Kane had a bodyguard.

"Sam, you remember Dan?" He paused, as the two men shook hands. "And this is Sage, my eldest daughter, and also Dan's wife. She and Kelly..." And he stopped mid sentence; Kelly was still his chink.

"Kelly and I are great pals. She is my best mate," chimed in Sage. And she leaned forward and threw her arms round Sam.

Immediately Sam liked Sage, and an instant bond was forged between the siblings of Kane.

"Well now, the greetings are over. Let's move into the lounge and get a drink." Kane had quit drinking for Kelly and now he had started again for the same reason.

Dumping their coats on a nearby chair, Kane offered Sam a seat next to him on the couch. This particular couch had seen a lot service and several children growing up. It was in stark contrast to the rest of the expensive furniture in the room.

Kane leaned back on the sofa. Immediately he asked for a whiskey and Hunter produced the shot in a glass. Kane emptied the glass in one go and handed it back for a refill. Hunter filled it again, handed it back to Kane, and then stood at the back of the couch and Kane.

Sam saw Sage glance at Dan disapprovingly. Her father was drinking again and that wasn't good, but worst of all Hunter was condoning it. When Kane was drunk, he was a handful...even for the AFP.

"Dad, you think that's a good idea..." Sage didn't get to finish the sentence.

Kane stood up. "Did I ask for your opinion?" Kane's steely eyes were electric. Two or three drinks and their comments were not going to faze him. "I will drink what ever I damn well please. Understand?"

"Dad, I was only pointing out that..." she pleaded.

"I don't give a fuck what you were pointing out! You are not my keeper..." And then he turned. "Nor are you, Hunter McLeod. I know you are here to monitor my drinking and to protect me...from what, Hunter? From myself? Is that the idea? Or from the people who took Kelly? I am right, aren't I? Someone took her, didn't they? She didn't just walk out on me, did she?" Kane looked around at the faces. Hunter, then Dan, his son-in- law, and ex- partner; Sage, his eldest daughter, and Sam, his son by Lilia, his first love in life. No-one could give him an answer. Kelly had been gone for almost two weeks and he couldn't deal with it. He missed her so...and he was falling apart in front of them. He hadn't only had three drinks. He had downed half a bottle of Scotch before they left the house that night. He had lied to them and himself. In the last few days, he had sought serious comfort in several bottles of whiskey.

Kane turned with such force and hurled the empty tumbler into the fireplace, sending a thousand splinters of glass into the crackling fire. He spun around to face his audience who were seated in various parts of the room. No-one moved. No-one dared to. Kane was in no mood to be contested. Big and powerful, almost sixty or not, he stood with his hands on his hips, his hair falling round his shoulders, his thick wool sweater stretched tightly round his body, and his gun clearly seen in the back of his jeans. His mood was dark and ugly and it was obvious to everyone that Kane had downed far more than three glasses of whiskey. But drunk or sober, Kane was not a man to mess with.

The glass hit the fireplace with such force that the mantel shook, rattling the pictures of Kane, Kelly and the kids. Seemed like an omen. The shelf was covered with pictures from all aspects of Kane's life, but primarily from the Kelly era. They were in stark reminder that she was not around. Kane walked to the mantel and lifted the offending picture from the ledge. He held it near his face and looked at the happiness it radiated.

As he replaced the photo, the lounge door opened wide. A small cherub of a child in a blue romper suit, sporting curly blond hair, burst into the room accompanied by a boy of much the same description, just an older model in regular blue pajamas. The younger boy that looked like a cherub broke free from the not-so-strong grip his brother Kene had on him. Kip Branson, just barely two years old, broke away and bounced across the room till he reached his father. His look was pleading and wanting. Two big blue eyes looked up and up till they reached Kane's gaze. He stretched out his arms, as the little sapling tried to reach the mighty oak.

From Kane's height, Kip looked like a little stick insect with a curly mop on top of his head.

"Daddy...daddy. We heard you shouting, Daddy," his bottom lip quivered and he pleaded with his eyes, feeling his daddy needed him.

Kane leaned down and scooped his youngest son up with one hand. Kip threw his arms around his father, buried his head in Kane's hair and began to cry. Small tears at first, becoming giant racking sobs as the child buried himself even further into his father's neck and hair.

Kane held his child in his massive hands and whispered to him. "Daddy's fine, son. I wasn't yelling at anyone...Kip, it's ok...daddy is fine." 'Daddy may never be fine again,' he thought.

Kip pulled back slightly so he could see Kane's face.

"No, daddy…we heard you. Me and Kene. We went to get mommy, but she wasn't there…" and the sobs escalated, yet again.

Sam watched from the side line as his baby step-brother broke his father's heart. He looked at the other little boy. They were clones of Kane, all with blond hair and good looks, all from the Branson stock.

At that point of time, Nanny Silvero put her head round the door-frame.

"Sir, I am so sorry. I was with Miss Star. I didn't realize the boys were gone." Nanny Silvero, donning a long nightgown and seemingly huge pink fluffy slippers, was an obvious threat to mankind, let alone young children. Sam decided she probably had a .38 hidden under her nightgown. A long, braided plait hung down the back of her and he thought she was the most unfeminine woman he had ever seen, but he had no doubt that she was damn good at her job.

"It's okay. My sons, and daughters," as he glanced at Sage, "are always free to come to me," and he cuddled Kip to him.

Kene clung round his father's legs and eyed Sam suspiciously. Kane felt it.

"Son," Kane said gently, as he looked down at Kene. "That is your stepbrother, Sam…and Kip, he is also your godfather. He saved your daddy's life once."

Kip stopped crying completely and turned in Kane's arms to look at this new person in his life. He didn't look like his brother, or his sisters. He viewed this man and just shrugged his shoulders in typical boy fashion.

All Kane's children were there except Star, and as if on cue, the last Branson child appeared through the door. A vision of a tiny Kelly came into view. Long curly hair with blond highlights cascaded down her back, with features that complemented both Kane and Kelly. Eight going on eighteen, Star was her father's favorite child. He looked across the room at her, an angel in a long white winter nightgown. Star was the most appropriate name for this child.

For a split second in time, Kane didn't see his child. Standing there, the same as that day in the hotel on Lantau Island was Kelly. He closed his eyes, hard, and then opened them. Still, he saw Kelly.

"Kane...sir...father." Sam had finally said it in front of his siblings. "Kane...are you okay?"

Kane blinked again and the image was gone. "I'm fine...I saw...," and he put his youngest son down on the couch and leaned on the arm rest.

"What did you see, dad," asked Dan, who had stepped forward to help with the children.

"You saw Kelly, didn't you, Kane?" Sam asked, knowing full well what the answer would be before Kane said it.

Kane raised his eyes to look at Sam full in the face. "Yes," he whispered. "I saw Kelly. She..."

And at that precise moment the phone rang. Every pair of eyes in the room looked at Kane. As he picked up the receiver from the coffee table phone, everyone also knew exactly who was on the other end of the line.

Chapter 2

Kane pushed his hair out of the way and put the receiver to his ear. "Kane Branson."

There was a hesitant pause on the end of the line. "Kane?"

"Yes," he was cautious and replied with care. "This is Kane." He knew it was her and his heart missed a beat.

"I want to come home, Kane." It was all Kelly said, as her voice got lower with every word.

"Really? Is anyone stopping you from doing that?" His reply was curt and to the point.

"You are," and her voice shook. "You won't want me back."

"Why won't I, Kelly? What did you do?"

"I..." and the line clicked into dead air.

While Kelly was speaking, Kane listened for other noises. He could hear several men's voices talking. His trained ear picked up distinct sounds of gunfire. Kelly was definitely not alone. It remained to be seen if that was good or bad. Kane replaced the receiver carefully with her voice still ringing in his ears. He raised his head high and looked at his family. There was total silence.

Kip broke that silence. "Mommy?" his little voice stated, and he slid off the couch.

"Mommy," replied Kane. "She's safe."

Safe was a strange term to use, but he had used it and he looked down at his son. His mind was in confusion as he answered his child.

"Kane, what did she say? Kane…what did Kelly say? She must have said something." Sam was right in front of Kane, almost peering into his face and questioning his father.

"I would rather not say," he replied softly.

"You would rather not say? What kind of bullshit is that, Kane? Your wife goes missing for two weeks, and you hear from her, and nothing? By your tone you sounded annoyed with her, and now you'd rather not say? Cut the crap, Kane. This is me, Sam, someone you ploughed down a fort with on Lantau Island. What did she say, Kane?" and he stood blocking him.

Kane stared at his son. "Move."

"What?"

"Move, Sam. Now!"

"I will when you answer me and…" Sam didn't get to finish.

"I said move. NOW! Out of my fucking space!"

Kane was bigger than Sam on all counts, but Sam didn't back down. If he did, he wasn't a Branson.

Kane's eyes sported blood. He didn't need this, especially not from Sam. It was at this point that Kane really saw red and brought his fist up high catching Sam fully on the jaw. Sam reeled backwards falling into Dan as he went. Dan grabbed him as he fell, helping him back to his feet. Hunter immediately moved to Kane's back and put his strong hands onto Kane's shoulders, stopping him from doing any more damage. Sam pulled away from Dan, and moved forward, as if to hit his father, but the look on Kane's face stopped him dead.

Both the younger boys started to cry, more out of fear than anything else. Star clutched Nanny Silvero's legs, and Sage's hand flew to her mouth to stem the scream that tried to escape. Her father had hit her stepbrother right in front of the whole family and that was wrong.

The two men faced each other like prize-fighters in a ring.

"Commander…Kane…let it go. Now is not the time. Your son is anxious, as you are."

Hunter still had a grip on his boss and was not going to let go.

Kane pulled in the grip, but the grip didn't budge.

Hunter whispered in Kane's ear. "He's on our side, Kane. Save it for the enemy," and he slackened his hold on Kane's arms just a little.

Kane nodded very slightly and glanced around the room. He had exploded far too quickly. Would they all notice he was not himself? Hopefully, they would attribute it to him missing Kelly.

Hunter let him go, and then, very slowly, Kane became much more controlled. "I'll be in my rooms," and as Kane strode away, with giant footsteps, he grabbed the half-full bottle of scotch, leaving his family standing in his dust.

"What the f…"

"Dan!" commented his wife rather sharply. "There are children present."

"Kane didn't think of them…" and he stopped. "Sorry…but what is going on here?" He turned in Sam's direction. "Did something happen in the car that we don't know about?"

"Actually, he was too quiet." Sam turned towards Hunter rubbing his now bruised jaw. "Hunter, is there anything you want to tell us?"

Hunter narrowed his eyes and looked from one to another. Sam would know the truth quicker than he thought, and possibly Dan, too. Sage and the children must never know that possibly Kane may not come back from this mission…and that mission was to find Kelly, and the hostage, and bring her out alive…whatever the sacrifice.

"I'll go after him. I…" Hunter didn't get to finish.

"You'll what, Hunter?" Sam exclaimed, pulling him by the arm. "Why you? Suddenly it's all you. Am I missing something here?" Sam was angry and he jerked Hunter by the arm. He wasn't happy at the run around he was getting.

Slowly and carefully Hunter removed Sam's hand from his own arm. "Sam, I need to talk to you in private…outside…"

"Why not here, where everyone can hear? Or is there some dark secret you want to share…"

"Sam, please a word…now," and Hunter all but herded Sam out of the room and closed the door firmly behind them, leaving everyone else in the room.

Sensing the tension running way too high, Nanny Silvero gathered up the off-springs and ushered her crying brood out of the room and up the stairs. Dan stared at Sage.

"I should go after him, I…"

"Let him go, Dan. My father is a grown man, and he has Hunter and Sam. I think we will find out very shortly, or you will, what is really happening."

Outside the large front door the cold stark air confronted Hunter first, closely followed by Sam.

"Now ....what the fuck is going on here?"

Where had Hunter heard that line before?

The night air swirled around them. From the rain had sprung a dense mist that was creeping around the Branson house and shrouding them like a blanket.

"Your father has been marked as a dead man."

"Explain, now!" There was a shocked look on Sam's face.

"Before he joined the AFP, Kane was in Nam, as you know. He was a very good soldier, very good. One of the best. Not afraid to take orders and when the time came not afraid to give them, nor was he afraid to kill, either. He was a born leader and moved quickly in the ranks, a natural killer you might say. A man of war. In the same platoon was a man named Ryan Holden. A big man, dark haired, worked out a lot. Both men were crack shots, martial arts experts, and both became top men in their own fields. Both men married twice, both had kids, Kane being a little more prolific than Ryan. That's where the similarity ended. Kane became commander of the AFP. Ryan is on the world's most wanted list for terrorism. One is the man of war, as I say, but one is the master of death."

"So there are comparisons. What about it? How does that affect Kane, and better still Kelly? Where does she fit in?"

"Recently, the military...that bit you don't need to know right now...contacted your father. Seems that out of the platoon, both Kane and Ryan are the only two fighting men left...and also, ones with rank. It became known to the right sources that Ryan was working with the Iraqi government. It also became known that the wife of an American diplomat had been kidnapped. The diplomat is a very powerful person and is a key witness in a drug related bust by the American government in Iraq." Hunter paused to let that sink in a little. The next part would be worse for Sam to handle. He started again. "The diplomat's wife is someone Kane knows...someone from his past making Kane the common denominator between the woman and Ryan Holden. But mostly, they contacted Kane because he knows Ryan's tactical moves and the way he thinks. And, also, because we suspect that Kelly is involved."

Hunter waited for the outburst which didn't come. Sam's face was blank, as he shivered in the dampness. He wasn't sure if it was from the cold or shock. The explanations did make sense, though, in fact the whole scenario made sense, but he did have questions.

"How is Kelly involved? Does she know the diplomat and the wife? And Kane...is that why he is acting almost violently. What does he have to do? And where does he have to go? And where is *there* anyway? Was he right when he said someone took her? And..."

"Whoa, slow down there, mate," and Hunter raised his hand to stop Sam asking more. "Too much...Kane wanted you with him. He knows from the past how good you are. You got his back, you helped him and you are his son. And, yes, he has to find Kelly. She is like the breadcrumbs Gretel leaves for Hansel, so to speak. That's what we think right now, anyway."

"We? Who are you, Hunter? And was that the first call from Kelly to him tonight?"

"Just who I say I am. Except I am working with the American government on this and so will Kane. What is a little disconcerting is that Kelly called him tonight right after you arrived. Someone else is monitoring his movements very carefully. The only thing we don't know right now is if Kelly went on her own free will or she was black-mailed into it. Even Kane doesn't know...and his anger is directed at himself because he isn't in control of the situation. A first for Kane, I would think."

Hunter fell silent and leaned back on the door frame. It was damp, but he didn't even notice. He watched Sam.

Sam reached into the back of his jeans and pulled out a pack of cigarettes. He slid one out and put it between his lips. He retrieved the lighter from his other pocket and lit up. He inhaled deeply and blew smoke out through his nose. Like father like son!

"This is too much to take in. What does my father think?"

"Why don't we go ask him?"
"Now?"
"Right now!"

In Kane and Kelly's rooms, Kane sat down on the king-sized quilted cream bedspread. He pulled his boots off, dropping them one by one on the floor, and put his gun on the solid oak nightstand, which is where it sat most nights. Kane stared at it, and then picked it up again. He caressed the gun barrel, and, yet again, images of the nightmare flashed before him. The only person he wanted to shoot was Ryan Holden. He set the gun in the back of his jeans, and then pulled the sweater up and over his head.

Kelly's perfume lingered in the air and her clothes and the empty bed were a constant reminder to Kane how much he missed her. He glanced around the room. Several huge teddy bears draped themselves over the white whicker chair that Kelly had used to nurse their children. The chair positioned itself in the corner where the summer sun frequently streaked itself across it through the paned glass windows behind it. Their oak dressers were over crowded with clothes from various trips round the world.

Kane could see his reflection in the large mirrors on the dresser. He decided he looked older with the beard. Maybe the moustache should go along with the beard. Maybe not. Kelly wouldn't like... He lay back on the pillows and looked down at his watch. Almost 1 a.m. His body was tired and he ached for sleep that would not come now, nor had done for days, except for fitful spasms of mind-blowing dreams. His head was full of thoughts and he knew sleep was not going to be his friend again tonight. As he contemplated climbing off the bed, getting the bottle from the table where he had set it when entering the room, someone banged hard on the suite door. He let them knock again. This time it was much louder and a voice came with it.

"Commander Branson? It's Hunter, and Sam is with me. He would like to talk to you."

Kane rose slowly from the bed and moved to the door. Passing the bottle of scotch, he went barefoot across the room, turned the key in the lock of his suite and opened the door. He stepped back a pace, widened the door and walked away.

Hunter and Sam entered through the opening. Not even Hunter had been this far before…the inner sanctum of the Branson dynasty. He glanced around. The room was huge by any standard, possibly once had been two. The far side housed the master bed and all its finery, where as this side had countless bookshelves, a writing desk, two huge couches in subtle dark cream colors and oak tables dotted round the room. Only the bed was half secluded, with drapes to give it more privacy. The biggest TV screen Hunter had ever seen adorned the wall opposite one of the couches. He could also see the bottle of very obvious scotch sitting on the middle table.

Kane followed Hunter's eyes as they rested on the bottle.

"You want one?" asked Kane, as he picked it up.

"I'm fine," replied a slightly embarrassed Hunter, because he had been caught staring.

"Mind if I have one?" Kane asked curtly. He walked to the table and picked up the bottle. Pouring himself a drink, he downed it in one go and slammed the empty glass down on the table top. He dared them to say anything.

For a man of his age, it was obvious he worked out. His chest was ripped, his arms strong and firm, and the hair on his chest light, and just starting to turn a slight shade of grey.

Sam watched his father carefully. He still had the mannerisms of a man in his forties and also the looks. It was hard to believe Kane was his father looking more like his older brother.

Kane sat down on the cream leather, not offering the two men a seat. He crossed his legs and his bare foot dangled in front of the couch. "Something on your minds?"

"Hunter and I have been talking…"

"Really? Can't imagine what about." Kane looked up at his son, and motioned them to sit down. Kane realized he was he was alienating the very people he needed on his side. "Sam…I am sorry. The pressure is way too much. I assume Hunter filled you in?"

He looked away from Sam to Hunter. "Did you tell him all of it?"

"No."

"Which bits did you leave out?" and Kane waited with abated breath.

"Two things. The diplomat's wife…and you!"

"Ah…well…then I guess you know most of it. So I should just tell you the rest." He sat back on the couch, but not before he poured himself yet another glass of whiskey. He leaned back against the soft leather, and as he did so, Sam could see needle marks in his arm.

Kane saw him look, and glanced down. Bad move not wearing his sweater, but as long as he had seen them, he may as well know. But first he needed to explain the other situation.

"The American diplomat is a very powerful man. His wife was once a U.S. Marshal. I worked with her a very long time ago. In fact the same time as I met Kelly, I met her." He hesitated, remembering what might have been. But it wasn't the time or the place. "To cut a long story short, she helped me out…a lot. And I had to betray her and actually, well…I killed her." He paused again.

"But if you killed her…*you killed her*?!"

Kane held his hand up to stop his son. "It was all part of a plan, which almost backfired. When I rescued Kelly from her supposed father's compound, the Marshal helped me get a wounded Kelly out of the place. Then as a favor to her boyfriend and American drug dealer, Miles Stratton, I pushed her over a cliff. The point is I owe her big time. I owe her Kelly's life. Her name is Reese Wade and she married the diplomat a couple of years after she came out of hiding. Now, she is being held captive to stop her husband testifying against these charming gentlemen in Iraq. Apparently, he was part of the group that busted the fuckers. Unfortunately, Reese was out there with him…so, she needs to be rescued." Kane changed position slightly, and tried to slide his hand over his arm. Maybe this wasn't a good time for the rest of the story. But he had a feeling that Sam should be in on this part more than the rest. After all, if he was going to die, Sam should know. He moved his hand away.

"Pin holes. I can see you noticed. Didn't know I did drugs did you?"

"You don't…" replied Sam.

"You sure, Sam?" Kane laughed sardonically. "Maybe I do, and maybe I don't. Guess you will find out for yourself. Anyway, you need to sleep. Been a long day for you…for all of us."

Kane saw Hunter looking at the bottle. "Don't worry. Not going to drink myself into a drunken stupor. Not tonight, anyway. Tomorrow we will work out what we are going to do about the situation. Hunter will show you to your room."

Kane stood up and moved to the door crossing thick plush carpeting. He stopped. "If you need anything to eat, Hunter can also show you where the kitchen is." He opened the door and stretched out his hand to Sam. "Thank you for coming, son. I need you…" and he stopped, and turned away, walking back into the room.

"Sam, let me show you where your room is," and Hunter escorted his new charge from the suite.

Sam was confused as he let himself be led down the hall to the room at the end of the lobby. His father needed him; he knew that, but why? That's something he would figure out tomorrow. Now, he needed sleep. It had been a 36 hour day.

"Anything you need, dial 2 on the phone and I will be here. One is straight to your father's room. I wouldn't call it tonight. Goodnight, Sam. My pleasure to meet Kane's son," and after opening the door, Hunter turned and walked away and back down the hall to his boss.

He knocked gently on Kane's door. It wasn't locked and the door opened as he knew it would. Kane sat on the couch with the needle in his hand. He injected himself in the arm, tossed the discarded needle on the table, and leaned back on the couch. Once again the pain was too much.

Chapter 3

Day came way too early for Sam. He wanted to sleep some more, but he was far more intrigued as to what was happening in this house. Certainly not normal things. He showered quickly; decided on wearing jeans and a cream sweater, and found that by now he was extremely hungry, having not eaten before bed. He closed his bedroom door, leaving behind the lavish guest room with expensive tastes. The room was immaculate, adorned with shades of light and dark grey. You didn't get this kind of luxury on a commander's salary. Sam had not been enlightened to the fact that Kane had inherited a lot of money from his ancestry. Sam could not help notice the photos on the walls. Pictures of the kids, pictures of Kane and the kids, but most noticeable were pictures of Kane and Kelly in far off lands. Asia, England, and Kane in a racing car, Kane flying choppers, Kane on his Harley. His picture-gazing was interrupted as Kane's door opened. Hunter stepped out first, followed by Kane. Was this the same man from last night?

Gone were the beard and the longer moustache. He now sported a very short moustache that could hardly be seen and his hair was pulled, as tight as possible, back on his head and tied with a band. He wore shades, jet black jeans and sweater and looked like he was going underground. Sam stared at him. Was this his father, or a commando?

"Morning, Sam. Sleep well?" Kane boomed.

"Fine, thank you. And you?"

"Like a baby," he lied, and Kane glanced at Hunter. "Let's go!" His tone changed, impatient to get down the stairs.

As they descended the staircase, very low laughter was coming from the dining room. Two boy's voices could be heard as they jostled for positions at the table. Two more children appeared to be there as well, and Sam wondered just how many more kids the household contained. The other two seemed to belong to the Lords, making them Branson's by heritage. The room was positively aglow with kids, and in the corner sat Star, as if waiting for her father. When she saw him walk through the door she bounced off the chair and ran to him. His new appearance didn't seem to phase her one bit. He leaned down and picked her up, hugging her to him as if she was his solace. Dan and Sage were already seated at the immensely large table that seemed to contain every kind of breakfast food imaginable.

Kane set his youngest daughter down and took his rightful place at the head of the table. An empty seat at the far end was the obvious vacant one which Kelly always occupied. Sam sat next to his new sister and she smiled at her older brother. Sage handed him freshly baked croissants and the smell of them made him realize just how hungry he was. He reached for the jam and took fruit at the same time. As he devoured them with relish, he noticed Hunter whisper in Kane's ear and Kane nodded slightly. Hunter immediately left the room, and Sam realized Hunter hadn't even sat down. Sam also noticed that Kane hardly ate, just played around with a glass of orange juice and pushed scrambled eggs round the plate from one side to the other.

"So, dad...you going to tell us what is going down here or do we have to guess?" Dan's tone started well. "We, Sage and I, are very concerned for Kelly and obviously for you. So..."

"So what? What do you want to know? When I know what is going to happen, you will." And Kane stared at his son-in-law.

"Dad, why is Hunter here? I know he is here for a reason, not just for social visits..." Sage didn't get to finish.

The dining room door opened and Hunter reappeared. He, too, was dressed in all black.

"Commander, the gentlemen are here from the Embassy." He wasn't so quiet this time.

"Right, let's go do it. Sam, would you and Dan join us, please. Sage, I think you should come, too, at least for a few minutes. There is something I want you to know."

Kane rose up from the table and looked from child to child. The Lord's kids took more after Dan, both children being dark haired and freckled. Making sure his gun was firmly in the back of his jeans, Kane turned away from the inquiring faces of the children and he left through the open door. Sam followed behind him, having not yet finished his breakfast, but deciding he would come back for more later. A wish he never got to fulfill.

"Commander Branson has quite a taste for the heroics I hear, and judging by the weapons he has on display in here, I think I would concur that feeling is correct." General Tucker was obviously impressed with Kane's collection of guns. He bent down and looked at the latest of Kane's weapons, a very polished ivory handled Colt, obviously from the American west era. The General continued to peruse the showcase of magnificent guns held captive there, and, moving towards the bookcases, to view history books on weapons, when the study door opened.

Hunter entered first, and then he stood back to let Kane through the door.

General Tucker was as impressed with the actual man as he was with the weapons he carried. He had heard of the Commander by reputation and by the looks of this man he was all he had heard and more.

Kane stretched out his hand to Tucker. "Pleased to meet you, General. I have heard a lot about you." First lie. He had only heard what Hunter had told him that morning, that he was a four-star general and on an errand from the United States Army and the American Embassy. He was here to make sure that Kane helped them out, and he wasn't to leave Sydney until he had completed his mission.

"Same here, Commander. Read your dossier, but it didn't include any of this er...extravagance? You must have guns from most eras of history. Very impressive, Commander. In fact the whole house is impressive," and the portly Tucker reciprocated the gesture of the handshake. "Over a hundred missions to your credit. You have traveled the world twice over, met with many heads of state, fought in Nam, worked with other governments over the decades, and made commander in record time. You were also on the 'Hunt down Drugs project', worked with Sam Branson on it, and the Chinese Government. I assume this is your son here," and he glanced at Sam, "and now we need you to work with us." The last statement was said with finality. He let go of Kane's hand.

Neither Sage nor Sam had heard some of this record and they listened with interest. Both were more than impressed with their father's reputation.

Kane had noted the word 'with' and not for. He respected that from the general.

"The name is Kane, general, and you have done your homework. And most of it is accurate which is unusual in military dossiers. The impressive lifestyle, in case you are wondering, was mainly left to me by my grandfather. Even a commander's pay isn't that good. He died a very wealthy man, which was mainly left to me. And, yes," and Kane turned to Sam, "this is my son, Sam, and this is my daughter, Sage, and her husband, Dan, my former partner in the AFP. You are obviously aware that they are by different women, as are my other three children." He paused. "And that brings you to the reason you are here. I am sure that my wife, Kelly, is part of that reason, aside from wanting me to work with you. Let's sit down so we can discuss the situation."

Kane moved to the leather couch and sat down. The general sat opposite Kane on a hard backed leather chair and his very prim and proper adjutant handed him the briefcase he had been holding. The adjutant stepped back out of the limelight and waited for orders, positioning his stiff and starchy self behind the leather chair. Hunter counter-positioned himself behind the couch, and Kane. This did not go unnoticed by Sam. Kane motioned Sam to sit down by him on the couch, while Sage and Dan stood. Kane never offered his daughter a seat, which indicated that she wouldn't be there too long.

Tucker opened the folder. "As I am sure Hunter has told you by now, the mission is to rescue a woman from the outskirts of Baghdad. She is the American diplomat's wife. You would know her by her former name of Reese Wade."

Sage could not stem the gasp that escaped rather loudly from her mouth. They all, except Kane, turned to look at her. "Oh, my god…I thought she was dead…we all did," she glanced at her husband. "Didn't we, Dan?"

"No, some of us knew she wasn't," admitted her husband rather ashamedly, and he turned to look his wife in the eyes.

"You knew? All that time? My god…does Kelly know? Does she? Reese was in love with my…" and she stopped dead and looked at her father.

"Say it, Sage," interrupted Kane, "so there is no misunderstanding here. She was in love with me. I knew it and so did Kelly. Reese heard you and Kelly talking that day in the hotel bedroom when Kelly confessed her love for me to you. I pushed Reese off a cliff for the great drug baron, and her boyfriend, Miles Stratton, and no one ever heard from her again, except me, until she surfaced to marry. And now, I believe, the general just asked me to rescue her, and I think, also, that if he keeps on reading the file, that my long lost partner, Ryan Holden, from my platoon in Nam, is involved. Am I right?" Kane raised his eyes and looked Tucker straight in the face.

"You are correct, sir. Ryan Holden is very much involved. Kane, the lady, well, that's not in the file…I didn't know…" The grey-haired general was apologetic, his face turning a shade of red that seemed to match the medals on his tunic.

"Of course, it's not in any damn folder…only the three of us knew. Not even Dan here knew all of it. I made my choice a long time back and it was, and is, Kelly. Right down to the night I supposedly *killed* Reese, she made a play for me, even in front of her boyfriend. She almost ruined the whole fucking plan with her jealousy. But that's in the past. I understand she has to be rescued. Her husband has to testify against those people. Ryan Holden was always a piece of shit even back in Nam. He would kill just for the sake of it. And he will kill Reese and anyone else that gets in his way." Kane stood up and moved to the mantle. He leaned against it, resting his elbow on the ledge. He turned to face them all. "There will always be a Ryan Holden in life. I remember him only too well. He terrified some of the men in the platoon into following him and threatened them with their lives if they didn't do just as he said. And he is still probably doing that. But that's not all, is it, general? There is more, right? You want me to go in for other reasons. Oh, you think I can get Reese out…no problem on that front. And I am sure you want Ryan Holden dealt with, which you are also pretty sure I can take care of. But you know something else, don't you, General Tucker." Kane's look became fierce, and he focused on the general. "You just lied, general. You did know, oh, not about it being in the folder. That was the truth. But you knew, because someone told you. And I know who that was. Like I said, only three of us knew that Reese was in love with me. And one of them is standing right over there."

Hunter moved from behind the couch and positioned himself very close to Kane as if he suspected something was about to happen. He was right.

Kane moved forward just a couple of steps and Hunter shot in front of him, and blocked his way. For the second time in two days, Hunter braced himself against Kane's chest with his hands.

"You fucking knew because the third person told you. Where are you holding Kelly, General Tucker? Where the fuck is my wife?" And Kane strained against Hunter's outstretched arm.

Sam jumped up from the couch and rushed to help Hunter. He knew, only too well, the havoc Kane could wreak.

"General Tucker. I hope to god my father is wrong in his accusations. Tell him he is wrong…please…General?" Sam begged him. "But if he is right, we may just have to let go of him!"

Tucker stood up from his chair and moved backwards and pushed his adjutant in front of him.

"I don't have your wife…why would I have her?" A very nervous general replied.

"Maybe not you personally, but you know where she is, don't you?" Kane pulled against the two men's grips, anger stretched across his face.

"General Tucker, I suggest you answer my father," put in Sage. "He is right. You had to be told that, and it was either Reese or Kelly. So, either you have seen Reese, which I doubt, as then you could rescue her yourselves, or Kelly told you. So, answer him, or I will ask my brother and his friend to let go of my father." Sage was a still a Branson, and even her husband was shocked. "The truth, General, and then I will leave you men to this discussion. My father asked me to be in here for a very good reason. I assume, somehow, he knew something about the line of this conversation," and she glanced at Hunter, "and knew I could back him up, or is there something else you have to say that he wants me to hear? Somehow, I think it was the first statement."

Kane looked towards his daughter. His anger turned down just a notch. She had come through when he needed her, and so had his son. He turned to look back at Tucker, who was still using a very pristine adjutant as a shield.

"Come on, general...you do know where my step-mother is, don't you? Answer Commander Branson," Sage paused, "I will leave you then. G'day, General Tucker. Gentleman, I bid you farewell," and Sage turned and headed for the door.

General Tucker was visibly perspiring. He tugged at the overstarched collar of his uniform. His highly decorated chest heaved under the new-found stress. He didn't want the lady to leave. "Mrs. Lord," he uttered. "Would you stay a moment?"

"Certainly, if you answer Kane..."

The General cleared his throat and his conscience. "Commander, I don't have Kelly...but Ryan Holden does."

"What?" hissed Kane. "Ryan Holden has my wife? Are you insane? He rapes women for a hobby. I've seen him...I stopped him once from..." Kane stared at Tucker and if it had been possible he would have killed him right there in the study. "How the fuck did that happen?"

The arms holding him pulled tighter on his chest. Kane tried to break the grip and with his strong hands prized Hunter's arms from his own body. He knocked Sam out of the way as he went.

"Kane, no..." pleaded his son.

But Kane wasn't listening. He flung himself at the general, hitting the adjutant first in the body, sending him sprawling, and then his fist connected to Tucker's nose. "You bloody bastard…you came here knowing that? You know Ryan has her and you walked into my home, her home? What kind of person are you?" he hissed, not caring that the general was staggering from the blow.

"Military kind of people, and before you rip me apart, your wife went to him voluntarily…"

"That's a lie!" and Kane lunged forward again.

This time both Dan and Hunter caught him. Sage stepped back by the door for safety. She was almost afraid that her father would kill someone.

"Kelly wouldn't go anywhere voluntarily, not without me," stated Kane.

"No? She called you yesterday, didn't she? And said something about you wouldn't want her back?" gloated Tucker.

"You were listening to that conversation? What else have you listened to? Is it just the phone that's bugged or the whole house? Answer me?" yelled Kane.

"She's working with us…has been for a couple of months. Kelly was upset that you wouldn't take her with you on the last assignment. Of course, we didn't exactly tell her the truth about who she would be working with, and she thinks she is undercover for us…which she isn't. She also thinks she is helping you. She thought that until…" Tucker paused. "Well, till she met Ryan Holden and he changed her mind…"

Kane was furious…more than furious. He strained in the two men's grips.

"General Tucker. You better explain before my father does kill you, and we let him," stated Sam.

The general gathered himself together and sat down on the couch. His face hurt and his nose was bloodied. Kane had hit him with force. He patted his face with a crisp white handkerchief that his adjutant handed him. Now, he blew his nose on the handkerchief and handed it back to the alarmed officer, who promptly threw it in the nearest trash bin.

"Would you sit down, commander, and listen to what I am going to tell you about your wife?" Tucker tried to compose himself as he spoke and regain some kind of control of the situation.

"Do I have any choice? I can listen and then kill you, or I can just kill you. You decide, general. This story better be good!"

The grip released on Kane as he cooled down a notch or two, but still all three men stood close at hand. Hunter, in particular, stood very near to his boss, while Kane's eyes held Tucker's stare.

"Explain! But before you do, it better be what I want to hear." He turned to face Sage. "I think you should leave the room."

"No, dad. I want to hear what the general has to say about Kelly." She shook as she spoke, but stood her ground.

"So be it," exclaimed Kane. "Now, general," as he turned back to look at Tucker, "the floor is yours!"

General Tucker looked around the room. It looked like a lynching party. Then he focused solely on Kane.

Kane sat down, and put his hand to the back of his jeans, and when it retuned to the front of him, Tucker could clearly see his .38. Tucker knew Kane would not shoot him, not now anyway.

Tucker began.

"While you were in Japan, we approached your wife," he droned on.

Kane listened. He'd heard this part before.

"We told her what we wanted her to know…what we needed to get her on our side so we could get you to help us. It seemed like a great idea. Kelly really thought she was helping you, especially when she couldn't reach you some of the time in Japan. Then we sent her undercover for real…to Iraq…"

"You sent her where? Did I hear you correctly? To Iraq? Are you insane?!"

"She thought she was going to meet you there when you left Japan…"

"Meet me there? Why the fuck would I be in Iraq?" Then his brain kicked in. They knew he wouldn't just risk everything to rescue Reese Wade; nor would he go there on their say so just to get Ryan Holden. But he would most certainly go in for his wife. And the

Americans knew that. A trump hand, one that seemed to be turning tricks. What Kane did know, and the general didn't, was that Ryan Holden would want payback against Kane for Nam. And that very obvious way, was Kelly. As soon as Ryan found out who she was, he would rape her like he had so many other women, and not just for the fun of it, but because he could. Only then would Ryan be sure that Kane would go to get Reese out, and also his wife: and then save the day like he always did.

Now, Kane knew why Kelly had said the words she had. How he wished he hadn't been so abrupt with her, and he didn't really know why he had done it. She was trying to tell him. Kane was angry, not just at the general, but at himself for falling for all this crap. It didn't just involve him, but his son, the department and the American government. He looked around the crowded room. All eyes focused on him and he knew he had to make a choice.

"When do I leave?"

"Commander, you cannot go on your own, not in your present…" Hunter stopped dead while withering under the ice king's piercing stare. He realized his mistake instantly. He didn't need to piss his commander off like that.

"What my associate means is, I have been drinking way too much in the last couple of weeks, but that will stop right this minute." He dared Hunter to contradict him or anyone else for that matter. Sam had seen the pinholes, but wasn't sure what they indicated.

"I meant when do *we* leave. My son and Hunter go with me."

"And son-in-law makes four!" Dan didn't look at Sage. He knew she would be furious. But he owed Kane one last debt, and he intended to pay it one way or another.

Chapter 4

General Tucker left by the back door, with his face still swollen from Kane's fist. Several frozen bags of peas had failed to bring the swelling down. At least the bleeding from his nose had stopped and the general was still in one piece.

At nearly five p.m., Kane, Hunter, Sam and Dan emerged from the study. All the men were hungry, with lack of food from breakfast to dinner. Sage discreetly removed any children from the men's field of vision. She knew right now they needed to be on their own. The only man she wanted to talk to was her husband, and find out what the hell he thought he was doing. But that could wait. It had to.

This time Kane ate. With a large rare steak sitting in front of him on the dining room table, Kane helped himself to a healthy, crispy portion of mixed salad and showered it with freshly sliced zesty lemons. He ate it with relish and allowed himself a half glass of red wine, and that was it. He sat back and watched the others eat dessert. Freshly baked apple pie with cream topping, and large slices, too. Now, he thought that was going too far. He thought about another glass of wine, but decided against it. They needed to talk and analyze the game plan. He waited till they had all finished eating. Dan seemed to be the last.

Kane pulled his cigarettes out of his back pocket and then the lighter. He lit one up, something he had not done in the house since Kelly had moved in with him. He saw Dan watching him, almost with condemnation. Kane thought about putting the cigarette out, but changed his mind. The smoke rings floated upwards to the ceiling and joined the rotary blades of the fan on its travels.

The cigarette satisfied his taste buds. A nicotine fix was one of the fixes he needed. The other only Kelly could supply. And she wasn't there. So one cigarette turned into two, and Dan's look of condemnation followed Kane from the table to the mantle where Kane had now moved to.

A large cracking fire in the grate heated the whole room, and the ceiling fan only dispersed the heat round corners that fires didn't normally reach.

Kane leaned his shoulder on the mantel and rested his boot on the hearth-step. He stared into the red hot flames. He reflected over General Tucker's words and his anger became as white hot as the coals. He didn't like Tucker on sight, nor did he trust him. His story seemed to change to suit the moment. However, he did trust the three men in the room with him, especially Sam and Dan, and it was time to talk with them and formulate some sort of plan. He finished his cigarette and dropped it into the fire. The small butt was consumed immediately much as were Kane's thoughts.

"Okay, gentleman…I suggest we sit down and discuss what we are going to do." Kane seated himself at the head of the large table. He noticed the half full bottle of wine in the middle of the table, and was sorely tempted.

Dan realized at that point he needed to rescue his ex-partner from any more temptation. He also realized that Kane had never really given up any of his addictions; they were just abated by Kelly. And Kelly wasn't around. He wondered what other vices Kane would succumb to without Kelly around, and shuddered to think. Kane wasn't a man to be without a woman for too long. Dan leaned over the side of the table and removed the offending bottle of alcohol. Kane had said he wouldn't drink again, but he already had at dinner. What Kane said lately, he didn't always do.

Kane frowned at Dan, but he understood his actions and perhaps he was right. He would let it go…this time.

Sam had watched his father light up the cigarette, so he followed suit, not knowing it was taboo. He glanced around the room for an ashtray. There wasn't one. That was the first clue that possibly smoking wasn't allowed in the house. He, too, put out the cigarette.

The four men faced each other and it was time to get serious.

"Much as I don't like Tucker, he basically told us what we needed to know. We know where Ryan is holed up, and that he and his people have Kelly and Reese, and how safe they are, who the fuck knows." Kane paused. Now, was probably a good time to enlighten them about Ryan Holden. He had their undivided attention. "Ryan Holden and I go way back…to Nam. As you know, we were in the same platoon. We fought together; we shared the same bunkers and we shared the same women." Kane continued. "We both rose quickly through the ranks, neither of us were scared of shit, and both of us could hand out shit. But Ryan had a fatal flaw. He thought that women owed him. If a woman didn't want to have sex with him, he raped her, just to show he had the power." Kane shifted in his seat. "I knew what he was doing. Most of the guys did. To be blunt, no one cared. They were just whores to most of the guys." 'Oh, that sounded real nice,' thought Kane. "That was the only female company for miles around."

Outside the big bay windows, the light was going fast. Lights in the room came on automatically. Another part of Kane's luxurious lifestyle. The room lit up and sported the warm and artificial atmosphere of a happy home.

"One night Ryan and I, and two other guys, headed into town in the jeep. We left base about twenty-one hundred hours. As usual, we were with women, only this night was not to be like any other night I have ever experienced. We were all drunk which was not an unusual thing, and we had all finished…as you might say…with the prostitutes. We were ready to leave and return to base when Ryan wanted a freebie. The girl had other ideas. When she said no, Ryan began to beat the shit out of her. I was getting into the jeep outside the cheap motel, when I heard her scream. By the time I got in the place, he had pulled his gun and shot her in the knees. Whore or not, she never deserved what he was doing to her. He was killing her slowly." Kane stopped mainly to get his thoughts together. He could remember every detail very clearly. He could still see the girl lying on the filthy bed, screaming in pain. She was all of seventeen. Kane realized that everyone was watching him, waiting for him to continue.

"I grabbed Ryan's gun from him and pushed him away. Told him I would report him. That this time he had gone too far. Ryan reeled back, drunk and laughing. He fell against the piss-stained wall of the scrubby little motel room. He was yelling at me that the other guys wouldn't back me up; that she was just a whore and the army wouldn't care less. Maybe he was right, maybe not."

Sam had already guessed what Kane had done. "So you were judge and jury?"

"Something like that. I beat him within an inch of his life, so badly that the other two guys had to pull me off of him. The girl needed help..."

Dan didn't want to hear the rest. He, too, had figured it out.

"She lay in my arms. She was just a fucking kid! And I had used her just like they all had!" Kane's face was lined. Suddenly, years of knowing all this was too much. It was though he was cleansing himself of the past atrocities. He shivered and they all noticed. "She was in terrible pain, screaming at me to help her. Ryan lay on the floor in his own blood. He was still conscious, staring at her with a fucking smile on his face. She kept begging me, trying to grab my gun. Not one of the other girls came to help her. No one came. I pulled my pistol out..." Kane breathed hard, "and shot her once between the eyes."

For the first time in forty years, he had told someone. Not even Kelly knew. There was total silence in the room, as Kane tried to compose himself. His hands shook. Dan grabbed a glass and poured some wine into it, handing it across the table to his father-in-law. He drank the alcohol down in one go.

Sam broke the silence. "You didn't kill that girl..."

"Peta. Her name was Peta...I had slept with her..." and Kane dropped his head slightly.

"Sam's right, dad. Ryan Holden killed her. You just pulled the trigger that freed her. But that's not your main concern, is it? You think if Ryan has Kelly and Reese..."

"I think he already did!"

Hunter intervened. "Commander, we should get the women out as soon as we can. With the drug ring disbanded over there, Ryan can't hold out forever in that fortress he is supposed to have there.

His men will only stay loyal as long as he can pay them. Only money or fear will keep them there, and right now it seems he has both. But when he doesn't have them, he will become desperate. Don't you agree, commander?" Hunter looked to his boss for backup.

"Totally!" Kane had regained control of his emotions. "Tomorrow, we will get maps of Samarra, right, Hunter? That's where Tucker said Ryan was holed up?"

"Correct, commander."

"We also need maps of the sewers, and railroad schedules. I am sure General Tucker's little army will fly us in to god knows where and drop us off, and then we go on by ground transportation. We should leave the day after tomorrow. Gives Dan and I a day with the kids. A day to say goodbye. I think, Dan, you should be with Sage. I have a feeling she isn't too happy with either you or me right now. And," Kane paused, "I need to spend some time with my son here."

All four men stood up from the table. Kane shook hands with each one, and then hugged Dan to him, something that Kane didn't do too often, and sent him out the door.

"Hunter, take a few hours for you. Sam and I need to talk awhile. If I need you, I'll call," and nodded to Hunter in a knowing way.

"Let's go to my suite, Sam. Need to explain something to you."

They left the room together and climbed the stairs. The house was eerily quiet of children and night had caught up fast to day. They reached Kane's suite in silence. He unlocked the door and paused slightly as if he was in pain. Then, Kane's hands began to shake, and he started to sweat.

Once inside the room, Kane spoke. "Excuse me. I have something to take care of." He moved to the bedside cabinet and pulled out a syringe and a small vile. He tipped the vile up and filled the syringe. Kane pushed up the sleeve of his sweater and plunged the needle in. He flinched just slightly and then tossed the needle in the nearest trash bin. This time, for some reason, Kane felt violently sick and headed to the bathroom. Out of instinct, Sam followed his father.

"Kane, you okay?" Sam yelled from an open bathroom door.

"No," was all Kane could muster through rounds of vomit landing in the bathroom sink, and he rested against the sink for support.

Sam stepped inside the bathroom. It was ultra lavish. Everything was in cream marble, only topped with gold tap handles everywhere. Sam was shocked. This was the Branson secret world. The giant Jacuzzi was obviously used for much more than taking a bath, with wine glasses and trays at the side of it. Sam wondered if perhaps Kane was moonlighting.

Kane watched his son's face. He could almost see his brain ticking over. "It's all gained by honest means, Sam. All of it!"

"Kane, I never thought…"

"Right, of course you didn't!" Kane took a beaker full of water and washed his mouth out, and then rinsed down the sink, till once again it sparkled. "I guess you are wondering what is going on here?"

Sam nodded.

"Let's go sit in the room, and I will explain to you." He ushered Sam out of the bathroom and to the couches. Sitting opposite each other, Kane enlightened his son. "You are fully aware that I was in Japan for the last few weeks on an assignment for the AFP. I was supposed to find out who was supplying China white from Japan to Australia. I found them alright. Unfortunately, they found me, too. A week after I had been there, I suffered a mild heart attack. Very mild. I had one years ago when I met Kelly. I could have dealt with it, but the Japanese took it seriously. I happened to be in a room with a bunch of Japanese business men that were entertaining a whole host of geisha girls. I kind of collapsed on the floor, and they freaked out, sending for a doctor; only a couple of them couldn't be seen with the girls, so they sent for a private guy.   Unfortunately, for me, this guy gave me an injection for the pain…heroin! Pure China white, mate. The pain stopped and the drugs took over. I remember waking up next morning feeling great, till it wore off. Then, I was promptly sick all over the bed. And so it went on. There it was easy to get the white… seemed natural. Too natural. They let me have it, freely. I should have questioned it. But I didn't. Kelly used to do it. Gave her a buzz. Kelly would have killed me…" he stopped. Kelly wasn't there. "God, I miss her!" And he held his head between his hands.

"I know you do, dad. I know you do! How could you not miss someone like Kelly? But you have to stop with the drugs, for her sake.

I know it wasn't by choice and if the AFP find out, commander or not, they will fire you."

"They already know. That's why Hunter is here, to help. Alcohol helps bring the symptoms down, also sweet things, candies, anything like that. I started on that the day I got home. Unfortunately, I liked alcohol a little too much in my past, so that's not easy. And I don't eat candies. When the pain is bad, I revert back to the heroin."

Sam knew it was bad for Kane to use the drug to cure the drug. He knew Kane's pain threshold was higher than most men could handle.

"So, now you know. You have a druggy for a father," and Kane laughed. "If I don't shoot up I go to pieces. If I do, I still go to pieces, and act like some crazy guy. God, Sam, what do I do? We have no choice but to go to Iraq and get Kelly and Reese Wade. I owe Reese. Without her, there would be no Kelly. They knew I wouldn't go just for Ryan or Reese. But they knew I would go for Kelly, and they knew if they kept supplying me with heroin I would do just what they asked of me. You see, the Americans were helping the Japanese get the drugs out of Japan. We have to go get them, Sam…before it's too late. I didn't know till today, when Tucker came here exactly where they were and what was going on, but he did. Of course, he did. He and his cronies had the whole thing planned, for me to do their dirty work and get Ryan Holden. You see Ryan isn't all Australian. One of his parents was American."

"You mentioned, 'before it's too late'…"

"Before it's too late to trade me…"

Sam jumped up from the couch, and yelled at Kane. "What the fuck are you talking about! To trade you? Is that why you are going in?! For trade? Have you gone insane? All four of us are going and coming back! We are not leaving you anywhere, for god's sake!" Sam was furious that his father would even consider the idea.

But Kane knew different. He knew he was going there to die!

Chapter 5

When Kane awoke the next morning, his mind was full of Kelly. He'd tossed and turned, throwing his bed covers to the floor. He was lying face down on the bed with sweat pouring down his body, as naked as the day he was born. This time it was not from the drugs, but from his dream of Kelly in the bed with him. He could almost feel her smooth body next to his rough skin. His fingers caressing her face and then her breasts; his mouth on her full round lips. Her soft moans of pleasure echoing in his ears, so much so that he called out her name so loudly that they heard him in the next room.

Hunter leaped out of bed, grabbed a robe and sprinted across the room, practically falling through the door and across Kane's bedroom.

"Commander...Kane. Are you okay?" Hunter reached Kane's bed.

Completely awake, Kane rose up from the bed, and sat on the side of it, still with a sheet attached to his lower body.

"I'm fine. Just hand me a robe, would you?" Kane asked.

"Sure, boss. Dreaming of Kelly? We could hear you halfway down the landing." Hunter handed Kane the black terry robe from the chair.

"God, I hope the kids didn't hear. Not that kind of dream, anyway," and Kane smiled to himself, and then the smile was gone. "What time is it?" Kane asked, as he wrapped the robe round his body, which left his chest slightly exposed.

"Almost six a.m. How do you feel?" Hunter was concerned.

"I'm fine. Before Sam says anything to you, I threw up last night, badly, and now he knows. I'm glad he does, in one way, makes life easier. No need, though, for anyone else to know. But, he thinks that the drugs are for the heart attack. He doesn't need to know anything else. It's party true after all."

"Boss, don't you think they have a right to the truth? They are your family..." Hunter was becoming exasperated by Kane's casual attitude to the whole thing.

"That's exactly why they can't know. And what is the truth? What good would it do? It won't stop anything. All I want to do is to get Kelly back, see her one more time. If I had known this was going to happen, I would have taken her with me to Japan. But, I didn't. And now the lying has escalated to where I can't go back to the truth. You have to give me your word that they will never know, not any of them, not even Kelly." He looked Hunter square in the eyes as he spoke.

"Don't you think she is going to notice? She knows you better than anyone. She sleeps with you, for God's sake."

"Then, I won't sleep with her..." Kane joked and moved to the couch, dropping the discarded sheet on the bed.

"Right, Kane. Everyone knows your reputation with women." And Hunter smiled, and tried to ease the tension. He sat down opposite Kane.

"Yeah, mate. Point taken. Then, I'll do it in the dark. Won't be the first time and maybe she'll be too busy to notice!" he laughed, and then became serious. "I had my sweater off, and Sam didn't notice. He did see the pinholes, though, which wasn't too smart on my part."

"True, but he couldn't see your stomach," and Hunter glanced very briefly at Kane's chest. "I guess if you are not looking for it, you don't notice. Does it bother you?"

"Only when I breathe. Seriously, not all the time. I guess that's what happens when you protect some Japanese ambassador who is not quite on the level. If only the needle hadn't contained heroin. No one would have ever known. Just regular pain killers would have been fine. Survived far worse than this little knife wound in my life, and without getting shot full of heroin, too. Damned heroin is worse than the wound. Hurt like hell, though, last night when I threw up. Sam, instinctively, followed me to the bathroom. I thought I was gonna bust the fucking stitches wide open from retching. That would have taken some explaining. Anyway, enough of my rambling, we have some work to do. What time are the Americans gracing our happy home?"

"Around three this afternoon. Think you can get through the day okay? If you need to leave the room suddenly, I can cover for you, and maybe Sam can, too." Hunter paused and changed the subject. "So what time do you want to meet downstairs?" Hunter started to rise from the couch.

"About two. I need to spend time with the kids. See if you can get breakfast sent up for me. And Hunter, thank you for watching out for me. I know I am not the easiest person to keep track of, and I know you have my back. Whatever happens in Iraq, get Kelly out of there and home safely." Kane stood, and stretched his hand to Hunter.

Hunter shook Kane's hand with force. "You'll be doing that part, Kane." He thought it was a very strange request, but he turned and left the suite and closed the door behind him.

Kane dropped the robe on the floor as he climbed in to the red hot water of the shower. He didn't even notice the temperature, as his mind once more filled with Kelly and making love to her. He wanted to hold her and tell her how much he loved her. He wanted her to be safe, and he wanted to kill Ryan Holden. He thumped his fist hard on the tiled shower wall in front of him. Kane was angry; angry because they had Kelly, and he didn't; angry because he wasn't in control of the situation; and angry because he had let this happen!

He slid his hand down to his gut, and searched for the stitches under his body hair. It was tender to the touch. What Kane had omitted to tell anyone, was that it wasn't a steel blade that he had been stabbed with, but part of a bamboo blade from a ceiling fan. The blade had snapped, and half of it was too far in him to remove without causing more complications, and that was the real reason the pain was so bad.

In the quietness of his room, Kane dressed once more in black, and then left the solitude for a nursery of countless children.

"Daddyyyyyyyy," yelled Kane's youngest, and he was more than excited to see his father this early in the day. The little boy flung himself at his father's legs and clung on. Kane leaned down and picked up the little boy. This was something Kane could still do without pain.

"Star, Kene, come over and sit with Daddy for a while. Maybe we can have an early lunch together, just us? Would you like that, guys?"

There was a unanimous vote in agreement to that comment. They played, they ate, and then they dozed together.

When Kane didn't show at two p.m., Hunter went to look for his boss. Opening the kid's bedroom door slowly, he was greeted with a very precious memory. Kane lay on the couch, his hair hanging down the arm rest; Star nestled into her father's arms as close as she possibly could get to his body, and his two sons lying across his legs. Hunter wished he had had a camera right then.

He hadn't the heart to wake them all and turned to leave.

"Hunter," whispered Kane, "one minute," and he put his finger to his lips to make certain Hunter did not reply.

Hunter nodded.

Kane rose up slowly with Star in his arms. As he moved, the two boys stirred. Kane whispered to them all, and laid Star back on the couch. He bent down and kissed her forehead, and with one last look back, he left his children. On the stairs, Kane bumped into Sage. He slid his arm round her shoulders, and whispered in her ear. She smiled, the same smile her mother had had all those years ago, and Kane could never resist that smile. Whatever it took, Dan would not go with them, even though in Dan's eyes he owed Kane big time. Both Kane and Hunter descended the stairs in silence. Kane knew that Sam was waiting for them in the dining room.

Sam sat at the dining room table pondering the future and their plans. It was several degrees colder today than yesterday, and in the cobbled fireplace a great fire warmed the room. Kane had never had heating or air-conditioning installed in the house. He thought it was a sign of weakness. Sam looked up at the mantel. Pictures of the family adorned the shelf, and Sam thought there were more pictures than there were yesterday. Amongst the kid's photos was one of him. He stood up and lifted the photo from its resting place. It was a picture of him leaning on a tree on Lantau Island, smoking a cigarette and taking a break. He had no clue when it was taken or who had taken it. Then, he remembered Kane's cell phone. He didn't know if it was a camera phone or not, but it would explain the picture. He was distracted as the door opened, and Kane stepped inside the room, followed as closely as ever by his shadow.

Today, Kane's long hair flowed down his back, in complete contrast to the shadow's black pony-tailed hair. It was like watching salt and pepper. The only similarity was the deep suntans they sported, and they were both AFP.

Kane stepped forward and shook his son's hand. "You slept well, son, and you have everything you need? We have to get you kitted out tonight; boots, clothes and anything else you want to take with you."

"I'm fine, and I am sure that Hunter will help me to get kitted out." He paused. "You sleep okay then, *Dad*?"

"Like a top. Great sleep," and Kane cracked a smile as he remembered back to this morning. The first night he hadn't dreamt of shooting Kelly. He shuddered.

They noticed.

Kane saw them both look at him.

"Now, did you get maps that I asked for? I think Baghdad and Samarra are the places to concentrate on."

"Got them, commander. Went to the station last night and procured them for us." Hunter picked up a role of maps and laid them on the table. "By the way, the department said they miss you. Maybe you should call them, sir. They haven't talked to you really since you got back from Japan." He still fiddled with the maps and put weights on each end of them. He glanced sideways at Kane.

Kane looked at his watch. Almost two-thirty. "Maybe I will go and call them now. Will only take a few minutes." Kane turned from the table and left the room.

Hunter waited till he was sure Kane had really gone.

"Now, while the commander is out of the room, he said you were with him last night when he was sick. I gather he explained to you about his health and…" Hunter was interrupted.

"Yeah, I was with him and he gave me some sort of explanation, half of which I don't believe. Is it all true? Did he have a heart attack?" questioned Sam, his eyes narrowing to more of a slant than usual.

"If Kane says so, then it must be. I'm just glad you know. Makes it much easier with two of us to cover for him." 'Even if it isn't all true,' thought Hunter. "Let's take a look at these maps while we wait for him. I guess the general will let us know today where they are taking us. Kane doesn't like him too much, better still, doesn't trust him. I have to admit I agree. Tucker had too many pat answers. Guess we will see what he says today."

"I don't trust him either," replied Sam. He looked Hunter straight in the face. "Have you ever met Kelly, Hunter?"

"Mrs. Branson? Yes, before Kane left for Japan. Couple of times, actually. Why?"

"Then you know what she is like, how much she loves Kane and would do anything for him? Kelly running off because she was pissed at him, and trying to get him to notice her, doesn't ring true. I was thinking about it last night. I don't think Kane believes that story either, if he's honest about it."

Hunter was taken aback. He hadn't thought of it like that before. He paused before answering. "You could be right."

Outside the door, someone had heard every word they both said, and leaned back on the wall to digest it.

At three sharp the American contingent arrived, this time escorted by two hefty black sergeants. Kane wondered if these two were going to Iraq with them; a question that would soon be answered. Introductions made in the dining room were fast and precise.

"Commander Branson, Sergeants Tyrone Rennick and Corey Miller." Both stood to attention. "At ease, soldiers. Stand down. Commander, these sergeants go with you in and out of the war zone. When Reese Wade is rescued, they will take her back to the States with them," stated the general.

After they were made, everyone still stood.

"Excuse me, General Tucker; if you have them why the fuck do you need me? Sergeant Tyrone Rennick looks like he could take out the whole fucking Iraqi army on his own, and Corey Miller, I believe, is a god damn woman?!" Kane was more than blunt. He was rude, and turned towards the fireplace.

"Commander Branson!" Tucker was very abrupt. "There is no need to be hostile and disrespectful to Miller. She is highly trained and speaks fluent Arabic, which, sir, I believe is more than you can speak. Don't let her being a woman fool you!"

"Oh, I won't," replied Kane very pointedly. Kane pulled his cigarettes and lighter from his back pocket and pointedly lit up his smoke. He faced Tucker.

Sam hid a snigger very well, but turned away just incase someone saw his face.

"What the commander meant was, that we already have two women to rescue and you just threw a third into the mix. Right, Commander?" asked Hunter trying to bring order to the conversation.

"No, it isn't fucking right! If I have to take Americans, I want two men. Then again, she…" and he stopped, mainly because both his son and Dan were staring at his unbelievable rudeness to this woman, one who was red in the face with embarrassment. "You are right; I can't speak Arabic, most everything else, but not that. Ok, she goes, but she better be good; and your boy here. So that makes six of us. Hunter got maps last night. We spent some time going over them earlier. Mainly depends where you are going to drop us off. I would imagine if we go from here to Kuwait, we would go by way of Abu Dhabi, then on to Baghdad, right?"

"Very good, Commander. You know your air routes." Tucker was doing his best to be pleasant. He had to get Branson on that flight tomorrow afternoon, come hell or high water, even if it meant kissing Australian ass to do it, and that's what he was attempting to do right now.

Kane puffed away on the cigarette, causing smoke to float round the room, and round the people in it. Dan had never seen Kane quite this arrogant. It was like he had some personal vendetta against Americans. In all the years he had known Kane, he was never like this.

"Of course, I know the routes! I've been all over the fucking world. So, are your guys flying us in or are we going the commercial route?" Kane's voice was tempered for now.

"Commercial…less obvious." He pulled the itinerary from his pocket. "You are booked on Etihad Airways flight 345 at 15.20 hours. You, Dan, Hunter, Sam and my people here. You arrive in Abu Dhabi at 23.10 hours, change planes, and then catch flight number 320 at 2.05 hours arriving 2.50 hours in Kuwait. A U.S. charter company will fly you to Baghdad. I don't have the times yet, but it will be organized for when you arrive. You, Commander, are obviously in charge of the whole operation. The only orders I have for you after you get your wife and Reese out, is to take Ryan Holden alive. But Reese Wade must be rescued, do you understand that?"

"Number one, I understand that I don't take orders from any damned American. Number two, my wife comes first, and hopefully we get Reese out, too. Number three, what I do to Ryan Holden is none of your fucking business!" And Kane stamped the cigarette out under his boot, like he was snuffing out a life.

He looked at Tucker. A four-star general, pushing retirement, giving him orders, him…Kane Branson, Commander of the Australian Federal Police. He looked at Sam, who winked at him mischievously; and then to Hunter, who was slightly red-faced. That puzzled Kane. He passed on by the two Americans. He would weigh them up later. Finally, Dan came into view. Dan smiled at his ex-partner, and Kane winked back.

Kane Branson was still a man whom one should fear, and right now more than one in that room did.

The group poured over the maps for hours. Kane lost his temper only once more in that time. Food came and went. Kane smoked a whole packet of cigarettes. He also asked for a scotch. Hunter fetched it. Tucker frowned. Kane had given his word he would not drink. Kane broke his word. When that one was finished, he asked for another. He also asked for a sickly sweet dessert. That was a sign he was weakening. He needed heroin. Hunter waited for Kane to make an excuse to leave the room. When he didn't, he was puzzled. Instead,

Kane drank another scotch, and then ate some candies that the kids had left that morning on the coffee table.

Sam watched his father, and he marveled at the way he was holding up. A normal man would have left the room long back.

"Warm in here, isn't it?" Kane opened the nearest window to him. He stood by it for a few minutes, breathing in the crisp night air. Sweat rolled down him and his black sweater clung to him. He tried to focus and it became increasingly difficult to do so. His hands shook, and he knew he had to get out of the room.

Sam moved to Kane's side. "You need to get out of that door. Tucker is watching you; hasn't taken his eyes off you for the last five minutes. I think he figures you are drunk," and he glanced back at the general.

"Good, let him think that. Maybe, he won't want to send his friends with me after all," he replied with a slightly slurred voice.

"And maybe he will send more of them! Go to your suite and do what you need to do. Hunter and I can cover for you."

"No!" Kane whispered.

"What?" asked his son.

"I can't let this stuff get such a tight hold. I won't be able to get a fix on the flight, so I may as well try and quit, now."

"You got some kind of death wish?" Sam regretted saying that. It was a stupid question.

Kane looked Sam in the face. "Yeah, I do…" and he laughed quietly. "I can make it; just let's get them out of here." He looked at his watch. Ten p.m. Kane turned slowly, leaned his backside on the window ledge and hoped to god he was speaking with clarity. "General Tucker, I don't think we can accomplish much more tonight. I suggest we get some sleep. It's going to be a very long day tomorrow."

"I agree," Tucker replied. "Commander Branson, I hope that tomorrow you will not be so…"

"Drunk, general? Is that what you were going to say? I am not drunk. Three drinks does not make a drunk. Drunk or sober, I can handle any mission, any day, anytime and anywhere! Always remember that!" Kane said it with finality, and turned back to stare out of the window.

"You know your way out, general?" stated Dan, as he ushered the military party out of the door. "We will see you here tomorrow, at noon, all ready to go." And he closed the door behind the trio of mumbling bureaucracy and walked across the room to face his father-in-law. "Now, Kane, what the hell is going on here?"

Kane opened his mouth to speak; instead he dropped to the floor, out cold.

Chapter 6

"Catch him!" yelled Hunter as Kane dropped. He managed to grab hold of one arm, which stopped Kane from hitting his head on the window ledge.

Sam reached for the other arm and together they hoisted him off the floor. He was a one-hundred-ninety pound dead weight.

"Dan," yelled Hunter. "Help us with him."

Dan moved to them at the window. The three of them struggled a little picking Kane up.

"What the hell is wrong with him? I have never seen Kane black out, not even from severe pain, and especially not from alcohol." He paused. "But it's not alcohol is it?" asked Dan.

"Not sure what it is." Hunter was loath to say what. If Kane had wanted Dan to know he would have told him and he hadn't, probably because it would have been repeated to Sage.

Taking arms and body, they lifted him onto a little couch in the far corner of the room. Kane lay there, not moving.

"Is he coming round yet?" asked Dan, very concerned.

"Not yet...he will. Is there any ice left in the ice bucket on the table. And pass me one of the napkins. Need something to wrap the ice in." Hunter seemed to know exactly what to do for the situation.

Sam handed him both, all the time watching for Kane to move. He didn't. "He's really out cold, isn't he?"

"Yep, he is. In a good way! When he wakes up, he is going to be in a lot better shape." Hunter retrieved a throw from the back of the couch and covered Kane. He also knew he needed to get Kane's temperature down, and get the sweat off him by dousing him with ice.

He needed to make sure, though, that no one could see the fresh scar. "Sam, can you put Kane up a little, so I can get his sweater off him?"

"Sure."

As the sweater came off, the sweat could clearly be seen rolling down Kane's chest.

"God almighty…he's on fire!" remarked Dan.

"Like I said, he will be fine. Dan, would you get more ice? There isn't enough here."

"Consider it done, mate," and Dan scooted off to the kitchen.

"Needed him gone for a minute. He mustn't see everything," stated Hunter, tending to his charge.

"Figured that," replied Sam.

"We need to get his temperature down. Some father you have there. He knew he needed heroin, but he stuck it out, and now he won't need it again. Hopefully, anyway. Takes some guts, mate. Can you hold him still, while I do this?"

Kane moved very slightly as the ice cold pack slid down his chest. Hunter was very careful not to go as low as the scar. Needle marks in view didn't matter in front of Sam.

"You sure he's your father," joked Hunter. "If you had said brother, I would have believed you. Kane's a good bloke. One of the best, but then you know that, don't you?"

"Yes, I do. One of the best," echoed Sam. "Wish I had known him when I was growing up," he mussed.

Dan came hurtling back through the door with a bucket full of ice, and handed it to Hunter. "He hasn't come round yet?" He looked astonished.

"Nope." Hunter was surprised that as an ex-cop, Dan had not guessed what was wrong with Kane. Then, again, Kane was so against drugs. Or, maybe he had figured it, and he didn't want to acknowledge the fact. He thought maybe the latter.

With the ice-pack changed, Hunter once more applied cold to Kane's body, and his temperature began to subside. Kane tried to turn his body and the cover slipped and the scar could clearly be seen. Hunter's eyes darted to both men to see if they had noticed. They seemed to be focusing on Kane's face more than his body.

Kane groaned, and his eye lashes fluttered. Very slowly he came round, and tried to focus. He was aware of three faces staring at him.

Hunter jumped in fast. "Some hangover you have there, Kane," and he laughed, and then cut his eyes to the two men near him, trying to force Kane to watch what he said.

Kane's focus improved and he realized he was flat on his back, with a cover wrapped round his lower body. He could see his snakeskin boots sticking out of the blanket. He wondered just how long he had been out. By the way they were fussing over him, may be some time had passed.

"Well, Kane that will cure you of drinking! You broke all records there!" Hunter added.

Kane also realized by what Hunter was telling him, he had broken the habit. The rest, he would grin and bear. He also realized that he wasn't wearing a sweater, and his chest was soaking wet. He tried to sit up voluntarily and succeeded, swinging his legs over the side of the couch. From there he stood up, albeit very shakily. He had to show them, especially Dan, that he was fine. The blanket fell from him and Kane realized that most likely anyone could see the scar. His put his hand down to cover it, and let his hand rest on his belt. As his fingers touched the scar, the pain shot through him, but he made no sound.

"Well, I guess that's what happens when you drink all day and mix it with candies." He laughed, a slightly waving laugh that indicated he wasn't a hundred percent yet, but getting there. "So what did I miss in the last few minutes?"

He was guessing at the time gap.

"Make it a half hour, Kane" stated Dan.

"That long, huh? I should have stayed out longer. Let you guys do all the work!" Kane moved to the table and retrieved his sweater from the chair back where Hunter had laid it. He shivered in the cooling air. "Ok, what did I do last?"

"You showed General Tucker the door!" remarked Sam.

"Oh, yeah, right. I remember that. Did he go quietly?" Kane smirked, while remembering the incident. He looked to Hunter who took the cue.

"We should get ourselves ready. I think I should go help Sam get his gear. You have some in the spare room right, Kane?"

Kane nodded.

"And then maybe we should sleep. Like you said, it's going to be a long day tomorrow." Hunter picked up the maps left on the table.

Sam could not miss the looks from Kane to Hunter and vice versa. There was much more going on behind the scenes than he knew about, a fact he promised himself he would remedy real soon. Sam followed Hunter out of the room, and Kane bid Dan a goodnight. Still a little shaky, Kane took himself to his rooms, fending off protests from Dan that he should help him up the stairs.

In his suite, he pulled a knapsack from the closet and stuffed it full of black sweatpants, tank tops, and a couple of thick grey sweatshirts. The Weather Channel said it was cold in Iraq right now, with unseasonable rains. Whatever he took, he would have to live with. He pulled out a spare pair of lace-up boots for hiking, a waterproof jacket, along with socks for the boots, and a pair of leather gloves. Confident he had packed enough, he stuck the backpack by the door to his bedroom along with coat and boots. Next, he went to the bedside table, picked up the heroin and syringes, took them to the bathroom, flipped the lid of the toilet and tossed the heroin in. He flushed the toilet and the drugs were gone as fast as they appeared into his life. He hoped he knew what he was doing, or he was a dead man.

Just then his bedside phone rang. He could see the internal light flashing as he picked up the receiver.

"Kane."

"Just wanted to see if you were okay. You gave us a nasty shock downstairs tonight. You were out for a good while. You sure you are okay?" asked his son.

"I am fine, really. But nice to know you are so concerned about me," added Kane. He meant it.

"Why wouldn't I be? You are my father. I don't know how you did that downstairs. Took some guts. Then again, no one ever doubted you had those." Sam paused. "I guess you didn't tell Dan the truth for some reason."

"He would just run to Sage and tell her and she would freak out." It was Kane's turn to pause. "Sam, how did it go with Hunter tonight? He say anything about me, or Kelly, when you blokes were looking for kit bags?"

"No, should he have done?" he replied.

"No, just wondered," stated Kane.

"Said he was going to check on you tonight, see if you were okay, but that's it. Why?"

"I was just curious."

Sam figured Kane was never just curious about anything. There had to be a reason that Kane asked him.

"Well, see you in the morning. You all packed? Dad, Kane? You there?"

"Yeah. I was just thinking. Say, you have everything you need to take with you?"

"Yes, sir, everything. Goodnight, sir." And Sam's line went dead.

Kane hesitated, and then hung up his line, too. He sat down on the side of the giant bed. He thought about a cigarette. He thought he had had enough. He wanted to sleep, yet he didn't. He needed Kelly, desperately. He stepped out of his clothes, entered the bathroom and took a long, cold shower.

Morning for Kane came round at five a.m. Dressed in his black robe, he stuck his head into the kids' rooms. He looked at their angelic faces, whispered goodbye, and then closed the door behind him. Back in his room, he dressed in tight black jeans, thick grey sweater over a black T-shirt and he pulled on his trademark handmade boots. Into these, he slipped the cell phone that seemed to reach anywhere in the world. He left his backpack and jacket by the bedroom door. He looked around the room. It was their room, his and Kelly.

Kelly.

Kane was first to the breakfast table, and seemed to be the first to be up anywhere in the house. Even the fireplace still slept with last nights embers. Kane sat down on the hard-backed chair. Sudden vivid memories of last night ran through his brain. He never wanted to go through that again, and hoped now he was in a position to handle any other side effect that came his way. Seven a.m. Kane was hungry. He picked up a nice green apple from the ever present fruit-bowl on the table. He brushed it shiny on his sweater sleeve, and bit hard into the juicy fruit. He finished the apple in six bites and tossed the core in the grate. Still, Kane was hungry. He chose a banana next for consumption, followed by a nice tangy orange. Only now, did he feel better. He still had the craving for sweet things. But with all that food he was thirsty. He got off the chair and rummaged through the drinks cabinet. He found soda water, wine and scotch. Scotch, now that sounded good even at seven-thirty. He poured himself a glass; just a small one. It went down in one go. Another sounded good. He poured it and took the small glass to the window with him. It was drizzling and looked wild outside, much like the thoughts in his brain.

He wanted to get on the road. He wanted to be nearer to Kelly. How was he going to face her after the way he treated her on the phone? And how would he react if Ryan had raped her? He had to put that thought from his mind. Kelly had been with many men before Kane, but none since. And he wasn't any angel, either. Kane had had his fair share of women before Kelly. That was all before…this was now. He knew Kelly would have put up a fight; what he didn't know, yet, was how much of one. She was his wife and he would stand up for her no matter what. Hadn't she stood by him so many times before? It was with these thoughts in his mind that he finished staring at the half full glass, and then emptied it.

His thoughts were disturbed as the dining room door swung open, and Sam entered pretty much the same time as Hunter.

Kane didn't hide the glass fast enough and both men saw it. Kane also saw the looks that passed between his son and Hunter. For some reason, today, Kane didn't care. Back was the brashness of Kane Branson. He had nothing to lose now, except his life.

By noon, they were all ready by the front door. Kane, Hunter, Sam and Dan. Sage hovered around Dan, her eyes red from crying. She did not want Dan to go. Kane watched his daughter with her husband. He knew, all too well from his first wife, how his daughter was hurting now. Dan felt he owed Kane for saving his life back in Hong Kong. Now, Kane was about to save it again.

"Dan, a word in private," and ushered his son-in-law into the study.

They were gone all of five minutes, when Kane emerged on his own.

"Okay, let's go. I can hear a car outside. Must be our transportation." He slid into his jacket, picked up his backpack and turned to hug Sage goodbye. "I love you, Sage, always remember that. Whatever happens, I love you. Look after my children for me." Kane hugged her unashamedly, and whispered in her ear.

Sage's eyes widened and she clung to her father. "I love you, too, dad. Thank you!" she replied through tears. "Be safe, and bring Kelly home. Tell her I miss her."

Kane could not take anymore. He let go of her, turned away, and headed out of the open door, with Sam and Hunter following close behind. The door closed tightly behind them and Sage disappeared into the study.

Kane never saw the lone figure on the stairs. A small child, eight going on eighteen, watching from the landing, hidden by the railings, her eyes streaming with tears and her hair hanging loosely around her.

"Goodbye, daddy," she whispered. "I love you."

Chapter 7

Outside the house, luxury transportation waited patiently, its engine purring in the drizzling lunchtime rains of Sydney. They had two or three hours before the flight and the airport wasn't so far away as not to make it in good time.

Kane turned his head to look up at his majestic house. Ivy now clung to the walls, and honeysuckle fought for a place among the vines. The chimney stack needed replacing. He would get that fixed when he came back…

"Commander Branson, we should be on our way, sir," Hunter gently reminded him.

"Yeah, we don't want to keep the general waiting, do we?" and Kane, after watching the loading of the luggage, climbed into the waiting limo.

Sam and Hunter followed suit, and with doors shut, the shiny black stretch pulled away from the house. Out of the tinted rear windows, Kane looked back at the upstairs windows of the house. He saw her there, her little hand flat on the glass, stretched out to him.

"Stop the car! Now!" yelled Kane to the driver.

Grabbing the handle, he swung the door open and climbed rapidly out of the car. Running down the path, his face wet in the rain, he saw the front door open and Star emerge, barefoot, clad in just her nightgown. She ran to her daddy and he scooped her up in one go into his safe and loving arms. He hugged her till he thought he would break her in half, and she clung to him desperately, their hair mixing together in the dampness. He whispered in her ear, and she cried for him and for a split second the two became one. Kane carried her back to the front door. By now, both Sage and Dan stood there.

"Why, Kane? Why did you knock me out?" asked Dan whose head felt like it didn't belong to him.

"You have to ask? Your place is here with your family and you once promised me that you would look after mine, remember?"

"I remember."

Kane handed his child to Dan. "Now, keep that promise."

Kane looked down at his wedding band, and pulled the ring from his finger. He opened his daughter's hand and dropped the ring into it, closed her tiny fingers around it, smiled at her one last time and was gone. This time, he never looked back.

No one spoke as Kane climbed back in the car. Words seemed unnecessary, as the limo turned out of the Branson drive and onto the street.

Sam figured that Kane was dealing with this his way. He allowed them to glimpse at a side of him that he never showed to anyone. A man leaving his child behind. A man going after the person he loved more than anything in the world, even his own life. But, never-the-less, a man. General Tucker needed to remember that fact.

"Where is Commander Branson?" Tucker paced up and down at the airport terminal. Today he seemed more obnoxious than ever.

"Sir, the flight isn't for another two hours yet," the adjutant reminded him.

"Right, that's right. Thank you." Tucker still wore a worried frown on his face.

The adjutant's cell rang. He flipped it open, and answered. "Right, thank you so much." He closed the cell. "It was the limo driver. Commander Branson and his party just left the car. They should be here any minute. In fact," he glanced around, "there they are now."

Kane strode across the tile floor till he could see Tucker and his merry band waiting by Etihad Airways. He cut a menacing figure, all in black with his long blond hair hanging loose on his shoulders. He was flanked by Hunter and Sam, all carrying backpacks, all dressed in black. Two salts and one pepper, with one salt worth far more than the other two condiments.

"General."

"Commander."

The two men shook hands out of sheer respect for their ranks, and to show a certain unity in front of the group. Tucker pulled out a package containing plane tickets and documents of entrance into Iraq.

"I assume you all have passports, and, of course, you have current shots?" asked Tucker.

Kane's respect of the general bottomed out yet again.

"No, sir. We left passports on the dresser, and shots? What shots! We need shots!" Kane stated as he rolled his eyes at the general, thinking he was extremely glad that Tucker was not going with them.

A grin spread itself across Corey Miller's face. Kane saw it. Maybe, she didn't care for her commander as much as he first thought. Perhaps Corey wasn't so bad after all. Kane smiled back, and then turned his attentions to the general again.

"Of course, we have passports. And as Federal Police that travel, out shots are always current. Sam just flew in from Hong Kong two days ago, so I guess that speaks for itself." Kane stopped speaking, took the package from the general and slid it under his jacket. "I would have thought, general, it would have been a little better to do this where prying eyes cannot see!"

Kane stared at Tucker. A four-star general standing by an Iraqi airline wasn't the smartest thing the Americans ever did. At least the sergeants wore sweats, albeit that they still looked somewhat military. That was something Kane would change before they got to Baghdad. He didn't want the whole Iraqi nation to know his group was arriving in the country.

The general was red-faced and about to explode, but said nothing. Kane could only imagine what Tucker thought of him, and he really didn't care. It actually amused Kane. To piss Tucker off just a little more, Kane stuck his hand out to Tyrone Rennick, and then to Corey Miller. They both reciprocated the gesture in turn. Kane purposely left his hand extended a second or two longer than necessary to Corey. He was trying the best way he knew how to apologize for his former rudeness to her. When he looked at her today, she didn't look so bad. She wore a little makeup; her hair was in a much more fashionable style, making her features more tempered, almost attractive in her own way. She smiled back at him as though accepting his apology.

"I think we should check in, and go through to the lounge and wait," Kane said, as he turned toward the ticket counter. There was only a very short line ahead of them and Kane was at the counter very quickly. He handed over his ticket and passport, got them back, declared no luggage, and then remembered his gun was down the back of his jeans. How he had forgotten it was there was a very convenient mystery!

"General," Kane tuned to him. "I inadvertently brought my gun," and Kane very surreptitiously pulled the piece out of the back of his jeans, handed it very carefully and partially concealed to Tucker. "Get this on the plane to Kuwait for me, would you?"

"You can't just hand over your gun at the airport, commander!" stated Tucker.

"I just did!" Kane replied, arrogantly. "Either of you two carrying?" Kane asked Hunter and Sam.

"Yes, sir," added Hunter, and he duly handed over his .38.

"There you go, general. Two guns to get to Kuwait. You have 'packages' going over right? Well, just add more to them, mate. Make sure we have extra ammunition, too, as I am sure Ryan Holden knows we are coming, and we will need plenty of bullets, too, won't we?" Kane finished his sentence and he and his backpack took off through the airport with his little band of soldiers behind him.

General Tucker watched them go, his fully-briefed sergeants, Hunter, an Australian Federal Police agent, Sam Branson, an unknown commodity, and Commander Kane Branson, a formidable foe. He wondered which ones would come back. His staff was expendable, so was Sam Branson. The other two were not. They were police.

At security screening, every backpack went through. Jacket, shoes, wallets, all went through without incident until Kane's boots. The cell phone hidden inside them caused concern. He was made to retrieve it, and put it through separately before he could continue on his journey to the gate.

Sydney airport, modern and very large, was bustling at this time of day. It offered extensive travel by many airlines. Etihad, located at A10, sported very comfortable seating and several kiosks were close by.

Kane tucked his passport inside his jacket, found a good seat near to the large glass window and sat down. Sam sat next to him, with Hunter taking the seat straight opposite his boss. Looking at Kane and Sam side by side, it was obvious they were related in some way. The two sergeants had not yet arrived, having stopped to buy candy at the kiosk.

"So, Kane, what do you think so far? Did you look at the documents?" asked Hunter.

"Took a quick peak while we were in line at security. Just papers, for 'in and out' of the country, that kind of thing," replied Kane matter-of-factly. He edged the cigarettes from the pocket in the back of his jeans, and was about to pull the lighter out, as well.

"You can't smoke in here, Kane!" reminded Hunter.

"Since when?" retorted Kane.

"Since a month ago when you were here! Since never, boss! You know that," added Hunter sarcastically.

"Speaking of vices, how much did you drink this morning?" added Sam.

Kane turned and stared at his son. "Since when has that been any of your business? If you must know, two, not that it is any of your fucking concern."

"It is my concern, if it affects you, or this mission."

"Well, I am not affected as you can plainly see, and I intend to have another drink on the plane, if that's okay with you? And, to put your mind at rest, it's nothing to do with the side effects of heroin, or lack of it. I just want a drink," he paused. "I have a lot of shit going on in my life right now. I just need..." Kane stopped speaking. He realized, himself, he had said 'need'. He didn't say anymore, but he could sense, without looking, that both men were watching him as he spoke.

Feeling like a caged tiger, Kane leaned back in the seat. He was like an animal ready to spring at the slightest provocation, a fact that Sam had not yet figured out.

The sergeants arrived on cue, and sat in the chairs next to Hunter. Tyrone and Corey looked more than happy to be away from the general. Fact being, they seemed happy to be with each other, period.

Sam noticed it, and thought perhaps they were dating. He guessed them to be in their late twenties, Tyrone possibly older. Corey, especially, was laughing and glanced at their commander to see if he was paying attention to that fact. She looked disappointed that his eyes were closed. She looked closer at this man that was to lead them to Iraqi territory. For a white guy, Corey conceded, he was very attractive, from his snakeskin boots to the long blond hair. He was built solidly, but not heavily, and his jeans fit him very well. She had never seen such long hair on a man, but to call him feminine would have been suicidal, and from the angle she was sitting, he was certainly all man.

Feeling he was being stared at again, Kane opened his eyes, and looked in her direction. He winked at her without even thinking about it. Corey smiled, and blushed. Tyrone missed it. Sam didn't and neither did Hunter and what it spelled…was trouble.

"Will passengers for flight 345 to Abu Dhabi please prepare to board, starting with first class, followed by rows twenty to thirty-five." The P. A. system echoed round the airport lounge.

The group rose up from their seats and headed for the ticket clerk and then the ramp to the plane. Kane made his way through the cabin till he reached row twenty-two. There he stretched up and pushed his backpack into the hold, peeled his jacket off and stuffed that in there, too. The two young blond girls in the row behind could not fail to notice him. Neither could the brunette in the row opposite them. He smiled politely at the admiring glances.

"You always get looked over like that, *dad*?" asked Sam.

"Mostly," answered Kane. Changing the subject, Kane said, "One of you guys want the window seat? I prefer to take the aisle. I have longer and older legs."

"Yeah and you can get in and out better, too!" muttered Hunter.

"Meaning?" replied Kane, almost playfully.

"You know what I mean, Kane," retorted Hunter.

Kane laughed, and sat down next to his son.

The sergeants sat in the row across the aisle. Tyrone on the aisle seat, and then Corey next to him.

With seat belts fastened, the flight took off into the afternoon drizzle. Once in the air, the plane leveled off after banking, and turned to head for the city of Abu Dhabi.

Kane pulled the magazine from the back of the seat in front of him. A few pages in, his eyes closed and the magazine fell onto his lap. He drifted into a contented sleep, his head falling back on the seat. He dozed peacefully for a while, when suddenly, without warning, he lunged forward in the seat.

"Kelly!" and his eyes were wide open. Sweat ran down his face and for a second he was disoriented.

"Kane, are you ok?" asked a concerned Sam. He leaned over to his father.

"Yeah, yeah. I'm fine. Just dreaming!" and Kane tried to get it together. "I must not fall asleep again. Every time it happens…" he muttered.

"What happens? What happens when you fall asleep?" Sam inquired, looking at his father.

"I dream…Never mind what I dream. Just nightmares." Kane became quiet. "Gonna find the bathroom," and he undid his seatbelt and left his seat.

Sam turned in the seat to Hunter.

"Has this been happening for long?"

"Ever since she left. He thinks I don't know what happens when he falls asleep, but I do," Hunter whispered. "Couple of times he has called out like that. The one time I asked him what the dream was about."

"And?" Sam peered at Hunter

"He said it was nothing. But I heard what he said." He leaned closer to Sam. "He said he killed Kelly."

"*What?*" Sam was astonished.

"He shot her. In his dream, he shot her dead!"

Chapter 8

S am leaned back in his seat. Would this nightmare never end for his father? He rested his head on his fingertips, and waited for Kane to return. Hunter was looking out of the window staring at nothing.

Kane returned in a few minutes, after stopping to share a moment with the two blonds in the row behind him. He just wanted to see if he had lost his touch with women…he hadn't. He glanced down at Tyrone, who looked like he wanted to hide. So, he had seen the outburst over Kelly. Kane wondered if Corey had heard. She turned her head from reading her magazine to look up at him. He figured she had.

Kane sat down and refastened his seatbelt. Even though the sign was not lit, he buckled it anyway.

"You okay?" asked Sam.

"Fine," and he dismissed the topic. "Did I miss the drinks?" asked Kane, knowing full well he couldn't have, and pulled another magazine from the seatback.

It was a hell of a long flight to Abu Dhabi. They all dozed, except Kane. He drank a couple of small bottles of wine, aircraft size. He read the magazines from cover to cover and went over the documents, again. He also pocketed the money that was in the envelope; something he omitted to tell the rest of the party about. Kane closed his eyes a couple of times, and each time his thoughts slipped to Kelly. He wondered why so much. Was it because they were on their way to find her, or was she trying in their typical way that he and Kelly had, to communicate with him? This time he wasn't sure.

Turbulence brought him back to reality. At almost forty-thousand feet, winds became increasingly stronger, sending the large plane slightly off course. It bounced on the air's current, and the thick steel fuselage shuddered under the pressure. The fasten-seat-belt signs popped on and the captain's voice echoed through the plane.

"Please return to your seats, fasten your seat belts, immediately. Flight attendants, take your seats. We have a very strong storm system."

Everyone in Kane's near vicinity seemed to be seated. He remembered seeing Corey head to the bathroom. He glanced at her seat which was still empty. As the plane lurched to the right, some of the passengers seemed to panic a little, and several children on the flight screamed. The plane lurched again the other way and dropped several thousand feet. There was a loud scream from the bathroom and Kane heard it above the other noise.

Kane didn't hesitate. Undoing his seat-belt, he slipped into the aisle and took off for the restroom, holding onto anything he could. He made it to the bathroom and banged hard on the door. No answer.

"Corey, open the damn door!"

No reply. He tried the door and found it to be locked tight.

"Corey, can you hear me?" Kane yelled. "If you can, move away from the door!"

Kane figured she had somehow leaned on the door and wedged it shut. The occupied sign was on.

When the plane lurched, Corey fell against the door, jamming it, and then fell back against the closed toilet.

From the outside, Kane could hear nothing from her. He braced himself and hurled his full body weight against the door, sending it off the track and to one side.

Corey sat on the closed seat, blood staining her forehead, and she was badly dazed. Kane reached in the doors, pulled her forward onto his body, where her long black hair dropped onto his shoulders. With his arms round her, he managed to get her into the aisle. The fresh lotions she had just used from the dispensers in the bathroom smelled good to him. *She* smelled good to him, and he was distracted for a moment by holding a woman in his arms. Her breasts were right against his chest, and Kane could feel emotions in him that he normally reserved for Kelly. He was shocked by his own feelings of lust.

Corey moaned by his ear, and Kane came back to his senses.

"You're safe. Don't panic. I have you," reassured Kane.

With her head resting on his shoulder, he edged his way down the aisle, with one arm round Corey and the other holding onto anything he could. As Kane reached row twenty-two, he could see Tyrone standing by his seat waiting to help.

"Move to the other seat! I need her in the end one," stated Kane.

Tyrone slid across as Kane maneuvered Corey into the aisle seat. He sat her down and she flopped backwards, her eye lashes fluttering. She was more in than out, but the gash on her head seemed pretty bad. Kane bent down in the aisle next to her seat, only letting his legs bend as far as his tight jeans would allow.

As quickly as the turbulence started, it quit.

"Thank god," muttered Hunter. "That incident even scared me! You need any help over there, Kane?" he asked, leaning round to get a better look at the situation.

"Think *my father* is doing just fine on his own!" Sam added sarcastically, staring a hole through Kane.

Kane had turned to look at Hunter, and flashed a steely-eyed look of disapproval, and resumed looking at Corey's wound. He ignored his son's comments, making his only concern one of his team member's condition.

Tyrone handed Kane some tissues from his backpack. As Kane dabbed Corey's forehead, the wound seemed more bruised than bleeding.

"Corey, are you okay?" asked Kane looking into her face.

"Yes, sir," she whispered. "My head hurts. What happened?" and she put her hand on the side of her head.

"Turbulence. You were in the bathroom and hit your head. I pulled you out. End of story."

"Right, sir. I remember now, I thought you…" and she stopped, realizing her boyfriend was listening to every word. She did remember, and far more than Kane had just told everyone. But, by the look on his face, he expected her to keep quiet about it.

"I remember falling against the door, then nothing till back here in the seat. I'll be fine, sir. Been through far worse things that this," she added.

"Of course you will, sergeant," he whispered, and handed her the tissues. "Tyrone, look after her for me, will you? Can't have one of the team incapacitated."

Kane moved to his own seat, sat down and turned to his son. "Don't you say one fucking word about what just happened," Kane hissed at Sam.

"No, sir," replied a rather amused Sam, and pulled a magazine from the rack in front of him and pretended to read it.

Normality seemed to come back to the flight. Once more cabin service, which was rudely interrupted by turbulence, was resumed. Kane was glad. He needed a drink or something to take his mind off the situation. Kane was ashamed of himself, knowing his only excuse was that he missed Kelly terribly.

When the drink trolley finally reached row twenty-two, Kane asked for two small bottles of wine. One went down right after the other. Now, he could sleep, more like slip into a slightly hazy wine-related slumber. While he slept, dinner was served. Sam thought about waking Kane, and decided against it. He figured right now he needed sleep more than food.

Kane finally awoke to Sam poking him in the ribs.

"We'll be landing shortly, Kane. You slept for a couple of hours. Feel any better?"

"Yeah, actually I do," and he glanced across to Corey to see how she was doing.

Tyrone was fussing over her like a mother hen, which only confirmed the group's thoughts that they were dating. Perhaps she didn't remember the reaction he had had to her, a situation that he certainly wasn't going to let happen again. Somehow, he thought she did remember.

The landing was far better than the flight and they touched down without further incident. The next flight from Abu Dhabi to Kuwait was very short, not even an hour, but there was a break in between of a good three hours.

Grabbing their backpacks from the overhead bins, and allowing the two blonds from the row behind him to go first, Kane led his party from the plane. Sam raised an eyebrow at his father. It never ceased to amaze him how Kane took centre stage. Sam also noted that Hunter seemed jealous of that fact, by the looks he gave Kane, when he thought no one was looking.

It was chilly when they stepped from the plane into the airport; and the air conditioning was in full swing even with temperatures low outside. The first thing Kane wanted to do was eat. The meals on the plane had been few and far between, due mainly to the turbulent flight and him sleeping. The first eatery Kane saw in the airport lounge was a McDonalds.

"That'll do, mate. Let's go eat," and he pointed his finger in the direction of the golden arches that sprung up to let him know the place was civilized.

"McDonalds? Can't we go somewhere a little more adventurous, Kane?" asked Hunter. "This is Abu Dhabi. They have to have more than McDonalds."

Kane was halfway across the marble flooring to the glittering food court.

"Kane, we have to have currency, we…" Hunter's voice trailed off in Kane's ears.

"Got that," Kane's distant voice came back to him.

"How did he get that?" asked Tyrone.

"You don't ask questions like that, sergeant. He is Kane. What Kane wants, Kane gets!" replied his son.

"I noticed that on the plane," remarked Tyrone with meaning.

So, he had seen the looks between Kane and Corey.

Later, he would mention that comment to Kane. All he could do for now was to follow his father. As he walked, Sam wondered if Kane had told them all about his son. He was pretty sure that Hunter would know, but Tyrone and Corey probably would not. Maybe, for now, it was better that they didn't. Kane normally played his hand close to his chest. Sam started to laugh.

"Something funny there, Mr. Branson?" asked Tyrone as they walked side by side.

"Actually, yes, but I don't think you would see the funny side of it," and Sam looked away as they continued walking. Sam had been on the right side of the aisle to see exactly what had happened at the bathroom door.

The party caught up with its commander at the entrance to Mc-Donalds. Kane handed his backpack to Sam, and pulled money out of the inside of his jacket.

"Second thoughts, let's keep the cash and use credit for now. What does everyone want to eat? Big sign up there on the wall…pick some food out. It's in Arabic and English. Thank god! Then again, we have Corey with us to translate and to order for us. Right, Corey?" he asked, not even looking her way.

"Right, comm…." she started to reply.

"Kane. The name is Kane from now on. Never know who is watching and listening from now on in and back home." He looked up at the sign declaring what tender morsels they could get to eat. There was hardly any line and Kane walked up to be waited on. "Three big Mac's please, with fries, and a large coke."

"We can't call you Kane, sir…" stated Tyrone, grabbing a tray.

"Why the fuck not? It's my name."

"I know that sir, but…" replied the sergeant.

"Then, what's the problem, Tyrone? Just do it!" added Kane with a hint of annoyance, and turned back to the counter to pay for his meal. "Anyone want anything while I'm paying?"

"Kane, your credit card is gonna give away your ID, sir," stated Hunter, stepping forward and into the conversation.

"Nope. Never does!" and he flashed it before Hunter's eyes. It read simply, Kane.

"Had this thing from way back. You didn't look at my ID properly did you? Some day I will explain why it's like that. Goes back to when I met Kelly, long story. Point is, it gives nothing away, and never will." He slid his card across the greasy counter-top and into the hands of a tall, dark gentleman, who looked like he had stepped out of a crime magazine.

The McDonalds had started to fill up a little with other flights landing, and folks needing food. All nationalities poured into the golden arches, most accompanied by screaming kids.

"Let's grab a table and eat this stuff, before there is nowhere to sit…" as he was finishing the sentence, the cell in his boot beeped. The cell phone didn't quit. He put his food down on the table, and retrieving the cell, answered it. He knew before he looked at the number who was calling him. He flipped the cell open.

"You arrived, commander," asked General Tucker.

"Not yet. Still in Abu Dhabi. Just about to eat. Need anything in particular, *Mr.* Tucker? And how did you get my cell number?" he whispered into the phone, his face creased in displeasure. "It's classified!"

"I have my ways." Tucker replied.

"And I have my ways of blocking you! So, goodbye, *sir.*"

"Don't hang up, Branson!" He yelled. "I have some news for you. Soon as you left, we received some information that you might want to know about."

"Can't imagine there is anything I would want to hear from you right at this minute. I need to eat!" Kane informed Tucker. He picked at the carton of steamy but greasy fries, pulled one out and ate it.

"You asked how I got the cell number. Dan gave it me. Right after your flight left, there was a package delivered to the house." Tucker went quiet on the end of the line.

Kane held his breath and the whole of McDonalds disappeared from his view. He knew what Tucker was going to say, so Kane said it for him.

"Show it me!" and he held the phone so only he could see the video come up on the screen. It showed Kelly, or what looked like Kelly. She was bloody, bound and gagged, with her head hanging down, and what looked like the dirt-bag of a man Kane remembered as Ryan Holden, pulling her head up by her matted hair. Two eyes looked at the camera, staring into his very soul, as she was searching for something she had lost. The video stopped abruptly. He put the phone back to his ear.

"Is she still alive?" he whispered, holding the phone close to his mouth. "Is she?" his voice got louder.

"I'm not sure, Kane. I am really not sure. All you can do is find out for yourselves," whispered the voice on the end of the phone.

"Is the 'package' in Kuwait?" Kane spoke with his brain and not with his voice.

"It will be when you get there. Kane, be careful!"

Kane, closed the phone, replaced it in his boot, left the food on the table, and walked silently and alone out the restaurant.

Now, the other side of Kane kicked in, a side the enemy didn't want to see, for a man had just lost his reason for living.

Chapter 9

"Kane, where are you going? Kane, I..." and Sam's voice trailed off behind him.

"What the hell happened on that call?" he asked Hunter. "Who was it?" He was utterly perplexed, and set his food tray next to Kane's and followed his father. "Kane, slow down...who was that?" Sam yelled.

Kane stopped walking and turned to look at Sam. Kane's mouth moved but his eyes were blank. "It was a video of Kelly. Ryan was holding her head..." he could not finish describing what he had seen. "I will kill him little by little till he begs to die..."

"Kane, was that Tucker on the cell phone? Was it?" asked Sam, his eyes near to slits, and his hand on his father's shoulder.

"Yes. Dan gave him the number. Why?" Kane peered at his son. "What are you thinking? Say something rather than standing there just staring at me? Not coincidence was it, that we were just off the plane and I was about to eat?"

"No, I don't think so. Either a damn good guess or someone is feeding info back to Tucker." Sam paused. "It isn't you, and it isn't me. That leaves Hunter, your new girlfriend Corey, and Tyrone."

"Cut the crap about Corey. What happened...happened. Nothing more to it than that.

I'm not dead!" declared Kane, very aware of his own masculinity.

"Obviously! But I hope she doesn't think anything of it...her boyfriend does. Apparently, he noticed, and he is not too happy about it."

"Fucking wonderful. Well, we can't worry about that situation." Kane looked at his watch. Two more hours till they would even board the plane. "I left food back there. I need to eat, I'm hungry..."

Sam produced the bags of fries and hamburgers he had grabbed when he left the trays behind. He handed his father his and the two headed for the nearest seats. Kane sat down and devoured the food like a refugee. He realized just how hungry he was. Greasy fries and an overcooked hamburger didn't quite fill the gap. He looked around for a trash bin.

"I'll get that," and Sam took the empty carton from his father. He nursed the trash.

"Aren't you going to dump that?" asked Kane, wiping a spot of ketchup that had dripped onto his jeans.

"Yes." He paused. This seemed as good a time as any to bring up the concern that Sam had. "Do they know who I am, Kane? I mean, aside from your son. Did you ever tell anyone, except Kelly?"

"That's a bloody funny question?" Kane paused. Maybe it wasn't so funny. "You think they know? How could they? The only one that could would be Hunter, and he is not high-ranking enough. I made sure he didn't find out through regular means. I doubt that anyone knows, not even Tucker. Unless..."

"Unless Kelly was persuaded to talk? Was that what you were going to say?" asked Sam.

"Yeah. Exactly," replied a concerned Kane, pulling his hair back with a band.

"Could they find that out from her? Would she give it away under pressure," his son asked, more than concerned.

"I doubt it. Kelly is tough, real tough. She has to be to live with me." For a brief second, he smiled. "It is a well kept secret who you are. Anyone else on that mission to Hong Kong is either dead or inaccessible. The AFP made it so, so did the Chinese government. With your mother dead, Inspector Chow covered everything in Lantau well, unless, someone has been watching you, too. Somehow, I doubt it. So, we will assume for now your cover is safe. And...you are the only one I totally trust out here," Kane said with finality.

"I have your back. You know that, don't you, Kane?" Sam glanced side-wards at his father.

"Yeah, I know that...bloody fine son I have." He placed his arm around Sam's shoulders, a gesture he did not make very often to men.

"I just wish that I had known I had a son. All those years, and I never knew. Thirty-five of them. Missed all that!"

"Yes, me, too. I always wondered what you were like. I knew that Colonel Cheng was not my father, only married to my mother. Lilia told me just enough, but I could never find out anymore than that. I do know she loved you more than her own life. She proved that to you in Hong Kong, when she gave her life for you." Sam dropped his head just a little. "You took her heart and never gave it back."

Kane had heard that before. "Yeah, real proud of that fact, too. I seem to make a habit of hurting the ones I love the most; Lilia, my first wife Sage Jay, my oldest daughter, you, and now Kelly. Is it some kind of knack I have or something? I can't get around women without leaving some sort of blazing trail. I wonder how many more kids I have that I don't know about? Sad, isn't it? My morals leave a lot to be questioned!"

"Yes, you do blaze trails, and I seem to be picking up that habit from you. Like father like son, *dad*," he blurted out. "You're gonna be a grandfather!" Sam had not meant to tell Kane like that. It just came out, and it seemed Kane could use some good news.

"I'm gonna be a what?" Kane looked staggered. "You got married and didn't tell me?"

"No marriage. Sita is a wonderful girl whom I met six months ago at a party in Hong Kong. Asian, dark hair, very pretty, a lot like my mother. Like father, like son!" and Sam smiled. "Only I will know this kid...I mean..." Sam could have bitten off his own tongue.

"It's okay," Kane smiled, "you're right...congratulations. Funny your kid will only be about three years younger than his uncle. Hope I get to meet Sita one day." He thought about that for a minute; his sons and his daughters, especially Star, lead his thoughts, back to Kelly, and he fell silent.

"We'll get her out Kane, and the other woman. Reese Wade? How does she fit in with you and Kelly? I know you said you killed her or pretended to, but there is more isn't there?" With Kane there was always more. Nothing was ever what is seemed.

"Reese fell in love with me. For once, I didn't think with my dick. I told her, another time and another place and things may have been different, but that was then, and Kelly was on my mind, and still is. Reese helped me get Kelly out of her own father's compound in OZ. I had gone there on behalf of the AFP, to bring down the five drug dealers responsible for my wife's death. But, when I didn't respond to Reese, she called Miles Stratton, American drug baron, one of the five men, and told him where we were hiding out, only she left my name off the list. It got complicated. I killed Kelly's father, because he shot Kelly, and found out years later that he wasn't her real father, that a man named Jimmy Rogers, head of Mercedes Racing, was. Kelly and I went to the States to find Miles Stratton, only to discover that Reese was his girlfriend. He had me *kill* her to prove I was a *real bad ass*. This deed let me get close to him and his little band, one that soon met their end. Stratton escaped. I chased him over half the world, and killed him. End of story. Kelly and I lived happily.... well, almost." Kane stopped abruptly. He said the whole thing so matter-of-fact.

"Wow, you don't do things by half do you, Kane? No wonder your life is so complicated. When you came to Lantau on the hundredth mission..." he had to ask. "Were you also looking to kill me?" He needed to know.

Kane looked into the face of his oldest son. "Yes. I came to kill you, because you were a Chinese agent pushing drugs into Australia, or so I thought. But, I was wrong. You were on our side. And you still are, and that's why the others must never know. They think you are just my son. They don't know that you are a double agent, or any kind of agent." Kane thought for a moment. "There is something else you need to know. The heroin and the things I told you about the heart attack...it's not quite the truth. I have a..." His sentence was cut short.

"Kane!" yelled Hunter as he and the sergeants caught up to them. "What the heck is going on?"

"Another time, son, another time," Kane declared forcefully, and stood up to greet the conquering heroes.

"Who was on the phone? Was it the general?" Hunter asked, almost agitated at not knowing.

Sam shot Kane a glance.

"Yeah, it was. Just something he wanted me to see." Kane did not want to explain exactly what he had seen. The least the others knew right now the better. He had confided in Sam and that was enough. "I need some more food." 'God, that sounded lame,' he thought. "Sam, you're still hungry too, right?"

"Of course. Let's go get some pie or something," Sam replied.

The two looked at each other like they were talking drivel, which they were. Sam raised his eyebrows to Kane, and father and son picked up their backpacks and started to another part of the food court. The others followed, not quite understanding what was going on.

Some kind of weird tasting pie and a couple of flat cokes later, they decided they had had enough food, and should probably start for the gate for the next flight. The hour was late, with their body clocks way off, and sleep was an after-thought now. They trekked through the seemingly never sleeping airport and found the right gate for the flight to Kuwait, and then sat down in the seats along with several other passengers.

Although only a short flight, it was a crucial leg of the trip. From there the U.S carrier would take them to Baghdad. There, they were on their own, literally. Kane knew where to pick up the packages, knew where to get a car, and that was it. They had a rough location on Ryan Holden, they would have guns and they had the sergeants, one of whom spoke Arabic. The rest was easy. Go in, get Kelly, get Reese and kill Ryan. Sounded easy, but it wouldn't be. Kane knew that.

He also knew that someone in the group was receiving information. Sam said it wasn't him. He was his son, but a son he had only known for five years. He wanted desperately to believe in this man. Hunter was AFP, through and through, but even they could turn out to be bad. He had no idea about the two Americans.

He did know that there was indeed a situation between himself and Corey, and there should not have been. He knew it at the house the first time he had seen her, and that was the reason he didn't want her on the mission. Kane knew it was only sexual, and he knew it was because there was no woman...he didn't have Kelly. But, it was no excuse. He was still trying to prove things to himself. He was on the plane with the blonds. Kane didn't give a shit about following

through on a situation, just that he could still pull it off. The reason...
Kelly was thirty and he wasn't. He was scared to death he would lose
her. When he was seventy, she would be forty, and these thoughts
had been nagging at him for a long time, even though to the outside
world he was so blatantly arrogant of his masculinity.

In his mind, Kane was formulating plans. Soon, they would be in
Kuwait. He had the name of the U.S carrier, and hoped that the carrier
really did know his team was coming. He wondered under what pre-
tense they were supposed to be traveling. So far, no one had questioned
anything about their travel. The cover seemed to be fine, and even if
it wasn't, Ryan Holden knew he was coming. Ryan had waited a long
time for just such a situation where he could get even with Kane.

When Kane shot Peta, Ryan had laughed insanely. Kane had
wanted to shoot Ryan to rid the earth of scum like him, but the
two soldiers that were with them that night had persuaded him not
to. They were both scared to death of Ryan Holden. Ryan couldn't
threaten Kane and he couldn't break him. How Kane wished he had
killed Ryan, and done the world a favor. One of the two men was Simon Harris, a man who was first cousin to Ryan, and a man who had
haunted Kane through most of his life. His brother was Giles Harris,
someone who had known both himself and Sam; and someone who
Kane had personally killed in Hong Kong, after Giles wiped out most
of Kane's team in Hong Kong, leaving just Sam and Kelly alive.

Simon died some years later, but Kane had had the pleasure of
bringing him down for committing murder in Nam, something that
Kane was blamed for and cleared of. The memory haunted Kane, and
so did Vietnam, and anything that was associated with it.

Kane considered his whole life maybe an episode of Vietnam. He
had never stopped killing from those days on, and here he was about
to do it again.

Kane switched his mind back from Vietnam to Iraq. With Ryan
holding Kelly, he at last had the upper hand. What he didn't have
was Kane, and he certainly didn't have Kane's son, and he wondered
had he done right by bringing Sam with him. He needed Sam to take
Kelly home, and he was the only one he could trust that task to, now
that he had left Dan at home to look after his children.

Kane watched his son. A blond Asian man, tall and slim, with porcelain skin like Lilia, tough as his father, Sam was all Kane could want in a son. How he wished Lilia had contacted him to let him know she was pregnant, and how he knew she couldn't. Missed opportunities.

Kane smiled at he sat watching Sam. Maybe, he had left a legacy after all.

Chapter 10

Kane closed his eyes for five minutes and was brought back to reality by the harsh tones of the loud speaker announcing boarding for their flight. Standing, Kane hoisted the backpack onto his shoulders, while the group approached the gate to board the flight bound for Kuwait. The flight was to be short and supposedly uneventful.

While waiting to board, Kane noticed a young woman a few feet in front of him. She was maybe twenty-seven, twenty eight years of age, not too tall, with blond hair that seemed to have endless curls in it. She was dressed in tight blue jeans and a low-cut T-shirt that, when she turned round in his direction, showed an extensive amount of cleavage. Kane could hardly miss this fact, but as his eyes moved upwards to her face passing pretty pink lips, her sparkling eyes danced on her face. At first glance, she looked a lot like Kelly. Even at a second glance, she did.

As Kane walked a little further, he commented to Sam. "When you get on the plane, take a look at the young blond woman in the jeans and T-shirt."

"Kane, for god's sake! Think more about your wife, than blonds walking…" Sam was stopped by Kane's hand on his arm.

"Sam…just fucking take a look at her!" Kane said with venom, and stormed away from his son and onto the plane.

Inside the plane, the seating was two and two. Kane's ticket showed a window seat and as he approached row 26, he could see a head in 26A where his head should be, and he approached the seat with a certain caution.

Sam took his seat next to Hunter, and yet again, the Americans sat next to each other.

Kane stuffed his backpack in the overhead compartment and leaned down to 26A.

"Excuse me, miss, I think you are in my seat," he stared at her as if he didn't believe the situation.

"I am sorry. It was empty and I didn't think anyone would mind." She pulled her purse and jacket together and attempted to move. Her Australian accent was very evident.

"My mistake. I am actually supposed to be in 26B," Branson replied and as he sat down, fastened his seat belt. He was still shocked by the girl next to him and felt someone tugging on his arm.

"My seatbelt seems to be stuck." The girl looked pitifully at him.

Branson had the distinct feeling that it wasn't, and that she just wanted to attract his attention. It worked.

"Pull the straps from under you," he suggested.

"They are stuck," she replied, as the blond tugged on them.

"'Scuse me," and Kane reached over her lap and tugged at the belt. It moved, like he knew it would.

"Thanks, Mister...?" Her well mascaraed eyelashes fluttered as she spoke.

"Kane. The name's Kane."

Kane felt as if he was playing back the past in slow motion, almost on rewind. He glanced across the isle to his son, who first stared at him, and then at the girl.

Sam screwed his eyebrows at his father, and mouthed the words, 'who is she', across the aisle to Kane.

Kane couldn't answer, just shook his head. He turned his attentions back to the blond in 26A.

"Need anymore help there?" Kane asked her.

"Yeah, the stupid thing won't grip properly. Am I doing something wrong here?"

From where Kane sat there was nothing wrong. "You just need to slot it in properly..." Kane stopped. Was she flirting with him? He wasn't sure.

She raised her hands in the air, admitting defeat, and smiled a precocious smile at him. *She was flirting.* He slid his hands across her and fastened the belt, and then sat back in his seat to wait for the next move.

"Thanks, Kane," and stuck her hand out to him.

He shook her hand. She was warm to the touch, and the more he looked at her the more she looked like Kelly. They were disturbed by the cabin crew announcing their departure. The aircraft took off at a good speed, was soon high in the sky and climbing rapidly. Kane looked back at Sam, who leaned towards him.

"You look like you have seen a ghost, Kane. Did you find out who she is? The resemblance to Kelly is staggering!"

"Yeah, I noticed. The dialogue that just took place, it was something like Kelly and I said when we first met. It's eerie! Can't explain it. Déjà vu." Kane stopped speaking, feeling that he was being watched. He was, by more than one woman. Corey was also watching with interest. He smiled at her and turned back to his new friend. She in turn smiled at Kane.

"So, Miss…Where are you heading?" he asked, undoing his seat belt, now that the sign was switched off.

"Baghdad," came the short reply.

'Interesting,' thought Kane "And what takes you there?" asked Kane cautiously.

"Thought I would surprise my father. He's stationed out there. Well, I hope he is still there, anyway." She paused. "Oh, sorry, I didn't give you my name. It's Sarah, Sarah Holden."

Kane's heart missed a beat. He stared at the girl. It wasn't possible. How many Australians would be traveling to Baghdad named Holden, and ones that looked like his wife, and were on the same plane as his group? Too much of a coincidence. He decided to find out more.

"Your father wouldn't be Ryan Holden would he?" Long shot, or so he thought.

Sarah Holden looked astounded. "Yes," she stammered. "He would. How on earth did you know that?"

God, how did he know that? "Wild guess…would you believe? Actually, I was in the military once. Knew a man by that name, that's how. When did you see your father last?" Kane asked, hoping to god it was way back.

"Over a year ago, maybe more. I was on a year's traveling spree in Europe with my boyfriend, and we split up six months back. Didn't tell my father because he would have made me go back to Oz. I am a big girl and can take care of myself."

From where he sat, Kane could vouch for that. He continued, "So you haven't seen your parents in a while then really?" Real long ball.

"I didn't know my mother. She died about a year after I was born. My father, apparently, never married her. There had been some sort of relationship between them, and my father brought me home to live with him, where I was raised by a nanny. I have a step-mom and a step-brother and sister. My dad was away most of the time while I was growing up, so I really don't know him too well."

"Ah," was all Kane could muster at that given second. Trying to make sense of this situation was impossible. Why would she be on that flight on the very day they were? Was she a plant, or was it pure coincidence? Right now he had no idea. What he did know was that he should tread lightly with this young woman, one because he didn't know quite who she was, and the other, he didn't need enemies in his own camp. The more he looked at Sarah, the more Kelly tugged at his heart strings. Could it be possible they were related? He really hoped not.

"Drink, sir?" asked the steward.

"What?" replied Kane, shaken from his thoughts.

"I asked if you would like a drink, sir. Water, orange juice, wine…"

"Wine, make it two," Kane wanted a drink. Correction. Kane needed a drink.

The steward handed Kane two small bottles of wine. Then, Kane remembered his manners. "Sarah?"

"Sure, I'll take one of them from you," and she pulled on the bottles from his hand.

"Not quite what I had in mind, but that's ok…" and he reached onto the drinks tray for another wine.

"Sir, I …" and the tall, lanky steward decided maybe it wasn't a good idea to argue with the man in seat 26B.

Kane's look was enough to stop the man in his tracks, and he hurriedly pushed the cart to row 27.

"Thanks for the wine, Kane," laughed Sarah.

"Most welcome," and undid the top on his first bottle of wine. It didn't last long. And the second one also went down well.

"You always drink that fast?" asked Sarah, as she sipped hers in a more sedate fashion.

"Only when I sit next to pretty women..." Had he really said that out loud? Did he consider that being careful?

Sarah blushed. Finishing her wine, she leaned back in her seat, and began fiddling in her purse. Kane had seen Kelly do that many times. All roads led back to his wife.

"So, Kane, what is your destination?" she said, while painting her lips a pretty shade of pink again.

"Kuwait." He didn't want her to know they were going on to Baghdad, not right now. Kuwait was the truth, and he doubted she would be on the same flight with them to Baghdad, not with a military company like his group was. Remembering his group, he hadn't introduced her to the rest of them. Maybe, that wasn't a good idea. He wondered if she had seen him exchange words with Sam. But, to announce to Ryan Holden's daughter that this was his son, may not be the best decision he ever made.

"On your own?" she asked him.

Was she reading his mind or something? "No. Might lay over a while there, might not. Depends what the others want to do," replied Kane.

"Others? How many of you are there? Sarah asked him, curious, while slipping her jacket round herself in the coolness of the aircraft.

"Couple. The two guys across the isle. We are archeologists. We dig up things!" Well, that was true. They were going to dig things up...her father!

Kane turned to his son. "Sam, I would like you to meet Sarah Holden. Sarah, Sam, a fellow archeologist."

Sam looked at Kane as if he had lost all reasoning, but nodded to the woman anyway.

"And the guy with the dark hair is Mr. Hunter..." and Kane shrugged his shoulders at them as if to say, 'what the hell do I tell her?'

Sarah leaned over Kane, her T-shirt dropping an inch down as she did. "Hi, guys. Name's Sarah Holden. Nice to meet you blokes. Kane tells me you are going digging in Kuwait."

"Right, yep, something like that," replied Hunter.

"Kane, aren't you going to introduce us," added Corey peering through the two seats in front of the guys.

"Oh, yeah, forgot about you two! Corey and Tyrone. They are helping us with the dig." He paused for effect. "They are a couple!" He hoped that had cleared him with Tyrone for good, and as he turned his head, he caught the look that Corey shot him.

"Glad to meet you all. I am going on to Baghdad. Going to see my father."

"Aren't we all," echoed Sam.

"Sorry?" Sarah asked.

"Nothing," commented Sam.

Kane leaned over to Sam. "It's not her fault she has a shit for a father. She may even come in useful later..."

"For you, Kane, maybe...sorry. That was unfair." Sam wished he had not said that. He remembered Kane and Kelly back in Hong Kong, and he knew that this was just an   act. Sam looked into his father's eyes, and could see the pain that lingered there. But there was more, something else that Kane had not told him.

If Kane could have smacked his son, he would have. If Kane could have told him the whole truth, he would have.

"What the hell is Kane doing?" whispered Hunter to Sam, leaning across the arm rest.

"I am sure he knows. Kane always knows. There is always a reason behind everything he does. I learned that from him in Hong Kong." This time, though, Sam wondered exactly what that reason was.

As Sam looked back to his father, Kane was refastening his seat belt. As he pulled the belt round him he caught it on his side. Sam saw Kane flinch, and for a second or two Sam thought he saw Kane hold his breath. Then, Kane continued to do up the belt. He felt a new concern. There was more. Something that Kane had not told him. He knew Kane had had a heart attack, he knew Kane had broken his ribs before. Maybe that was it, and maybe it wasn't. But he knew now to watch his back even more than before. He wondered how much Hunter knew, and maybe he should find out.

He turned to his traveling partner. "Did you tell me everything about Kane outside the house the other night?"

"What the hell is that supposed to mean?" replied Hunter with caution.

"He was going to tell me earlier tonight in the airport and you all appeared from nowhere." Sam pushed his long hair from his eyes and continued. "What else is wrong with Kane? Something with his chest."

"Heart attack. He told you that didn't he?"

"Yeah, he told me that. And right now, I don't believe that's what's wrong with him. Tell me what else, god-damn-it." Sam was angry. He couldn't get any sense from this man next to him. "I am his son," he whispered near Hunter's ear.

"His son you may be. Confidant, obviously, you are not!" replied Hunter.

"You think you are?" retorted Sam, his Branson temper heating up a notch.

"Through and through," and Hunter smiled more than just a knowing smile.

"What are you to my father?" Sam sensed something and he was not quite sure what.

"What the fuck is that supposed to mean, *mate*?" asked Hunter. "You think I want to be more than an aide to your father?"

"You said that, not me. Do you? Kane's a good looking man. The *ladies* think so, anyway," retorted Sam.

"I wouldn't go saying that out loud, mate."

"I just did! You got a problem with that?" and Sam peered into Hunter's face, animosity growing.

"Yeah, I do! It's something you and I will settle later, my friend. Count on it!" and Hunter stopped speaking mainly because Kane was staring straight at him.

Sam turned towards his father, the arm rest getting slightly in his way, and forced a smile. "Should be landing soon, Kane. We should probably discuss the next stage of events." Sam picked his words carefully. He knew that both Hunter and Sarah were listening.

Sensing tension, Kane said, "Wanna take a quick stroll down the plane then, Sam?"

"Good idea, boss," and Sam undid his seatbelt and followed his father to the end of the plane. Sam also noted that more than one of the group watched Kane's walk.

"Shit!" said Hunter more out loud than he wished it to be. This wasn't how it was supposed to be. He hadn't wanted Sam there in the first place, but Kane had insisted that his son fly to Australia, and Hunter didn't have enough authority to stop it happening. Now, he had to contend with an offspring, something neither he nor the U.S. government wanted.

Chapter 11

"I wish we could still smoke on these tin cans." Kane felt the cigarettes in his back pocket.

"Bad habit, Kane. One of the ones you should really give up, amongst others!" stated his son.

The back of the plane wasn't that far from their seats, but far enough that they could not be heard.

"Point taken," Kane paused. "So, what were you and Hunter *discussing*? I could hear you. Not sure who else could. What the fuck is going on?" Kane raised his voice to slightly more than a whisper, but loud enough to get his point across.

"Hunter has his eye on you," joked Sam, looking at his father.

"Yeah, he is supposed to. He's a watch dog. After the heroin incident…" Kane stopped, aware of the look on Sam's face. "You don't mean what I think you mean, do you? Fucking hell, you do! Don't be so fucking stupid, man!" Kane happened to glance at the woman in the aisle seat. She was staring at him as if she wanted either Kane or his language to go away." Kane nodded apologetically at her and turned his back to her seat. "You are fucking joking, Sam. What do you want me to do about it? Are you sure? You must be mistaken," Kane added half glancing back at Hunter.

"I might be," he paused. "I called him out. Told me we would settle it later."

"Fucking wonderful. Jesus Christ! Corey, Sarah, now Hunter? A guy? Am I some sort of *homing devise*? This is getting fucking stupid, and…" Kane was obviously upset.

"Kane, calm down," said Sam. "It came up in a roundabout way. I asked him if he had told me everything that happened to you in Japan."

Kane flinched. Just for a second his father's guard was down, and then it was back.

"There was something you were going to say at the airport, and I saw you visibly flinch when your seatbelt hit your side. So, tell me." Sam waited for the usual curse words. They didn't come.

Kane dipped his head just slightly, and then raised it and looked into Sam's eyes.

"Remember in the house, I said I was going to trade myself?" asked Kane.

Sam nodded.

"The trade is easy. I am going to die."

"Now you are joking. Stop it! You're not joking are you?" asked Sam, not quite convinced.

"I think in the short time you have known me that I would not joke about something like that! You know me better, I hope." Kane leaned against the side door on the plane. "You want the truth about Japan? I didn't have any heart-attack, not then anyway. I was stabbed protecting someone, and if it had been a knife, I could have handled that. It was a shaft of a bamboo ceiling fan. Unfortunately, some of it broke off and when they tried to pull it out it moved nearer to my lung. So it stays there. Prognosis, there is a chance it will rot, and also the chances are it will move, and if it does…All *ifs*, I know…well, you get the gist of the conversation."

"And Hunter doesn't know all this because?" Sam asked, very curious why the right hand man didn't know.

"Because till now, no one knew, except the doctor who stitched me up and who also gave me heroin. Drugs are nothing to them in Japan, every day occurrence. I just wasn't used to them after all these years."

"Were you going to tell Kelly?" Sam looked Kane straight in the eyes, as he reached for the back of the seat, as the plane rocked just slightly, and started its descent.

"You mean had she been home?" responded Kane.

Sam nodded.

"I don't know. Am I going to tell her when we rescue her? No and neither are you. Are you?" Kane leaned towards his son, almost threatening.

"No, sir. But I also won't let you die out here either. It took me all those years to get a father," Sam paused, "and I am damned sure I am not gonna let you go that easily, you son-of-a-bitch!"

Kane was visibly shocked at his son's outburst. He didn't know what to say, an unusual occurrence for Kane. He shifted his stare away from his son and looked out of the plane windows. All he saw was blackness. He cleared his throat. "Good to know. Fucking good!"

Being the original tough cop, Kane, Sam figured, wasn't used to such emotions.

"Sam, promise me one thing."

"Depends," replied Sam.

"Just fucking promise me!" retorted Kane, lips curled in anger, not waiting for a reply. "Get Kelly home at all costs. No matter what it takes. You get her home. She is worth more than even my life."

Sam looked at his father. A man desperate to get this resolved, just in case.

"You have my word." Sam fell silent.

"The captain has turned on the *fasten seat belt* sign. Please take your seats for landing." The loud speaker echoed round the plane.

Father and son returned to their respective seats. Kane was extremely glad he wasn't sitting next to Hunter, as he had the feeling he may have just punched him out. For now, he had to shelve any feelings, hostile or otherwise, and focus on the task in hand. He turned his attentions to Sarah.

"Where were we? Any more problems with that seatbelt?" Kane asked the girl, as he fastened his belt again.

"Seems to be okay now." Sarah replied, trying to think of something to hold Kane's attention. "So where are you going to dig in Kuwait?"

"Did I say Kuwait, I meant Baghdad." More prudent maybe to keep her where they could see her.

"You did say Kuwait." Sarah looked confused.

"We have to stop in Kuwait. Get some things and then fly on." Sounded like a logical response.

"Then I can fly on with you. Great! I was worried about being on my own in Kuwait looking for a flight to Baghdad. It is okay to go with you, isn't it Kane?" Sarah was excited and it showed. She tugged her T-shirt down a tad to show him more cleavage.

He was stuck. Why hadn't he kept his mouth shut?

"Sure it is, right, Sam?" and he turned to his son and made a face at him.

"Anything Kane says is fine," Sam smiled at the young woman.

"Great! Say, you can meet my father!" and she laughed.

Kane almost choked. He regained his composure very well, and said, "Wonderful. You can introduce me." It really was deja vu. Hadn't this same thing happened with Kelly years ago?

"Of course, Kane. You look out for me and I look out for you," said Sarah as she applied yet more lipstick. "That's if it's okay with you, Kane?" She asked him almost bashfully. She had met this man only a couple of hours ago and she was throwing herself at him, and she knew it.

All Kane could do was agree. Out of the frying pan into the fire. Blazing trails yet again.

It was a good landing and an even better departure from the plane, fast and methodical. In the airport lounge in Kuwait, Kane's party regrouped. Hunter pulled Kane to one side.

"What are you doing, Kane?" asked Hunter. "We can't take her anywhere with us. We are going on a military flight. What are you thinking?"

"I think it's rather what you are thinking that worries me, Hunter. Worries my son, anyway, and if he is worried, so am I."

"Whatever he said to you, it is not true. You are my boss. That's all, I assure you!" Hunter lied, and turned his head away slightly.

"Then there is no problem is there? Just make sure it stays that way. And for your info, the girl goes with us. Better to have her in my sights than have her somehow get to her father before we do, don't you think?" Kane never faltered.

"Well, I guess you have a point, Kane. I'm sorry. I wasn't questioning your authority, but isn't she going to be in the way…" Hunter didn't get to finish the statement.

"Not in mine, she isn't! In fact, I think she may come in very useful, both she and Corey, but especially Sarah. She's pretty, blond, great figure, you know, just my type…" Kane rubbed in the fact that he was totally into women even further, and left Hunter standing alone with his backpack.

Sarah was gathering her bags together, when her purse, which was sitting very precariously on top of her backpack, spilled half of its contents onto the floor; lipstick, perfume, passport. So intent on picking up her toiletries, Sarah didn't notice Kane pick up her passport, and pocket it, when he helped her with her other fallen articles. Sam noticed and said nothing. Obviously, Kane was doing some checking on the girl other than seeing how great her body was in the tight clothes she wore. Even Sam noticed.

To the right of them, slightly away from the others, stood Tyrone, and Corey, who still looked a little confused at the day's events. Sam figured Corey was trying to understand Kane, something Sam couldn't even do after five years.

"Right then, mates, lets go find this airline that is gonna take us to Baghdad," and Kane swung his backpack, and Sarah's, up onto his shoulders, and headed towards the terminal entrance and baggage claim.

Sam smiled to himself. Kane's act was almost too good, and he hoped the others believed it. He watched Sarah take extra steps to catch up with her new found friend. Corey stared at her boss. As he passed by, Kane turned his head in her direction and winked at her. She blushed. Kane was playing both women and only Sam knew it. He hung back just a little mainly to watch his father's performance, but also to see how Hunter handled a rebuff from Kane.

Hunter turned to Sam with angry eyes. "What the fuck did you tell Kane?"

"Told him I didn't like you too much! And, I don't trust you, either! Too many things don't add up with you," stated Sam very plainly.

Hunter stared at Sam. He thought about hitting him, and thought better of it, especially with two army folk standing right there. He leaned towards Sam. "You *Chinese* don't mince words do you?"

It was all Sam could do not to punch Hunter out right there and then. Instead, he smiled.

"At least I know who and what I am, and like we said earlier, we will settle this later…one way or another, my friend!" and Sam walked away to find his father.

Kane and Sarah reached the baggage claim first.

"Don't you have to pick up some stuff from here?" Sarah asked, dumping her purse on the floor.

"Yeah. Should be at baggage claim waiting for us." He dropped both backpacks next to her purse and he took off round the carousel. One could not mix the bags up. His was grey and black, and hers was pink!

"Left you already, has he? Not surprised," stated Corey smiling, as she slipped up next to Sarah.

"Kane went to get some things…" and Sarah Holden realized she had competition. "Said he would be right back," as she primped her long hair.

The three men arrived together; Tyrone, Hunter and Sam, in that order.

"Where's Kane?" asked his son, looking round the people at the carousel.

"Went to look for some things," and from her purse Sarah retrieved a package of gum and unwrapped a stick of it. She popped the stick of delicious fruity gum into her mouth. Chewing it for a few moments, she blew a bubble out of her mouth, popping the gum just as Kane appeared around the corner of the carousel.

Kane stopped dead, and his pallor changed. All he saw was Kelly standing there, and was visibly shocked at the habit.

"Didn't I ask you not to do that…" He never finished the sentence. '*My god, she's not Kelly. No wonder they are all staring at me like someone in a freak show.*'

"Not do what, Kane?" asked Sarah looking slightly puzzled.

"Move away from your bag like that." He closed the sentence, and turned to his son. "Nothing waiting for us, not a fucking thing.

I thought Tucker said here!" Kane was visibly angry. He removed his jacket and threw it on top of the backpacks, revealing the thick tight sweater, and more of his tight jeans.

Sarah noticed.

"Maybe it will be in Baghdad, Kane," Hunter's voice responded to his boss.

"I fucking doubt it. I thought it was supposed to be here with the other luggage, which isn't here either." Kane was becoming agitated.

"Maybe it just hasn't come off the plane yet…" Sam said.

"Wasn't on our plane, Sam. Was supposed to be waiting for us here, wasn't it?" Kane looked puzzled. Maybe, he had remembered incorrectly the other day when Tucker was there at the house. It was a heroin day after all. But he thought he was correct about the subject. In fact, he knew he was. "We need those fucking packages, especially the one," he paused to see who was listening, "the ones with the maps. Hunter, would you go to the main desk and see if you can track them down?"

Hunter faced Kane, "Sure, boss. *Anything you want!*" Hunter took off across the airport back to Etihad Airlines to see if they knew anything about the missing packages.

"He's being a smart ass!" remarked Sam.

"Yeah, I know he is! But we do need these things big time. I think it may be our friend Mr. Tucker is two timing us," and Kane cut his eyes to the Americans, "right guys? Mr. Tucker didn't follow through on my request, did he? And he is now in possession of some very valuable items that we need. Did you know he was going to do this? Or is it just as much as a surprise to you two?"

"Surprise, s…, Kane. He has a lot of our stuff, too," and Tyrone glanced towards Sarah and back to Kane.

Kane knew Sarah was listening. If she was going to listen then he would make sure she heard what he wanted her to hear.

"Why don't I give him a call?" Kane retrieved the cell from his boot. Much to the amazement of Sarah, who had never seen a cell in a boot before. "Hand made, you know!"

"What?" she asked startled that he knew she was watching.

"The boots. Hand made. Special order!" Kane winked a serious wink at Sarah.

Sam smiled. His father was a master, and if Sarah had been listening carefully, Kane had imparted a very personal piece of information to her.

Kane redialed Tucker's number that was on his cell, and just as he figured, the line was no longer connected. He folded up the phone and replaced it back in his boot. "Line was busy," he lied.

As he spoke, Hunter appeared back across the floor from the Etihad desk. His look said it all.

"Let me guess. Nothing was on the plane, nothing is on any other plane, and nothing will be sent out for us. And as far as we are concerned, we are on our own. Right? No, don't answer! I know the fucking answer. We have to get our own stuff, because they don't want a paper trail, so to speak. Tucker's number is never going to work again, and we have been disowned by the U.S. government," Kane paused, "and they never heard of these two guys," he said looking at Tyrone and Corey.

Sarah looked from one to another. "What's going on, Kane? You aren't who you say you are, right? And what's the U.S. government got to do with anything?"

"Do we really look like archeologists? Course we aren't!" and he showed her his hands; rough, tough hands that certainly didn't caress porcelain remains. "We are mercenaries employed by the U.S. government to get hostages out of Baghdad, right Mr. Branson?" he asked his son.

"Right," replied Sam, somewhat stunned this time by Kane's antics.

Sarah laughed a precocious laugh. "Sure you are! I can tell that by the accent. You two are Australians like me! What the heck would you be doing with the U.S. government?"

"You don't believe me?" laughed Kane. "Just you wait and see. This, young lady, is gonna be the adventure of a lifetime. You, Sarah Holden, are gonna help us. You up for it?"

Now, Sam knew his father's game. He was gonna let Sarah Holden lead them right to her father, by one means or another and whatever it took. He had an ace up his sleeve, and what better way to secure that stacked deck was to take the leading card, and it just switched from the Queen of Spades, to the Queen of Hearts.

Chapter 12

Two hours passed wasting time looking for the missing packages, and Kane's patience deteriorated by the minute. Now, Kane had a problem. Not only were his and Hunter's .38s in the hands of the Americans, but he didn't have a weapon, period! None of them did. Kane excused himself from the group, left his stuff with Sam, and headed for the bathroom. After doing what he had to do, he now needed to call Dan to establish some kind of contact with Australia and to let him know what was going on, or not, as the case might be. He also needed a cigarette.

Kane slipped out of the bathroom and into an alcove in the terminal. The airport seemed unusually quiet for this time of the morning. He retrieved the cell from his boot, flipped it open and called home. The phone rang and rang. Kane snapped the phone shut. He tried again. This time someone answered it. "Dan, is that you?"

"Kane?" asked Dan. "Where are you? We were expecting to hear from you a while back. Are you there yet? Kane? I can hardly hear you. Where are you?"

"Dan, is everything okay there? Dan...Dan," Kane yelled down the line. He turned the volume up on the cell. "Is everything okay? Are the kids okay? Dannnnnnn..." and he lost the connection. He closed the phone and redialed. This time the answer machine came on in the house. "Fucking hell!" In all the years he had had the cell, he had never had this problem. He tried one more time. This time he left a message, and then tucked the cell back in his boot, pulled his jean's leg back in place, and took off towards the group. He was more annoyed, if that was possible, than before.

Arriving back at the group, Hunter was missing. "Where did he go?" asked his boss.

"To find you. I will say one thing for him, for whatever the reason, he is dedicated to you…or his job." Sam sat on a seat with bags cluttered around his feet. Sarah was reading a pamphlet on the schedules for the next flight, and the two Americans were eating some strange looking things on sticks. "You okay? You don't look too happy, not that you looked that pleased before you left here."

"Tried to call home. Could not get a good line." Kane paused. "We are on our own, literally. Tucker never intended to keep in touch. Oh, he called me in Abu Dhabi, but that was it. That call was to make sure we kept going. Sam, I am not sure that…" he stopped.

"Not sure what, Kane?" Sam followed Kane's gaze to Sarah.

"Not sure who our friends are…" Kane stared at Sarah. Why had she shown up on that flight? Who was she really? He remembered her passport in his jacket. Time to take a good look, and he picked up his jacket from the seat where Sam had things stacked, and searched in the pocket for the passport. He slid it out and handed it to Sam, who didn't even look shocked. "We need to know who she is…agreed?"

"Agreed." Sam took the passport from his father and waited till Kane set his jacket down again. Then, he handed it back to Kane, who turned his back to Sarah, and opened the passport. Name read Sarah Kelly Holden.

Kane almost dropped it in shock. Sam saw his expression. Kane read on. Birthplace was the same as Kelly's. The age was as he figured. Blue eyes, blond hair. 100 lbs. Kane looked hard at the picture. There was something wrong with it. He kept on looking. He didn't know what it was, but something was wrong. He needed to get it back to Sarah and right now he wasn't sure how. Her over-stuffed pink purse sat on the floor next to the backpack, and Kane needed an excuse to open it.

"You got any more gum?" asked Kane of Sarah.

"Sure, in the top of the purse. Help yourself," she offered, not even looking up from her brochure.

Kane picked up the purse. It reminded him of something his wife would carry, and he began to wonder what other similarities there were. If Sarah was a plant, she was a good one, and she knew her job well. Kane unzipped the bag and sure enough the gum was on the top. He pulled the pack out; let a stick slide out onto his hand. He palmed the gum and passport back into the bag in one go. As he did so, his hand touched something hard in the bottom of the purse. Kane leaned a little closer and looked into the purse seeing the glint of steel looking back at him. He knew immediately what it was. How the heck had she got that on the plane and why didn't she care that he saw it? Now would be a good time to find out. He set the purse back where he found it.

"Sarah, a word with you, darling," asked Kane.

"Just a minute. I…" She didn't get to finish her sentence.

"Now, Sarah!" demanded Kane. And he took hold of her right arm, hauling her up from the seat to a standing position. "I said now!"

The brochures fell from her hands onto the floor as the she looked up into Kane's face.

"Sam, watch the stuff. Miss Holden and I are going for a walk," and they departed across the floor just as Hunter reached Sam.

"Where are they going?" asked Hunter, watching Kane lead the girl away.

"Kane found something in her purse. Wanted to talk to her about it. Not sure what though," Sam lied.

"Getting awfully friendly in such a short space of time, aren't they?" stated Hunter, still watching. He sat down a couple of seats away from Sam, closer to Tyrone than Corey.

"Not from where I am sitting, they aren't! Kane wasn't too happy when they left." Sam thought Hunter was jealous.

He was, and it showed, but not for the reasons Sam thought.

Kane marched Sarah to the terminal windows. Night was turning into day, and as the moon disappeared, and the sun strived to light the morning, Kane leaned down to Sarah Kelly Holden, and very forcefully, still with his hand on her arm, kissed her.

Sarah responded passionately to Kane. When his mouth closed on hers, Sarah could hardly breathe. It was a deep, lingering kiss that Sarah wanted to last forever. Unfortunately, it didn't. But the hand on her arm seemed to.

"Your passport is back in your bag, and please, darling, be more careful. What if someone else had found it, and then opened your purse?" His hand tightened on her arm and he turned slightly, glancing back towards his followers, their mouths gaping. Mission accomplished!

Kane let her go immediately, turned and walked away, and left Sarah standing looking out of the window, tears welling up in her eyes.

Sarah wiped them away with shaking fingers before she could rejoin the group. She had to regain her composure, and for her that was going to be hard. She had thought about getting out. Now…it was too late.

Kane sat down next to Corey, and winked at her. She stared at him as if he was the biggest lecher in the world. He moved closer to her, and she could smell his scent like last night on the plane. This time, though, she was aware of him, and it scared her. She had just seen him kiss another woman, and he was grieving for his wife?

Sarah stood at the window. As she looked in the glass she could see her reflection. Slim, blond, pretty, tight jeans, high heels, and T-shirt; dressed that way on purpose. She reached up with her fingers and pulled the T-shirt down another inch, and let a pink and purple butterfly reveal its hidden wings dancing on her breast. Sarah pulled the shirt back up and once more hid the tell-tale trademark that Kelly Branson always wore. Sarah could see the group through the window. She watched Kane. He was making a move on Corey. Sarah knew he would; he needed to keep both women happy.

Kane slid his arm round the back of Corey's seat. She noticed, and so did Tyrone.

Sam wondered just exactly what his father was doing. He thought maybe it was still the effects of the heroin, but he doubted that. Sam wished he had looked at the passport when he was holding it. He felt sure that Kane had seen something at that time.

Whether Kane knew Sam was watching or he saw him look, didn't really matter.

"Sam, we need to go. Miss Holden says there is an eight a.m. flight on Cyprian airways. We can easily make that. Obviously, no one is going to contact us, send us anything or claim they know us.

Not even Dan called me back. We are incommunicado," and he stood up to his full height.

Hunter stood upright from the crouched position he had been in the seat. "Ready when you are, Kane. Would like to be finished with the flying bullshit, and all the other bullshit that's going on around here!"

"Meaning?" asked Kane, flexing his authority.

"Nothing!" and Hunter brushed past Kane maybe just a little too close.

"Problem, Hunter?" Kane asked him, catching him by the arm.

"No problem, Kane. Just want to get out of here, like you should be thinking of doing," replied Hunter, not even looking down at his arm or Kane's hand.

Kane put pressure on Hunter's arm and his look was fierce. "You will never know how much I want to get out of here. Never!" and Kane felt the muscles in Hunter's arm tighten, and he leaned forward and whispered in Hunter's ear. "Remember you work for me and for the AFP, and I can make or break you!" and Kane let go of his arm.

Hunter walked away with an air of arrogance that Kane had not noticed before.

As Kane leaned down to get his jacket and backpack, Sam caught Kane's stare. Sam's look was serious.

"What? Trust me. I know what I am doing. Okay?" stated Kane.

Sam nodded. He did trust his father even if he didn't understand what he was doing right now.

Once again he picked up Sarah's backpack and waited for her to come back for her purse.

As she arrived back to the group, she felt everyone was staring at her. She was right, they were. Picking up her purse, she swung it over her shoulder, and then turned away from prying eyes and marched herself, with clicking heels, across the floor. Corey actually felt sorry for her, for as much as she wanted Kane's body close to her again, she could see what she thought was hurt in Sarah's eyes.

The group moved out as a unit plus one, dressed in black and grey, except for the very obvious Sarah colors, they moved to Cyprian airways. Through the glass windows day light was much in demand to brighten the skies. Kane realized that the group had not eaten properly since yesterday and now they passed a small café serving some kind of breakfast. He pulled his credit card from his jacket.

"Go grab some food. Sam, take the card, get everyone what they want. Get me some nuts, water and a sandwich full of meats, and a couple of small bottles of wine."

"Kane you don't need..." Sam stated quite exasperated that his father needed wine at seven a.m.

"Yes, I do. Trust me," and Kane lightly touched the side of his chest. Sam understood.

With various packages of nuts, sandwiches, fruits and liquid, the unit set off towards Cyprian. It wasn't quite what they thought the airline would be. Expected to be there were military flights. Instead it was a civilian airline harboring military personnel. Kane noticed the high level of security round the airline, one that he hadn't noticed quite so much before. It wasn't just police, but military forces that seemed to be in hand round the terminal. The thought occurred to him maybe that was why there were no packages waiting for them, which made him wonder if they even had tickets for that flight. Maybe time to check.

The everlasting credit card came in handy to buy five one-way tickets to Baghdad. Kane bought everyone's, except Sarah Holden's. He watched her buy hers and then they headed for the check in. They all went through, except Sarah Holden.

"Is there a problem?" Kane asked the ticket clerk when he held Sarah back.

"Just a slight one, sir. Is the lady traveling with you?" the tall, dark gentleman asked him.

One wrong answer and they were all in trouble. "Just met her on the other flight. Had never seen her till then," commented Kane, fiddling with his own backpack and not looking up as he spoke.

The check-in clerk looked again at her passport. "But she is Australian, too. You might have known her?"

"Australia is a big place, mate. Never seen her before today." Kane was beginning to tire of this, and looked up to see the rest of his party boarding the plane. Now, he was uncomfortable. "Can I get on the plane, or do I have to stay with this girl?"

"You can go, sir. We can deal with this lady," stated the clerk.

"Kane, don't leave me here! I came a long way to see my father, and this flight's my only chance."

Kane could see the panic on her face.

"Tell him I am with you," she whispered. "Please?"

He looked at her standing there. Sarah Kelly Holden. He whispered to her. "*Please* has a price, lady!"

"Anything!" she replied.

"Anything?" he asked looking her up and down.

"Anything. Just name it!" Sarah replied.

Kane nodded.

"I guess she *is* with me now, mate," and Kane laughed, as he slipped the clerk some currency, and winked at him. "I'll carry her pack back on with mine, okay? Probably full of clothes and female crap. As long as it's full of things for bed! Let's get on the plane, Miss Holden," and they disappeared through the gate and headed with some haste to catch up with his group. One man, two backpacks, and a woman in tow. Pink was not his color.

"Like I said, Miss Holden, please be careful," and he took her hand in his and led her onto the plane."

She looked down at the hand, but didn't pull hers from his.

"Just play along for now, so that you can get on the damn flight. What you do then is your own business, darling," he didn't say it too loud, but loud enough to have the desired effect on the rest of the group, which had just now caught up with them.

He ushered her down the plane and into two available seats. Stuffing the backpacks up into the overhead bins, he sat down next to Sarah, and leaned towards a very nervous woman.

"Now, Miss Holden," Kane whispered. "When we get off this plane, you really are with me, whether you like it or not, and like I said, there better be some things in that bag that really will interest me, or you will find I am not the gentleman you thought I was!"

Chapter 13

Kane watched Sarah's reaction to his statement. She never flinched, as if she knew what he was going to say. She pulled her purse tighter to her and leaned back in the seat.

"Your wish is my command, Kane. Didn't I prove that when I returned your kiss?" Sarah responded to him.

That caught him off guard. "Yes, you did. But like I said, there better be what I want in that backpack of yours. I know what's in the purse."

"Do the others know?" she asked, looking into his face.

"Know what? That I intend to make love to you? Not yet." Kane laughed. To him it was kind of ironic.

"Not quite what I was thinking. I meant do they know anything about me?" she asked, a little flustered by his blunt statement.

"No. Not sure whom I can trust. Know who I can't, though. Watch out for Corey. I can only keep her happy to a certain point. She should not be on this trip. Knew that back in Oz. A chemistry that shouldn't be there, and not sure why it is. Not like with you, a business arrangement. You give me what I want, and I give you what you want." Kane stopped speaking and thought for a moment. "You give me Ryan Holden..." his face muscles tightened.

"And I get you!" Sarah stated emphatically.

"Yeah, something like that," he conceded.

"Something? It's exactly like that, Kane," she said, turning to get a better look at him. "Eye for an eye! Ryan Holden is a bastard. Top of the ten most wanted. You know that! Do I really look like her?" she asked changing the subject.

"Yes," was all he could muster. He was thinking and wondering why they just didn't swap her for Kelly. It could have been done rather than this entire charade. But then he would not have had the pleasure of killing Ryan. It was hate that neither of them had gotten over, and now was more intense than ever.

"Your wife is a very lucky woman! But then I guess I will find out, won't I?" her eyes flashing at him.

"Maybe! It's not real, Miss Holden. Don't take the personal part too seriously, neither should Corey," and Kane glanced across the aisle to the young woman in grey sweats. He did find her attractive, and he really didn't know why. She wasn't even his type. Perhaps, it was her grit he admired. A certain part of him, though, had apparently liked her for more than her grit. He studied her more carefully. With her hair down, a little makeup, she really was pretty. How he wished he had not been so rude to her back in OZ. But he had. Corey was the first women he had had those kinds of thoughts about since he met Kelly, not that he would have followed through on it, just that, even the thoughts shocked and surprised him. His thoughts returned to Sarah and the situation in hand.

"Kane, are you with us?" Sarah asked.

"Yeah, sure." He fastened his seatbelt ready for take off. "Suggest you do yours up. By the way, meant to ask, how did you know how to pick me up with the seatbelt routine?" Kane questioned her.

"What seatbelt routine? Her look was honest and her answer was real.

"Nothing," and Kane turned away, a little shaken.

Sam, seated behind Kane, heard most of the conversation. Now, he understood a little more.

The other three dotted themselves round the plane, a move that Kane felt was rather strange. But each one had their own thoughts to sort out.

The plane taxied down the runway, and headed into now clear and bright skies. This was the last leg into destiny. One last flight, and then they were grounded till they found Kelly, and Reese Wade. Kane figured they would rent a car and drive from Baghdad to Samarra. From there, find the girls…

Kane dozed with the motion of the plane. His dreams once again were filled with Kelly. He could see her, touch her, and smell her. He awoke with a start to Sarah spraying perfume on her wrists…Kelly's favorite kind.

"Scuse me," and Kane climbed out of his seatbelt to go to the bathroom. He needed to take a piss after all the liquid he had consumed. Opening the door, he went inside, closed the door, raised the seat, took a pee, washed his hands, and was about to leave, when he felt the phone vibrate in his boot. Kane never turned his cell off on planes, just to vibrate mode. He immediately closed the door and fished in his boot for the cell. By the time he retrieved it, it had stopped ringing, but he flipped it open anyway. He didn't recognize the number on the screen, and while he was looking, the phone beeped with a message.

As he was about to listen, someone banged on the door.

"Wait a minute, mate," Kane said loudly.

They banged again.

"I said fucking wait! And don't bang on the door again!" He put the cell to his ear and listened. He heard one word on the message. 'Kane.' The voice was soft and very feminine.

His heart skipped a beat. He had missed a call from his wife, and at that moment in time, he wanted to die. He stuffed the cell back in his boot and opened the door.

When the man outside the bathroom saw Kane, he flinched. He didn't expect six feet of angry Australian to come bursting out of the bathroom.

"Mate, would you get in my grave that fast, or would you like me to help you get into your own?" and Kane positively glared at the cringing little man with the balding head, who was backing into the panel behind him, and praying to his god that Kane did not hit him.

Kane pushed past him and strode down the plane and back to his seat, pushing the seat belt out of his way in the process. He had wanted to dial the number right back and couldn't. Now, he was angry. He also knew that by the time the plane landed it would be too late to get her back on the phone.

"Kane?" Sarah asked with some caution.

"What?! What the fuck do you want now?" he yelled at her. He hadn't meant it to come out like that, but it had and the more he looked at Sarah, the more he needed Kelly. He longed to hold her, make love to her, and tell her he loved her. For the moment he had to play out the charade. He turned back to Sarah. Not only was there a dull ache inside, but one in his heart. "Sorry. I should not have lost my temper with you. It wasn't your fault," and he reached across her lap and put his hand, very fleetingly, on her knee.

Sarah looked up into his face, into his eyes, that were steely blue, icy pools, frozen with contempt and despair. She knew for Kane this was all business and she needed to remember that fact.

The flight was not long. A little turbulent. Eventful, most certainly. Each time Kane looked at Corey, she shared a smile with him. He knew he was still in there, as he knew he was with Sarah.

Kane wanted the plane to land so he could make the call, as his cell was burning a hole in his boot.

Sam leaned around the seat to his father. "You okay?" a concerned look on his face.

"Fine. Just want to get off this piece of crap. Need to make a call!"

"I gathered that. We all heard you. Half the plane heard you." Sam lowered his tone. "Kelly?"

"Yeah, Kelly." Kane whispered, and turned back in his seat.

Sam knew his father was in pain by the look on his face. But to question him now would not be a smart move, with ears listening hard. He wanted the plane to be on the ground, too.

They got their wish faster than they anticipated.

"Ladies and gentlemen. Please fasten your seatbelts. We have reports of gunfire in Baghdad airport and the surrounding area. This flight has been diverted to a private airstrip south of Baghdad, where buses will take you on to the city. Please bear with us on this, and there is no cause for alarm."

The passengers reacted to the announcement with anxious alarm. Though not a full flight, there were several women and children on board, and a couple of very military-looking folks not far from Kane's seat.

Kane turned back again to look at his son. If this had been planned to delay them it could not have been at a better time. The two exchanged looks.

"Could not be, could it?" Sam asked.

"Ryan Holden was always cunning, but I doubt that he could even go so far as to disrupt a whole airport. I do know that this slows us up even more than we needed to be, and I still need to make the call, too. Would like to know where this fucking airport is. I notice they didn't give us a named location, just a private airstrip. Very convenient." Kane changed pace. "By the way, you notice some of our traveling companions?" asked Kane.

"I noticed. You think they are keeping tabs on us?" Sam questioned.

"Maybe," his father answered. "I noticed that Hunter kept to himself on this flight. It's time to find out which side he really is on, before we get too far into hostile territory."

"You want me to ask him? From you, he will expect it; from me, he won't."

"Go ahead, Sam. Just do it where no one else can hear you," and Kane tipped his head very slightly towards Sarah.

Kane returned himself to the upright position in his seat, and started to fasten the seatbelt. A thought occurred to him. He needed a gun. He leaned down and reached under the seat in front of Sarah, and pulled out her purse.

She grabbed his arm. "What do you think you are doing, Kane?" and pulled him back from her purse.

He looked at her hand with such a piercing look, that she let go like her fingers were on fire.

"Want the gun you have in there." No please or thank you from Kane.

"You don't know for sure it's…" she didn't get to finish.

"Cut the crap! You and I both know what's in the purse, and the backpack." And he continued to pull the purse open, and stuck his hand inside it. Pulling the gun out, he slid it round on her side and stuffed it down the back of his jeans.

"Loaded?" he asked, not having checked the gun.

"Does it look like it?" Sarah replied like he was nuts. "No, it's not! Even I can't get a loaded gun on the plane!"

"Magazine?" Kane whispered, and he put his hand out flat in front of her.

She fished in her purse and produced a magazine for him, dropping it into his palm.

"You always carry them like that? Loose in your bag?" he questioned.

"Mostly! What business is it of yours?" she frowned at him, not caring who she was talking to.

"My business, if things get screwed up. And, they are screwed up enough right now. Don't complicate matters, darling!"

"That's funny coming from you, don't you think?" and she laughed quietly. Sarah leaned closer to him and whispered in his ear. "So, you remember what you have to do, right?"

"How can I forget? You won't let me!" and he breathed a heavy sigh.

"You want Kelly back, right?" she whispered, leaning in on him.

"More than anything! More than my life is worth."

Sarah thought for a moment. "What's it like to love someone that much?"

"No words can explain it," Kane murmured.

"You just did, Kane," and Sarah found herself both jealous of Kelly and sad all in one go, and she leaned back in her seat to reflect on this.

Kane glanced at her. She should not be here. None of them should. This was an International incident, and they were involved in it. They were also expendable. Kane leaned back in the seat. He was warm, and noted that the temperature in the plane made it a little stuffy. He pulled his sweater off over his head, which then joined the jacket under the seat in front of him.

If Sarah was not impressed before the removal of the sweater, she was now. Kane's tight black T-shirt left nothing for her to imagine about him, and that was the effect he was trying to create. He watched her cross her legs, and her heels hung seductively from her foot. He suppressed a smile, but it also reminded him that heels were not a great thing to be wearing in Iraq.

"Sarah, I assume you have boots in your backpack? Because you sure are not gonna make it in those shoes, darling!"

"Don't plan to. I have boots and shorts, and some skimpy T-shirts, all the things to seduce you with," she laughed at him.

"Right! The only thing that would seduce me is more guns!" Kane retorted.

"Well, we can arrange that, can't we? Boots don't weigh *that* heavy. Have a Beretta 9mm hidden in one of my boots, and one in the other, besides the gun I just gave you. Would that make you happy?"

"Maybe," he replied and looked past her and out of the window to a cloudless blue sky.

Feeling she hadn't quite got him where she wanted him yet, she turned her body towards him and leaned against his arm.

He felt her body pressed against him, and this time he had the same reaction as he had when Corey's body touched his.

Sarah looked at the cut of his jeans and smiled. She had succeeded in having the effect she wanted on him, or so she thought.

With Kane, everything was an illusion, except when he wanted a woman, and right now, he did.

Chapter 14

As the plane touched down on the runway, Kane could see cracks made by mortar shells, some old and some much more recent. It was not the smoothest of landings, and the airplane's wheels snagged in the cracks, pulling the plane slightly to one side.

Sarah fell on him, yet again, and this time he caught her by the arm, slid his hand onto her shoulder, and gently rubbed his hand down her back.

The plane finally came to a complete stop after lurching to the right a couple more times.

"You okay?" Kane asked Sarah in a concerned tone.

"Yeah, fine. Just bumpy. Never get used to *bumpy*," she laughed nervously and her fingers turned white as she clutched the arm rest.

Kane glanced round the plane at the crying children, who definitely did not appreciate the landing. Immediately, he thought of his own children, especially Star, and the way he had left her. Inadvertently, he went to finger his wedding ring, and realized he had given it to Star. Probably, by now, it was hanging on a chain round her neck. He smiled to himself. She would be such a big shot wearing her daddy's ring. His thoughts were rudely interrupted.

"Ladies and gentlemen. You are asked to disembark at the front of the plane, and take all hand luggage with you."

Kane watched as three burly Arab-looking fellows pushed the solid steel steps to the plane for disembarking.

Kane undid his seatbelt, stood up, and reached up into the overhead bins for the backpacks. Sam stood up at the same time, mainly to talk to his father.

"How are things going? You still in pain?" Sam asked Kane, while lifting his own belongings from the bins.

Kane was going to deny it, but what was the point? Sam would know he was lying. "Yes, I am. Don't say anything about it to anyone, especially not to our dark-haired friend over there," he added, glancing at Hunter.

"Oh, yeah. Might make his day if he had to touch you…" remarked Sam casually.

"Stop it! That wasn't funny. Makes me cringe though, mate. Not the right sex for me!" added Kane, with a smirk on his face.

"Speaking of sex, looks like it's going well with Sarah…" commented Sam.

"Business only, Sam." Kane replied.

"Right!" and Sam turned his head away in mock gesture.

As Kane started to pull the second backpack down, he felt a severe pain in his chest, which he had not felt before. He knew immediately that the shaft had moved slightly inside him. For a second, Kane could not breathe, and he held onto the overhead bin.

Sam turned back to look at his father. "Kane?!"

"I'm okay! Ignore me. Bags stuck! Get them all off the plane. I'll join you in a minute." He was breathing way too hard, and his speech was staccato.

"Kane, I…" and Sam moved closer to his father.

"Get the fuck off the plane…now!" and Kane's lined face said it all.

"Miss Holden. Let's get out of Kane's way and get off the plane. I have your backpack. Let's go," and Sam ushered her down the isle and off the plane to the waiting tarmac.

Sam turned to look at Kane, who had his free hand on his chest. Sam's first thought was to go back and help his father, but he had been given an order. Fortunately, everyone else was off the plane except the two military-looking gentlemen Sam and Kane had spotted earlier. The situation worried Sam, but he had to let it go.

Kane released his death grip on the overhead bin and sat down on the armrest of the seat for a few seconds. To Kane it felt like he was being stabbed all over again. He looked up briefly and the two military-looking men were coming towards him.

Outside the plane, on the potholed tarmac, the rest of the unit waited for its leader. Sam thought Kane was taking way too long.

"Where is Kane?" asked a perplexed Hunter. Today he had left his hair hanging loose. It made him look older and very menacing. Aside from his accent, he definitely could have passed for an Arab.

The whole group appeared anxious as to where Kane was.

Corey whispered to Tyrone. "Where is Kane? He looked tired on the plane."

"Of course you noticed that?" stated a caustic Tyrone, as he, too, removed his sweatshirt, and threw it down on the backpack.

"Why shouldn't I? He's our boss," Corey replied, not looking up at Tyrone.

"Right! A boss that wants into your pants!" he replied without any hesitation.

"Don't be so ridiculous! He does not!" But the statement was almost a question. "He's a married man."

"Married, maybe. After women, for damn sure, and he doesn't have to try very hard, does he? He has women falling at his feet, apparently. The other Australian guy isn't like that!" said the American.

"Course not, he's gay!" laughed Corey.

"What?" Tyrone asked her, looking at her like she was nuts.

"Said he's gay!" she repeated.

"How the hell do you know that? And keep your voice down. He's right over there."

"How do you know I meant that one? Could have been the blond?" she asked, turning her face to Tyrone.

"Kane's son? I doubt that. Not one of Kane's sons. He would kill him first!" Tyrone finished the sentence and looked across at Hunter. He hadn't really noticed before. But Corey could be right. All that long hair on a guy; then again, Kane had long hair and he certainly wasn't gay. Tyrone had been so busy watching Kane make passes at his girlfriend, that he hadn't noticed, and if he was really honest, Corey had encouraged Kane.

Sam was concerned. Kane should have emerged by now. The two military-looking gentlemen came down the steel steps, and kept on going. Now, he was really concerned, as aside from the pilot and crew, Kane was the only one left on the plane. Sam decided he would go back in the aircraft and see what was wrong.

At that moment, Kane emerged through the aircraft door, backpack hanging from one arm, hair tied back, and dark shades on his face. On his feet he wore the blackest desert boots Sam had ever seen, and ones that could not have been in the backpack. Gone was the pain from Kane's face, no hint of five minutes ago, and in his belt the gun could clearly be seen, and Kane looked like he could take on the nation.

Kane didn't use the handrail as he came down the steps. Sheer arrogance propelled him, and he wasn't feeling any pain.

Sam couldn't take his eyes off his father. He had seen him like this only once before, and that was when they had first met each other in a parking lot in Hong Kong. They had come face to face, and Kane had protected his friend, Giles Harris, from a bullet from Sam's gun. Now, Sam looked at his father. He wore the same look of defiance. He had never flinched then, and he didn't now. Kane looked ten years younger than he really was as he walked down to the waiting group, removing his shades as he did, and hung them from the T-shirt neck.

"So you blokes ready?" asked the man of war.

"Waiting for you, Kane," Hunter stated, and he stared at his boss.

"Yeah, well I am here now. So, let's go." Kane stated the obvious.

"We can see you are here." Sam whispered the next sentence. "What happened back there? They make you the bionic man or something?"

Kane flashed Sam such a look. "Let's just go to work, shall we? We need to find this bus they are talking about? Anyone know anything about it?"

"Yeah, right over there. Everyone else is onboard. One bus already left. We need to get on it if we want to leave here, wherever here is!" interjected Hunter. "I can't find a name for this private airstrip," looking around at the buildings.

"Don't suppose you will either, mate! Not on anyone's map." As Kane spoke, the bus started up, and the driver blasted its horn in the morning air.

The temperature had changed a little and was turning warmer than should have been so early before noon. Kane tucked his sweatshirt and jacket through his backpack straps, and carried the backpack in one hand. With his other hand he reached for Sarah's pack, and lifted it like it was filled with gold-dust. To Kane, it was.

He strode across the potholed tarmac with the same air of arrogance he had when he won the British grand prix, the same arrogance he always had had from an early age. Youth was not on his side, but arrogance and a gun were.

They watched him walk away. "Never changes…" murmured Sam.

"What?" asked Sarah.

"Said, he never changes. What ever life throws at him, Kane is Kane," and Sam followed after his father like he always would.

Sarah watched Kane. Her job had just become more difficult. She was beginning to admire this man very much. She was leading him to Ryan, who was her father. It was no lie, and he was a bastard. And Sarah had been overseas traveling; she had not lied about that fact. Should her father die by Kane's hand? She wasn't sure about that. What she did know was that Kane would kill him to get his wife back. Did she want Kane to get Kelly back? Now, she wasn't sure. For the time being she had to follow his orders. That was for now, so she took off after him, her hair blowing out behind her, and sporting a great shape in a pair of jeans.

Sam could not help but notice Sarah watching his father. He had seen Kelly do the same in Hong Kong. The two women had to be related in some way, that much Sam knew. Was that why Kane was paying so much attention to Sarah Holden? He thought not. There was another reason, one that he had not been told. But, he sure as hell was gonna find out, one way or another, and he, too, followed Kane.

Hunter pulled back out of the way, and slung his backpack over his shoulder. He had to watch his boss, that was his job, and make sure he didn't get his hands on any more heroin. He, too, felt that Kane was holding back. He had noticed on the plane that Kane didn't look that great, and now he was superman. Something had happened in that short space of time when no-one was around. He glanced at the two Americans. Corey was staring at Kane like she had never seen him before. Hunter glanced at the last member of the party, Tyrone… who appeared to be sulking about his girlfriend watching Kane. It kind of amused him. They were all watching Kane. And that was the idea. They would watch him and follow him, if not to find out what was to happen, just to watch him. The women wanted him, and the men wanted to be like him. Hunter was no exception.

Kane stopped at the door of the bus and yelled to the driver. "This the only bus left? And where the fuck are we anyway?"

The driver of the dirty, ramshackle old yellow bus yelled something in Arabic. Kane hadn't a clue what he said, a very unusual situation for Kane to be in, and looked round for Corey to translate.

"For god's sake, Corey, stay right by me. I haven't a fucking clue what he said, and that's what you are here for anyway!" Kane paused. "Get him to repeat it for you!" and he pulled her by the arm and stuck her right in front of him, resting his hand on her shoulder. In the other hand, he clutched the backpack straps. "Do it!"

Corey was afraid not to do it, and yelled at the driver to get some kind of reaction. Once again the driver waved his arms in the air and spat out some kind of words to her.

She turned back to Kane, twisting slightly in his grasp.

"He says that this is the last bus, and we should get on it now or we will be stuck here!" Corey reported back to her boss pretty much what the driver had said, give or take a few curse words.

Kane looked at the group who had just about reached the bus. "Get on that fucking bus. We can't be left here. Corey, from now on you are with me! Where I go, you go. Tucker was right about that. You will come in very useful to me," and Kane smiled through the hassle of the situation. "Good job, Corey."

She smiled back at him, and the situation between herself and Kane increased, as the rest of the party started to climb on to the bus.

As Sarah passed Kane, he whispered to her. "Get me a seat. Try and get the ones at the very back, if you can."

She nodded her head in acknowledgment, and climbed up behind the rest of the group.

The driver was still waving his arms and spitting out words that Kane could not understand. Kane propelled Corey to the steps, and followed her into the bus. The first thing to hit him was the stench. The bus had not been cleaned for decades, or so it seemed, and had obviously been used as a toilet on more than one occasion. The seats were filthy, with vomit and food stains collecting on them.

Kane pushed Corey to the back of the bus, much to the disgust of Tyrone and the stare of the doe-like eyes of Sarah, who figured she had Kane to herself for a spell. She figured incorrectly.

The backseat, which had been free, was now occupied by Sarah, Kane and Corey on his other side, and backpacks rested at the end of the seat. Half the bus was empty, and no one ventured to the back. Kane and his friends were soon to find out why.

Kane shifted in the seat to get comfortable and as he did a spring shot through the material.

"God damn son-of-a-bitch! First class travel all the way!" remarked Kane, trying, with no avail, to push the spring back through the seat. It made a pinging noise as he did.

"What happens if one has to pee?" asked Sarah fairly timidly.

"You hold it!" snapped Kane. "Or you piss on the floor like everyone else has! Why, you need to pee, Miss Holden?"

She fidgeted in her seat, obvious to all that she had to. Sam, sitting in front of the trio, turned to talk to Kane.

"I wonder how long we are going to be on this bus? And did anyone figure where we are?"

Kane shook his head, went to lean back on the seat and changed his mind rapidly when he noticed gum stuck to the back of the seat in front of him. He looked up in time to see two very armed policemen boarding the bus and chatting to the driver, who then pointed to the back of the bus.

"What the hell do they want?" asked Kane, putting his shades back on.

"Passports and visas, maybe?" explained Sarah.

"We cleared them in Kuwait, and I paid passport control off so you could get on the damn plane, darling!" added Kane.

Sam gave Kane a very questionable look.

"Yeah, I paid them off. So what? She had to get on the plane, didn't she? Gonna lead us to her father!"

No one had time to answer. The policemen were right in front of Kane, and half the bus had turned to look at the Australian.

Kane found that the police officer's gun pointed at his chest, and the tall, thin Arab in the uniform yelling at him, was enough to keep his attention.

"What does he want, Corey? What is he yelling about?" Kane asked, already knowing the answer.

"You, Kane. He wants you!" she replied, her eyes darting from the policeman to Kane. "He wants you!"

Chapter 15

"Ask him why he wants me? I am not getting off this bus without good cause, and a god damn gun in my chest sure as hell is not just cause! So ask him what the hell he wants!"

Corey did "He says he wants to see your passport," she repeated the words back to Kane.

Kane very carefully reached into his jeans pocket and pulled his passport out and opened it, but kept hold of it.

The policeman stared at it. "You Australian?" he asked.

"You speak English?" retorted Kane, still not letting go of his passport.

"Some," the policeman replied, still with the gun fixed on Kane's chest.

"Good. Understand this. I am not giving you my passport, and I am not getting off this fucking bus! You can see by my passport who I am! Every right to be here and you are in the driver's way of leaving here, and we need to get going."

"I see who you are. You come with us!" and the policeman pressed the gun even harder into Kane.

"Not on your fucking life, mate," and Kane was about to pull his gun from his pants.

Hunter came down the bus behind the policemen, and intervened before his boss took his gun, and shot them dead where they stood. He uttered words in Arabic.

Kane was shocked. That wasn't in his dossier. The policeman turned away from Kane.

"What are they talking about?" he asked Corey in a quiet voice.

"Not sure! You think Hunter is on our side?" questioned Corey.

"Beginning to wonder about that!" replied a suspicious Kane.

"Think he is telling him who you are!" Corey said with a bemused look on her face.

"What?! I would rather shoot the fuckers than have them find that out." He paused. "Now, what is he saying?" Kane was becoming agitated and his hand rested on top of the gun.

Sarah saw it. He could not get arrested now. That was not the plan, but then again, neither were the police.

She leaned closer to Kane, flopping her arms round his shoulders, and directed her conversation to Corey. "Tell the police that I can't be left alone. My husband here needs to be with me, especially in my condition!"

"What? Are you insane?" Corey stared at her.

"Just do it, Corey. Tell them!" demanded Sarah.

Corey touched the policeman with her hand, and he turned quickly. She gave him the story.

The policemen laughed. "You are alright. You go to Baghdad. Have fun there. Take the lady, er, your wife."

Sarah leaned forward, and pulled the T-shirt down slightly for more effect. It was then Kane caught site of the butterfly tattoo. He stopped dead in his tracks. Sam saw it, too, and looked at Kane's face.

"That's like..." and Sam stopped speaking.

"Yep, it is." Kane replied, as he tried to get over the shock.

Sarah nestled into Kane, and as he removed his hand from his belt, slid his arm around her waist, pulling her to him.

Sarah smiled at the policeman and winked at him. It had worked, far better than Hunter's little explanation seemed to have done.

"Sorry about the hold up, sir. Bus can go now," and Mr. Policeman stepped away down the bus and through the doors. As soon as he hit the tarmac he reached in his tunic and pulled the radio from his belt.

Kane watched out the window at the goings on, and then he turned his icy stare onto Hunter. "You and I need to talk..."

"No, Kane. I will talk to Hunter. About time we found out what the hell is going on here," emphasized Sam.

"I know what we agreed, Sam, but I need to find out a couple of things," and as Kane looked at the half crowded bus, "but now is not the time and place."

A look of relief spread across Hunter's face. Had he been caught out? He didn't think so. And what if he had? He was there to protect their identities and that's what he was doing, whether they liked it or not. All he had told the policeman was that Kane was his boss, and that he was Kane's right hand man; his bodyguard, if you like. The truth! Kane was traveling with a unit of folk so that his cover would not be blown. Hunter never mentioned they themselves were police and military. But, now Hunter knew that Corey's translation capacity was not perfect. Was she someone Tucker had planted to monitor Kane and the group?

As much as Kane wanted to talk to Hunter, Hunter was as eager to talk to Kane. Instead, Hunter returned to his seat, a few rows down the bus, and watched through the window as the cop used his mobile phone.

Mr. Policeman appeared to be relaying info back to someone.

"Why aren't we moving? We are just wasting time with this fucking shit!" and Kane rose up at the same time that the cop waved the bus on. "About fucking time!" and Kane sat down again, and turned to Sarah. "Where did you get that tattoo?" Once again, he rested his arm round her shoulder.

"Tattoo parlor!" and she pouted her pink lips.

"Don't get cute with me, lady!" Kane answered her as he leaned closer to her and looked her in the face, his eyes creased in a semi-angered fashion. "I know that! I asked where?"

"Sydney, why?" she asked innocently, her eyes looking into Kane's.

"Because my…I know someone else with the very same tattoo!" he replied, glancing at the others. Sarah knew he was married, they all did, but they all didn't know Sarah knew. Kane was having a problem keeping the situation straight in his own mind. Now, he doubted things. Of course they would copy Kelly. But to go this far?

"Pretty, isn't it? Lady said she had done one like this once before. Maybe it's the person you mentioned? Could be, huh?" Sarah wasn't letting it go, and the T-shirt stayed low so the butterfly could be seen clearly by everyone.

"Maybe," and this time Kane's face showed great displeasure. Sarah was pushing him, and he couldn't do anything about it, but he was beginning to be annoyed by her antics. His hand tightened on her arm almost to the point of hurting her, and he knew it. He had to shut her up. She was taking it all too far.

Sarah grimaced under the pressure of Kane's hand, and this time the sarcastic words she was thinking didn't make it to her mouth. Sarah realized she may be pushing Kane too much. That wasn't her job.

Sam watched the whole proceeding. Kane was definitely keeping something secret. A man didn't push Kane around like this, let alone a woman, and Sarah Holden was pushing his father, like she had a hold over him. Sam couldn't quite figure out what. Wasn't sex. Kane could get that from Corey if he wanted it badly enough, and Sam figured that Kane really loved Kelly enough to abstain from such side-lines till he could be with Kelly. Sam was puzzled. He watched his father's face. He hadn't let his defenses down, if anything they were more in tact than ever. But Sarah had a hold; that was certain. He wondered if anyone else had noticed. He glanced at the other faces in the unit. If they had, they didn't give anything away. He leaned back in the seat, aware it stank of something. Of what, he wasn't quite sure.

Kane also leaned back, taking Sarah's body with him. She leaned against him, and closed her eyes. Tiredness was catching up fast, to all of them. On his other side, Corey also became sleepy. As the bus trundled from first gear to second and on up the gears, Corey fell against Kane, much to the disgust of Tyrone, who sat bolt upright in his seat and stared ahead of him. Kane moved his other arm so that Corey might rest also. God knows, they all needed it.

Half an hour into the trip, most of the people on the bus had fallen asleep. It was hot and dusty and the bus lacked air-conditioning, along with good, balanced tires and suspension. Most of the folks on there had drifted asleep as the bus ploughed on. The roads were not the best and it was seemingly taking a long while to get to the destination.

It was turning noon, and the sun was high and much warmer than it should have been. As the bus entered the outskirts of the small village, the vehicle came under fire. As bullets ricocheted off the side of the metal, the occupants of the bus ducked down and tried with futility to hide themselves from being shot. The seats were low to the floor and only the children from the flight could get under them.

The taller of the two military gentlemen shouted out. "No one panic! It's a sniper. Stay down!" and he pulled a gun from the back of his dark pants, clutched it between both hands, and moved down to where the driver was crouching behind the wheel of the now stopped bus. Pushing the driver out of the seat, he yelled at him in Arabic.

The driver scooted into the empty seat and sat there cowering and quivering with head buried in his hands while asking his god to save him.

Suddenly, the bullets increased in numbers. Not one sniper, but two. The second sniper seemed to be targeting the back of the bus. Kane pushed both Corey and Sarah down underneath him, almost covering them with his body. Sam also flung himself onto Corey, and between the two men they made a shield for the women.

Kane's head shot up as soon as the round of bullets stopped. Just in time, he ducked down again as another round launched itself upon the bus. "To the right of that building! See the angle? There!" and Kane pointed with his finger to where he figured the bullets were coming from.

Sam looked in the direction Kane was pointing. He was right. It was the only place on that side of the bus they could have come from. How he wished he had a gun.

Kane slid out from between the girls, and sat on the filthy bus floor, his back facing the other end of the bus. He pulled Sarah's backpack down with him, and unzipped it with some haste. Reaching inside, he fished around looking for the two Berettas. Finding one, he handed it out to Sam, and then he stuffed the other one between his legs. He tossed the backpack, now a little lighter, up and onto the seat.

Sam didn't flinch as he obtained the gun. He thought maybe he should have wished for something bigger, and the thought amused him.

"Something funny, Sam?" asked Kane, slightly accusatory.

"Nope. Just thinking I should be careful what I wish for in future!" and Sam stuck his hand out for the magazine, then slithered across the seats to get a better view of the window and the buildings outside.

Tyrone moved in beside Sam. "See anything, and where in hell did you get the gun?"

"Same place as Kane did!" replied Sam, his eyes scanning through the window.

"Where did he get his from?" asked Tyrone as he leaned against the seat.

"Didn't ask!" lied Sam, and he shifted positions to get a better view. "Anyone ever tell you that you ask too many damn questions?"

"Fuck you! I'll ask as many as I like! Such as, how come you are armed and we are not, and why didn't Kane say he had guns?" Tyrone was pushing Sam.

"Why don't you ask Kane? Sure he would be glad to tell you, right Kane?" and Sam leaned back to include Kane into the conversation.

Kane turned and as he did he tossed the other gun to Tyrone, and then the magazine right behind it. "Happy now? All the little boys have their guns to play with?" And Kane turned his attentions back to the window as another round hit the bus.

The military gentleman at the wheel shoved the gun back in his jeans, started the bus back up and revved hard. "Everyone stay down. We're going to make a run for it." He glanced back at the passengers. Everyone was down except the commander. "Sir, would you get down on the floor, please?"

The military gentleman was ignored, not for any reason, just that Kane and his unit could not hear him yelling above the seemingly instant crying of the children on the bus.

He tried again.

"Sir, would you stay low..." yelled the military man.

"Kane, I think he means you," stated Sam. "Why is he so concerned about you?" he questioned. Sam looked from the driver to Kane. Mr. Military was very worried now, and yet he wasn't when the policemen got on the bus. Maybe, Mr. Military figured Kane could handle that, but for some reason they didn't want him shot.

"I know he does. I can look after myself back here. He should be more worried about others on here, like the lady…" and Kane stopped. He could not show concern, and turned to look back through the window.

Sam was trying to figure out just what was going on. He couldn't stop thinking about the relationship between Kane and Sarah. It had sprung up way too fast. He looked at the girl. She was leaning down as far as she could on the seat and had covered her ears with her hands. If she was Ryan Holden's daughter she would have been brought up in military surroundings, and should be used to far worse than this. Sam turned his attentions to Corey, who was also down on the seat but in a more tactical position. He glanced at Tyrone, who was crouched behind the seat, gun at the ready and a steady eye looking out of the window. Only Hunter was not participating in some form or other with the unit. He appeared to be consoling some of the kids that had never seen or heard gunfire before. Sam decided he hadn't seen this side of Hunter expressed to anyone except Kane. Maybe, he had misjudged him, maybe not.

His thoughts were rudely interrupted as bullets shot through the windows at the front of the bus, shattering glass over anyone that happened to be in the path which included the new bus driver and also the old one. Mr. Military ducked down low and as he did the bus swerved violently to one side sending passengers to the far side of the vehicle. The bus stalled, and Mr. Military didn't move. He lay there on the floor, as blood seeped from his mouth, and gushed from his chest in a crimson red geyser.

Kane leaped from his seat and moved quickly down to the front of the bus. Leaning down by Mr. Military, he didn't even feel for a pulse as there was no doubt he was dead.   Kane all but fell into the drivers seat while brushing the broken glass from the torn leather seating and trying to get a grip on the situation. He stuffed his gun on his lap, took a hold of the wheel and put his foot down on the pedal.

The bus shot forward and Kane took off at the usual Branson speed of one to sixty in the same amount of seconds, or at least as fast as the bus would go. He cleared the area and sped on through the town, the bus twisting and turning under its new handler with a lease on life the rickety bus had not seen for years. It screeched to a halt along the dusty road, and Kane jumped up from the seat and started back down the aisle. Applause rippled through the passengers on the bus, all except from one man, who stood in Kane's way in the aisle.

"What the hell do you think you were doing, Comman...?" He didn't finish the sentence, as the blow from Kane's fist sent him flying across the seats.

Chapter 16

"What the hell was that for?" asked the military man, now staggering under Kane's blow.

"You were about to give away my identity, you stupid idiot!" and Kane shook his fist. It hurt. He hadn't meant to hit the man quite that hard, but he was angry, and that was the only way knew how to vent anger.

"Damn that hurt. I didn't know your party didn't know! Why is it such a secret now?" asked the military.

"Most of them do know, but you don't know who else is on this bus, and that wasn't smart. I had to shut you up. Now everyone will be wondering why I hit you. Great!" Kane glanced around the bus. Everyone was watching, making it a lot more obvious that something was going on than before Kane hit him. "I'm sorry about your friend," Kane whispered and carried on back down the bus to the unit. "We seem to be safe for now," Kane told them.

"Safe?" stated Sarah, wide-eyed. "Do you always drive like that?" she asked him.

"Mostly...right Sam?" asked Kane, never flinching, while stuffing his gun down the back of his pants.

"Right! He does. And he's right; we should be safe for now. I'll go outside and look around. But away from the town, we should be okay." Sam bustled down past the seats and gave a sideward glance to Mr. Military number two, cut his eyes to Hunter, and carried on to the door of the bus. Stepping outside, Sam looked around him. All he could see was dirt roads and nothing else. They were clear from trouble for now, but Sam had a feeling that wouldn't last too long. He stepped back up the dirty steps into the bus, and made his way back down the isle. This time Hunter stopped Sam.

"So what was that about with the military guy other end of the bus?" asked Hunter.

"He's dead, that's all." Sam tried to be patient.

"Not that one. The other one that's alive and well, and about to give our boss away to the whole bus." Hunter was blunt and to the point.

"Oh, that one…not sure. By the way, I need to talk to you. You wanna take a walk?"

Hunter laughed. "I don't think Kane would be too happy about that. He said he wanted to talk to me, and I want to talk to him. Some things need to be settled!"

"You got that right!" retorted Sam. "Ok, so lets all go talk. Right now!" and Sam squeezed past him and moved to Kane's side. "Your man down the bus wants to talk to you. Think we should both go, mainly for your safety and temper, and possibly my temper, too."

"Let's do it before we get interrupted again," and Kane left his backpack and the rest of the unit standing, watching.

"What's going on?" pestered Sarah. "Where is Kane going?"

"As if you don't know!" muttered Corey under her breath.

"You say something, Corey?" Sarah asked with pursed pink lips. "I thought I heard you say something?" as she picked up her purse and sat on the seat in a far better fashion than she had been doing for the last few minutes. As she rearranged her seating, she tided her clothes, pulling her T-shirt back up to hide the butterfly.

Kane ushered Sam in front of him and they collected Hunter on the way, almost propelling the man out of the bus. They passed over the dead military on the floor and Kane made a quiet note that they should cover him on the way back. He could at least do that for the man.

Hunter stepped off the bus first. Kane and his son followed, and the three walked to the back of the bus, moving behind it, away from prying eyes.

"Now, Hunter. Few things we need to clear up here." Kane ploughed right in. "You gay?" He stared at Hunter as Sam almost choked.

"What?" Hunter peered at Kane with a most unbelievable look.

"You heard me. Something wrong with your hearing, too? Yes or no? I don't care if you are, but I need to know!" Kane thumped his fist on the bus.

"Is that what you think?" and he started to laugh. It humored Hunter that's what Kane had said. "Don't think I have to tell you that, Commander. Not required in my job description to divulge that," and Hunter leaned back carving a figure on the dusty bus.

Kane looked down at his boots. Jet black once, now dirty brown from the dust. "Look, my books got dirty," and Kane looked up into Hunter's face. "On my watch, it's in the job description. Yes or no, and if you call me commander again out here, you are a dead man! Understand me?"

This time Hunter didn't laugh and came back at Kane right up in his face. "You know, *sir,* you are an arrogant son-of-a-bitch and if it hadn't been for me the heroin would have destroyed you! You were damn glad of me then. Now, you have your son, you don't give a fuck about me! Did you tell Sam the rest of the story? Did you? I doubt it! You tell him you came to die? You told him about the wound, and Corey, she isn't who she claims to be…" He watched Kane's face.

Kane gave nothing away as he looked into Hunter's face. Sam looked from one to the other in total disbelief that his father would let Hunter talk to him that way.

Without any warning Kane brought his arm up under Hunters chin and pinned him against the bus. It made a loud thumping noise as he did so, and faces appeared, looking out of the back window. Kane held him there.

"You fucking bastard. You are done! How dare you disrespect me like that, and how dare you share things that were supposed to be confidential. You are gone from this mission and from the force. Sam, get him his backpack. He can find his own way from here!" Kane still had him pinned. "I don't ever want to see you again, you understand me? Get out of my sight, NOW!" Kane dropped his arm and turned to walk away.

He felt Hunter grab his T-shirt and he knew Hunter was going for the gun in the back of his jeans. Kane spun around and hit Hunter as hard as he could in the stomach, dropping him on one knee to the earth. Hunter didn't get up. He was completely winded. By now, Sam had returned with Hunter's backpack, and set it down on the ground next to him.

"Let's go," and Kane walked away, with his son behind him, back into the bus. Kane never looked back, and manually closed the doors to the bus. With some help from the bus driver, he moved military man's body in between the seats, covering it with the driver's coat, and then stood up.

"Corey," yelled Kane down the bus.

"Right here. What do you need?" she asked him, scampering down the bus at his master's voice, and dying to ask what had gone on outside and knowing she dare not.

"Tell the driver to reclaim his seat and get moving again. This delay has set us way behind. Damn it!" and Kane waited impatiently for her to do that.

The driver didn't need to be told twice. He started the bus, put his foot down on the pedal, and took off at a fairly good clip, leaving Hunter standing in the dust.

Kane took his seat between the two women at the back of the bus. He sat down with an air of confidence that exuded from him. If he had looked back through the window, Kane would have seen Hunter pick up his backpack and step to the side of the road.

This time Sam joined them on the backseat, seating himself next to Sarah, who looked a little surprised at the move. In Sam's old seat now sat Tyrone, who thought by sitting there could keep a closer eye on his girlfriend.

Sarah turned to Kane and whispered in his ear. He listened.

"Told you before, use the floor." Kane dismissed her.

"I thought you were joking. I can't do that!"

"Why? If you have to go that bad," he quickly replied, getting tired of her moaning.

"Cause I can't!" she insisted.

"God damn it! Okay, I will ask him to pull over. Our friend, Mr. Military, can go with you. You might even know him. Keeps looking this way."

"Yeah, Kane, at you!" Sarah retorted. "You punched the guy. What the hell was that for?"

"Cause he was gonna say something I didn't want anyone to hear. That satisfy your ladyship?" Kane quipped. "You want the bus stopped or not?" He peered round his companions and looked through the murky window. "There are some trees coming up on the right. Can you make do with those? Or is there something wrong with that location, too?"

"Sarcasm is the lowest form…" and she screwed her face at him.

"Of wit…yeah, I know. Been accused of that a lot of times," said Kane, before Sarah could finish her sentence. "You wanna go or not?"

"Yes, I want to go. Probably by now half the bus does!" Sarah gestured to the other folks.

Kane flashed Sarah a look, stood up from his seat and moved back down the aisle of the piss-stained bus. Halfway down there he remembered he couldn't talk to the driver. "Corey!" he yelled back to her, almost annoyed with himself for forgetting such a major thing.

She scuttled down to where he stood.

"Stay with me. Everywhere I go, you go, no exceptions!" and it flashed through Kane's mind what Hunter had said about her. "Tell him to pull over by those trees," and Kane pointed to the large group of trees that the bus was about to trundle on by.

Corey told him. The driver applied the brakes and screeched to a halt, and Corey turned to the rest of the bus, yelling to them what was about to happen. After she told them in Arabic, she finished it off by telling them in English. Half the bus rushed on by Kane and Corey, almost pushing them out of the way, including Sarah, and all but fell into the arms of the welcoming trees.

"What the hell did you do that for? I was gonna go down there first to check it out, make sure there weren't any unforeseen guns waiting there." He peered out of the door. "Bit late for that now! Hope no one gets shot!"

"Shit! I didn't think about that!" Corey looked mortified, realizing she could have got someone killed.

"Guess you didn't…you need to go?" Kane asked her.

"Yep." Corey had forgotten that she did indeed need to go to the bathroom.

"I'll come with you. We don't want to lose our meal ticket down there. Miss prim and proper!"

"Thought you liked her, boss?" and as they climbed down from the bus and walked across to the trees, Corey looked sideward at him, her long eyelashes hiding eyes that held a certain jealousy.

Kane heard it. "I like her only as much that she will lead us to her father, and to my wife."

Reality check for Corey. "Right, your wife."

They had reached the trees. "Remember, stay by me back on the bus. I mean right by me. We'll square it with your boyfriend later."

"Kane, he is not my boyfriend. He just thinks he is," she stressed.

"Ah, ha," and Kane disappeared behind one of the trees to join the men. The field was wide open.

Kane joined several men and a couple of little boys all relieving themselves behind a large patch of trees. Kane did what he had to do, zipped his jeans back up and stepped back out into the clearing. He waited a few seconds, and then turned to look in the area that both Corey and Sarah had disappeared to. Sarah appeared first.

"Better?" asked Kane, not knowing what the hell else to say.

"Yes, thanks for asking. You?"

"Much," and Kane started back towards the bus. He needed to let Tyrone and Sam take their turn. Kane glanced back down the dusty road. There was no sign of anyone following them, not even Hunter. He felt no guilt at leaving him behind; in fact, he felt nothing for anyone lately, least of all himself. He wondered why?

"Kane," yelled Sam from the bus steps. "Swap?"

"Sure, sorry…be right there!" and Kane hurried across the grass to the parked bus. "Sorry, mates. You two go. I'll stand guard," as Kane jumped up the steps and onto the bus in imitation sentry duty. He watched them go. Two totally different men; and two men that were light years away from each other.

Sarah joined Kane on the step, and standing next to him, slipped her arm round his waist.

He looked down to his waist. "A little familiar in public, don't you think, Miss Holden?"

"No one is looking, and what do you care if they do, Kane? You don't exactly hide the fact that you like women. I saw you talking with Corey. You fancy her or something?" Sarah was pushing him again.

"If I did, what business is it of yours?" Kane was more than blunt.

"None, but I don't think your wife would like it? Do you?" and she played with the back of his T-shirt.

"How is she going to know unless you tell her? Anyway, if I was going after someone it would be you. I would have more to gain, wouldn't I, Miss Holden?" Kane rested his hand on her shoulder, and fingered her long hair, feeling it was soft to his touch.

"What do you think you would gain there? Or are you gonna punch me out if I call you anything but Kane?" Sarah stated, trying not to respond to him touching her hair.

"Well, let's see. You can lead me to your father. You can also get me amnesty, and then I would be safe, for the time being anyway."

"You give me too much credit, Kane. They sent me to lead you to my father, a father that is also expecting you. He just doesn't know I will be with you and he doesn't know what you know. Then again, no one else on this trip knows what you know." As she spoke, she slid her hand lower on his waist, just into the top of his jeans. She touched the gun very lightly in the back of his jeans, and her hand carried on going to his side just below his belt, and pressed gently. "Still hurt?"

Kane winced slightly. "Only when I laugh or make love; and I haven't done much of either lately."

"Perhaps you need to remedy that, Kane," and she left her hand lingering on the top of his jeans, her fingers playing with his leather belt.

"Maybe I should, after all, I don't have much time left, do I, Miss Holden?" said Kane, trying not to pay too much attention to the very obvious pass she was making to him.

"No, Kane, you might not. Fan splinters are very dangerous things, and so are Australian agents working for American and Japanese governments, especially when you are not quite sure which side they are on. Right?"

"Right, Agent Holden, so maybe I should be just a little bit nicer to you, shouldn't I?"

"Maybe you should, Commander Branson. Maybe you should!" and Sarah looked up into his face and smiled a precocious smile.

Chapter 17

Sarah let go of Kane's waist, as Corey appeared from the trees, and walked over to the bus. Kane stopped playing with the end of Sarah's hair, but the dishonorable thoughts stayed with him. She looked so much like Kelly...

"Everything alright, boss?" asked Corey as she mounted the steps to where Kane stood, glancing at Sarah, who was turning to leave Kane. Corey noted the smug look Sarah sported, like the cat that had tasted the cream.

"Fine," was the first, and the last, word that came to Kane's mind. He turned around and headed for the back of the bus, all the time watching Sarah's backside in motion.

Corey followed him. He had told her one thing and now his actions screamed another. Was this man always this confusing?

Instead of taking the usual seat in the back, Kane sat in the seat in front of Sarah, who seated herself next to the window and propped her feet on the back of Kane's seat. Corey chose not to sit by Sarah, which was what Kane was forcing her to do, either that or to sit right next to him. She chose the latter, which was received with a smile from Kane.

"Is anyone else hungry, or is it just me? Seems like hours ago when we ate. Fact it is hours ago!" Sam was yelling to Kane, as he joined their group back on the bus. Sam pushed his hair from his eyes, walked towards Kane, and pulled his back pack to the floor. "Must be something in here to eat," and he rummaged through his stuff, pulling out a candy bar he had stuffed in there some time back. He ripped the wrapper from it, went to put it in his mouth and stopped. "Anyone want a bite?"

Various heads shook no.

"Good, more for me!" and Sam tucked into the candy bar with relish, which went down in a total of three bites.

"Hungry, Sam?" inquired his father.

"Yeah, thirsty, too. I wonder how far we are from Baghdad?" Sam had finished his candy bar and was stuffing the empty wrapper into his backpack.

"About an hour," answered Mr. Military. "I looked at a map. It seems we are going through a neighborhood that is known for terrorist activity."

Everyone looked at Mr. Military, including Kane. "And you would know that because?" asked Kane trying to make a point that he didn't really know Mr. Military.

"Name is Kirk, Captain Kirk, United States Airforce. And before I get the usual comments about the Enterprise, I had the name first." This darker-skinned man, with hardly a hint of an American accent, made his presence known to them at last. Aside from the much shaved head, there was no other sign that he was military. His clothes were black and formal, but not totally unbelievable for the area. His build was stockier than his friend, and he appeared to be about Kane's age, maybe older.

"Nice to meet you," stated Sam. "And, of course, you already met Kane." Sam glanced at his father and back to Kirk.

"Yes, sir. I already met him," and a look passed between Kane and Kirk, "when his fist connected with my jaw!"

Sam had the feeling that wasn't the first time they had formally met. He figured they had been introduced back on the last plane, when Kane became the new superhero. He still hadn't figured what they gave Kane, but it had certainly stopped any pain he was in and heightened his senses.

"I have to get to Baghdad for a meeting. I was supposed to be there an hour ago! Then this stupid crap happened. They can't take a plane in because there is gunfire? Geez…back in Nam you just flew the sons-of-bitches in, never mind the gunfire. Shoot back at the fuckers, I say!" And Kirk stopped, aware he had mentioned Nam.

'So that's the connection,' thought Sam. "You were in Vietnam, sir?" Sam asked him.

"Right, son. Saw plenty of action." The new found friend sat himself down on a seat close to Kane. "If you are still hungry, I have some food in my backpack, and a bottle of water. You are welcome to it. Trying to diet, myself." Kirk replied. "It's the black one on the seat," and he pointed to the place he had been sitting previously.

The Captain seemed to be making a point of Sam getting sustenance.

"Thanks. I'll grab some. Anyone else like any?" Sam asked as he turned.

"Please," replied Sarah. "Some water."

"Coming up," and Sam headed for the backpack. As he unzipped the top, he could clearly see water and some crackers. He dug deeper and found nuts. Not very well hidden underneath was a gun, and then another gun. Sam recognized them immediately. They were Hunter's and Kane's .38 standard AFP issue. So, this was how Tucker meant to get them to Kane. Now, they had two more guns. How had Kirk known to have Sam find them? Unless Tucker had told him that he was Kane's son. And now, for sure, Sam knew that his father and Kirk had met. Maybe, if he dug deeper, he might find some kind of drug...

"You find what you were looking for, son?" Kirk shouted to him, half-turning his head. "Yeah, sure you did! Take what you need," and continued talking to the unit as a whole.

Sam stuffed the guns down the back of his jeans, along with the other gun, making him a walking arsenal. He grabbed the water and food and turned back towards the group.

"Here, Sarah. You first," and handed her the rather tepid water.

Sarah grabbed it, opened the top and guzzled down a quarter of a bottle.

"Save some for the rest of us," put in Corey, licking her thirsty lips, and reached around the seat, trying to snatch the bottle from Sarah.

"Ladies! Ladies," interjected Kane. "There is plenty enough for you both, and some left over for Sam."

"Hell, what about me?" asked Tyrone, looking fiercely at Kane.

"What about you? I'm sure you've been on missions before without water, right?" asked Kane, totally unconcerned about Tyrone's feelings.

"Just because you don't need water doesn't mean I don't."

"Ask your girlfriend for her share then," added Kane.

"He's not my boyfriend, Kane," Corey jumped into the conversation.

"That's right, you just told me that!" Kane retorted, really stirring the pot, and he leaned over the seat and took the bottle from Sarah, handing it to Corey without even a second thought.

Corey swigged it back, more than wetting her lips, and then purposely handing it to Kane, who took it from her and took only one sip. He smiled at her, and then handed it across her to Tyrone. "One sip only. You and I can do without till we get to Baghdad. One! Then hand it to Sam."

"I thought Hitler was dead," mumbled Tyrone, but did as he was asked, taking one giant sip from the bottle, and handed it to Sam.

Sam grabbed the bottle and glugged it back till it was empty.

"You really were thirsty, son," Kirk declared. "So, where are you guys heading?" Kirk plunged right in there.

"Baghdad," Kane's reply came fast. It irritated Kane that Kirk kept calling Sam son, as though he was making some point about it.

"I know that. I meant after that. You are together, right?" Kirk once again pitched in.

"I think that's obvious, mate," and Kane raised his legs up on the back of the seat in front of him, his boots resting on the armrest, and he slumped down in his seat. He was pretending to rest.

The captain took the hint. "Well, I guess I will go see if you left me any food, er? Didn't catch your name, son," and stared hard at Sam.

"It's Sam Branson." Sam said it on purpose. Tyrone and Corey already knew, and he figured somehow that Sarah did, too, so now was the time to find out if she really did.

Kane's feet dropped to the floor with a loud thump and the look on his face was one of amazement.

"Well, *dad*, you must have told your new girlfriend by now!" Sam was flippant in his comments. "And I am sure everyone else knows. We god damn look alike, *sir*! Not sure why it's such a state secret. It's fact!"

Sarah was crimson. She did know, but Kane had not told her. It was in his file. The captain also knew. Again, it was in Kane's file. But no one knew that everyone knew. Now, everyone did know.

"So, I am your new girlfriend, Kane. Thanks for letting me know," Sarah said, leaning over the back of the seat and whispering to Kane. "Guess we should consummate that fact!"

Kane shot her a scornful look. "If, I had a new girlfriend, I would know. And, if I had wanted everyone to know you were my son, Sam, they would, and they didn't."

"Well, they do now," commented Kirk. "And I was calling you *son*," he laughed, looking at Sam. "Funny. Well, I don't see what harm there is in knowing. Makes no difference to me!"

Sam realized that maybe Kirk really didn't know, or he was a damned good actor. Maybe it had been wrong not to consult with Kane first, but he wanted to smoke some things out, and he had done just that. He had noticed both Kirk's and Sarah's expressions. They had made one mistake. They had glanced at each other before Sarah had leaned over to talk to Kane. He thought maybe Kane had seen Kirk's look but from his position in the seating, he could not have seen Sarah's. It was obvious they knew each other. Now, Sam was confused. How could they? But he had also begun to realize that Kane knew Sarah, too. The only ones that didn't seem to know the captain were Tyrone and Corey, and they should be the people to know him. He realized Kirk was still babbling away to the others. Maybe, he was just the messenger.

"So your name must be Kane Branson?" asked Kirk, looking straight at Kane's face.

"Would appear so," replied Kane, purposely glaring at Sam. "I just usually go by the name Kane. Saves a lot of problems." Kane turned away from Kirk and looked directly at Sam. "Sam, let's go see what is holding the driver up. We should be almost where we are going, instead of just sitting on this fucking bus. Everyone is back onboard, aren't they?"

Not the statement Sam was expecting from Kane. He glanced around the bus. Seemed full enough. Sam stood up and backed down the bus. Kane thought that was kind of odd, but excused himself past Corey and followed him down to the driver.

"Give!" demanded Kane, his right hand stretched to Sam.

"What?" replied Sam, with a nonchalant attitude and his back still away from Kane.

"You know fucking well what…he's American. You went in the backpack. He made sure you did. Now, you have our guns!"

"I do?" Sam was smug and glanced away from his father

"Yes, you fucking do!" Kane was getting irritated.

"And if I do, why didn't you get them back on the other flight, *dad*?"

"Because I wanted to get the ones away from Sarah first, which I did. And why the fuck am I standing here explaining to you. Just give me mine and Hunter's guns."

"But they are working together, or didn't you know that?" Sam was a little puzzled.

"I knew it. I didn't want them to know I knew."

"And she is your new girlfriend, right?" Sam kept pushing.

"Kelly is the only women I want! You god dam know that!" replied Kane.

"Then what's with you and Sarah?" Sam replied.

"I can't tell you, so don't keep pushing it. You understand?" Kane was menacing and raised his voice above the whisper it had been when he first started the conversation.

"You gonna screw her?" Sam didn't flinch in his questioning.

"What?!" Kane's eyes creased in anger. He had had enough.

"You heard me!" Sam moved closer to his father.

"Yeah, I did. I'll do what I have to do. Now, unless you want to go the way of Hunter, give me the guns. NOW!" Kane hissed about three inches from Sam's face.

"Hunter," pondered Sam. "Makes me wonder now why you got rid of him. He wasn't gay, was he? That was a cover. You just had to find a reason for him to go. How much more does he know that I don't?"

"Enough, Sam. I mean it!" and Kane's clenched left hand started to move from his side.

Sam saw it. He didn't think his father would follow through, but right now he wasn't sure about that. He reached around to the back of his jeans. "How are you going to explain three guns in the back of your pants?"

"No one will see me when I sit down. And who said they would be in the back of my jeans? I have other places to put guns!" Kane's toned mellowed a half degree, and he sat down to the side of Sam, and raised his jeans leg up past the top of his dirt boots. "Now, one last time, give!"

Sam handed both .38's to his father. He watched as Kane undid the laces on the boot, stuffed one gun inside, laced the boot back up over the gun, and replaced his jeans over the top of everything. He still had his other gun tucked neatly in the back of his pants.

It was right now that Kane wished he had his jacket or his sweatshirt, but he didn't. They were with his backpack. He turned from the seat and glanced back down the bus. No way could he get the other gun back unseen. The rest of his clothes were way too tight to hide anything they didn't already cover. "Damn it!" he cursed under his breath. Thinking he would have to do the same with the other, he stopped. His cell was in the other laced-up boot.

"Need any help, Kane?" Corey leaned over his shoulder.

Sam had seen her approaching, but decided not to tell his father. He wanted to see just what would happen next.

"Yeah. Stuff this down your pants," and he handed her the spare gun.

"You look surprised Special Agent Branson," and Corey took the gun from Kane, and put it inside the front of her sweats. "You looked shocked, sir that I know who you are."

Sam stared at her. She wasn't talking to his father, but to him. He looked from one to the other. Hunter had tried to convey not to trust Corey. Now, he wondered exactly which side Kane was on.

Chapter 18

"How on earth did you know?" asked Sam. "My father must have told you in one of his geriatric moments, right?"

"I don't think you should be so rude about the Commander, Agent Branson, especially as there is still doubt which side you are on?"

"Which side I am on? Which side is *he* on?" asked a very confused Sam, squinting with his mother's Asian eyes at Kane.

"Think you know the answer to that, *son*, and if you don't by now, you should. I didn't make commander for nothing, and if you have anything to say, say it to my face. Nothing has changed," Kane said fiercely as he stood up to his full menacing height.

"Might not have changed, just seems like I wasn't aware of all the facts. You told me no one knew who I was." His look was one of betrayal towards his father.

"I lied!" said Kane nonchalantly.

"Why?" Sam was more suspicious than ever.

"Cause I wanted to see who was on which side." Kane was good under fire. He had years of practice under his belt.

"That include yourself?" Every word was aimed at Kane.

"Absolutely!" he shot back at Sam, his brows furrowed in disgust that he was being questioned.

"You son-of-a-bitch, Kane! What are you playing at? And more to the point, what does Sarah Holden have over you?" Sam had to find out.

"Nothing!" replied Kane all too quickly, and his eyes averted his son's gaze.

"Give it up, Kane. She does, and we all know she does. I saw your face when I said new girlfriend. That's what she is pretending to be. Only Corey here knows she's not, from when? Or is it Corey you're gonna screw? Is that why she is so close to you so suddenly?" Sam was running close to the limit and he knew it.

Kane took a step forward. It wasn't just Corey's honor at stake, but his own reputation.

"Let me explain to you, once and for all." Kane was angry now and it was going way past the joking stage. "In the past, I have been known to take what I wanted," he conceded, "and once before, I had to create a situation that almost led to someone getting raped, and that isn't gonna happen again. Corey is smart enough to know that what happened by the bathroom was just that, something that happened. Right, Corey?" Kane looked her in the face, hoping she gave the right answer.

She did. "Right, Kane." She said what he needed to hear; knowing full well that's not what was going down. "Why would you think otherwise, Sam?" She pulled her sweatshirt on the top of her pants. "Perhaps I should go back to our end of the bus and leave you two to talk?"

"Good idea," Kane said with a sideward glance at Sam. "I'll be right there. Just need a couple of minutes with my *son*, here."

Kane waited till Corey was out of earshot. "Just go along with whatever I do. I trusted you with my life once in Hong Kong. Now, I am asking you to do the same. Trust me, no matter what happens. Okay?" he whispered.

"Do I have any choice? I am stuck on this damn bus with you! But you seem to switch from one side to the other in the blink of an eye! Sometimes, I don't know you. You are not real!" Sam was becoming exasperated.

"Sometimes, I am not! Tell the driver to get a move on and let's get to where we are going," and Kane sauntered past Sam and back up the bus to talk to the rest of the unit.

Sam stood in Kane's dust, where he figured he would always be standing; two steps behind him. He couldn't figure out what was going on in Kane's head before; now he certainly couldn't. But he did trust him, god knows why, but he did. Sam motioned to the driver to get going and then followed his father, just like he would always do. He watched Kane slide in the seat next to the window and Corey sat down next to him.

As he approached his seat on the end of the row, Sam could hear Corey whispering to Kane and it wasn't in English. Wasn't Arabic either. Sam could have sworn it was Chinese! He could understand everything they were saying, so it had to be. He knew Kane spoke the language, but it was news to him that Corey did, then again, Corey seemed to be in on most things. She was sitting so close to Kane, that there was no space between them. They obviously didn't want Sarah or Tyrone to hear what they were saying, and had discovered a common language to converse in.

Sam noted Sarah's look of jealousy, and Tyrone appeared to be extremely agitated by the whole proceedings. Sam thought that maybe Kane didn't want to piss Tyrone completely off. He may need him in the days to come. Then again, Kane never needed anyone.

The pair stopped whispering as they realized that Sam was right next to their seat. He glared at Kane, and Kane winked back at his son, as if to try and ease the tension that had sprung up between them.

Sam sat down abruptly on the aisle seat opposite Corey, as the bus lurched forward and began its travels once more at a much steadier and deliberate pace.

Kirk leaned over the back of his seat to talk to Sam. "I did not know he was your father. I hope you believe that. I just knew to get the guns to you, not that it matters. I am sure Tucker had his reasons for not telling me." Kirk picked at the plaid threads that still managed to hang onto the seat back. "What does worry me is that there was gunfire at the airport. Someone else knows that Kane is coming, someone other than her father!" and he inclined his head towards Sarah.

"You know her, don't you?" Sam asked Kirk, knowing full well what the answer was.

"Of course. She's an Australian agent, like you." Kirk looked at Sam like he should have known.

"She's what?! And you also know who I am?" His eyebrows raised in horror, as did his voice. He glanced over his shoulder to see if anyone had heard him.

"Of course I know who you are. Sarah doesn't know though. But didn't you know that about her? Strange, I thought the commander would have told you. Sarah is working with us, too. Has been for a year now, but to be honest, we have been watching her. Maybe her own agency is watching her, too. Something doesn't ring true about her." Kirk paused and sighed, as though he was really thinking about that angle.

"You sure Kane knows who she is? He doesn't meet every new agent that joins the academy. Maybe he never met her before," questioned Sam.

"Quite possibly he hasn't met her. I don't know everyone in my own squad, and she may not have told him she is on an assignment for us. Sarah is helping us get to her father, but we couldn't just take her in there. And she doesn't know Ryan Holden like Kane does, nor can she kill him either. He is still her father!" Kirk pulled a handkerchief from his pocket, and wiped the sweat from his face.

Sam wondered if he was just hot or the sweat was from nervousness.

"Can I ask you where she was overseas? Sarah mentioned she was on a trip for the last few months. Do you know where?" Sam dreaded the answer.

"Of course. Japan! Why do you ask?" It was Kirk's turn to look confused, and he patted his forehead some more. .

Suddenly, for Sam, everything fell into place. Kane had met Sarah Holden in Japan. Had he slept with her? He wasn't sure. Did Kane trust her? Of course not! Kane didn't trust anyone, not even himself. Kirk knew Sarah. He didn't seem to know Corey or Tyrone, yet they were both Americans, but two were army and one was airforce. Still, seemed strange they didn't know each other, and yet they both knew Tucker.

"Why are you telling me this information? I could tell Kane?" Sam questioned.

"You could and you probably will. He will either tell you he knows or he will be shocked. Somehow, I think he knows. He is playing it low key on purpose. We think she has some kind of hold on him and we don't know why or what it is. Something must have happened somewhere to them both. Something none of us know about."

Now, Sam's ears pricked up. He turned around in his seat so that only Kirk could hear him. "You think so, too?"

"Tell me. Does she look like Kane's wife?" asked Kirk, wondering if he was hitting too many home bases.

"How the hell do you know that? Have you seen pictures? Are you working *with* Tucker or *for* Tucker?" asked Sam.

"With...he tells only what we need to know, and why am I telling you? Because, since my partner was killed, I have to have backup. I really didn't know you were Kane's son. Tucker just asked me to give you the guns. Now, I know why. It appears that you are the only one on this mission that can be trusted. It would seem that whatever Miss Holden has on your father has top level clearance. There are giant pieces missing from the puzzle."

Indeed, there were. Kirk obviously didn't know that Kane had been stabbed. He also didn't know about the heroin or he would have brought it up by now. Yet, he was the one who supposedly had given something to Kane on the plane...or had he? Maybe Kane had it in his bag the whole time. Maybe, Sarah or Corey gave it to him. No, that couldn't be it. Sam was confused.

Sam turned back to look at Kane, who was leaning against the seat, pretending to be asleep. He knew his father well enough to know he wasn't. Suddenly, he felt very protective towards Kane. He was obviously hiding something from everyone except Sarah. She seemed to be the puppeteer, and Kane the puppet. But why? What had they done in Japan that would cause this, and why had she been there?

An idea so absurd came to his brain. Why did she look so much like Kelly? And why was she with Kane in Japan, and instead of Kelly? Kane told him that he wouldn't take Kelly with him. Was it because Sarah went with him instead? Kane had looked shocked when he had seen the butterfly on her breast implying he had not seen her without clothes. What if he had seen her before the tattoo and it was a recent addition? What if the girls were so much alike to outsiders that they could switch them? Was that the plan? To switch them under Ryan's nose, and then Ryan to find out later he had his own daughter there? Unlikely. But there was a huge piece of the puzzle missing.

Sam turned even further in his seat and looked back to Sarah. She was sulking, and not hiding it too well, either. Her pretty pink lips pouted, and her feet kicked just slightly on the back of Kane's seat, showing her jealousy.

Kane totally ignored her, and carried on pretending to sleep. He was very tired though, but at this moment he could not afford to sleep. He needed his eyes wide open.

Corey leaned back in her seat, feeling like Tyrone was staring a hole in the back of her head. She smiled to herself. There was no competition between him and Kane. But he wasn't hers for the taking. At least she was near him for now, and she found it comforting that he needed her for whatever reason.

Tyrone's eyes darted from one to the other like a caged animal. He didn't like Kane. The more he was around him, the more the animosity built up. Maybe he would make a play for Sarah? She seemed to be the 'other woman' and something that would possibly irritate Kane. He moved along the seat towards Sarah, and pulled gum from his pocket.

"Gum? Not bad tasting stuff. We haven't talked much, have we? You wanna talk?" Tyrone shook the pack and a stick slid out onto the palm of his hand.

Sarah turned to him. In an instant she figured what he was doing. He hadn't spoken two words to her the whole trip and now he was sidling up to her. "Sure, why not? Got anything else I might want?" and she picked the gum from his hand, letting her fingers linger there a second or two longer than needed, tossing her head in such a fashion as if to come on to him there and then.

Tyrone caught the implication immediately. He whispered in her ear and she laughed very precociously.

Kane heard it, just like he was supposed to. He hadn't thought of that combination. Now, that could be a dangerous liaison for Tyrone. Sarah would eat him for breakfast, but it would keep them both occupied for a time. Kane smiled, opened his eyes, and looked at the window. With his right hand, he rubbed the glass to get a better view of the outside. It was now late afternoon and the sun was going down. He had hoped to be leaving Baghdad by now, not just arriving on the outskirts of the city.

"See anything?" Corey asked him while peering round the side of him and looking through the windows as buildings seemed to loom into sight.

"Sun is starting to go down. Over there…look…a mosque. Looks kinda like a finger pointing up to god in anger!"

Corey had never heard Kane speak like that before. "You're right, it does." She watched his face, while Kane pulled a band from his wrist and pulled his long hair back into a ponytail. She figured Kane had a side that only Kelly and his children saw.

Without warning, Kane stretched his arm round the back of her and pulled her closer to the window. "Look…Baghdad!"

Corey leaned on him as she looked to see what he was seeing. Like Kane, she had traveled the world, and could see the things he could see in the sunset. Powder puff skies, leaving way for the darkness which concealed many things, including humans. And then there it was; large, overcrowded, bustling as the sun sank, looming before them, enticing them into its arms and folding them into enveloped wings.

From outside the bus, noise became a reality with car horns, yelling street vendors, and people heading downtown for the night. No one noticed as the bus carrying death slithered into town. No one cared. In Baghdad, death was a way of life. The only difference was that this was not home grown, only the best imported kind…headed by one person, the man of war.

Chapter 19

Baghdad's traffic was congested and the bus took another half hour to reach its terminal where finally they could disembark; tired, dirty and much disheveled.

"Can you ask someone where the bathroom is?" Sarah muttered to Tyrone.

Tyrone was only too happy to help his new found friend out.

"I'll come with you," interjected Corey, and the two girls took off behind Tyrone to find the restroom.

"God, it's good to be off that bus." Sam said, while stretching his legs, and then turned to Kane. "So where to now, dad? We need a car don't we? Some sort of transportation to get us to Samarra."

"We do, but I think we need to get a room, get a shower, and change clothes." While he was speaking, Kane was looking around the street near the bus terminal. He spotted a small inexpensive looking place only a block from where they were standing. "Right there, see it?" Kane pointed to the place. "I'll walk over and see if they have a room. We only need one. We are not staying!"

Sam didn't have a chance to answer him. Kane disappeared into the flow of traffic and crossed the street. Sam figured he better wait there with the bags, and for the girls to come back. He looked down at the floor. He was surrounded by backpacks of all colors.

"They left you then, son?" asked a weary looking captain.

"Appears so, sir. Where are you going from here?" 'Think before you ask such damn stupid questions, Sam!' he thought.

"Following you guys, but at a distance. Holden doesn't know the air force is here. Even Sarah won't tell him that. I'll say goodbye for now. Say goodbye to the commander for me…and wish him luck."

"Quick question." Sam needed to know.

Kirk nodded.

"Does Ryan know his daughter is coming in with Kane?" Sam cocked his head sideward.

"No," and Kirk turned on his heal and walked away, waving as he went.

"Where's Kirk going?" asked Tyrone, who had returned without the girls, leaving them on their own after they found the ladies room.

"Back to his job." Sam changed the conversation. "Kane has gone to get a room so we can shower and change. Guess we smell funny!" and Sam laughed. He wasn't keen on Tyrone either.

"Really? Just one room?" questioned Tyrone.

"We aren't staying, just resting and showering and there are only five of us. Why waste money?" questioned Sam.

"We wouldn't want that would we, Sam? Your father must have plenty to spend, but not on us!"

Sam thought that a very odd statement, but decided to ignore it, and looked across the street hoping that Kane would appear on cue, which was pretty much what he did.

"Hotel was pretty full, but managed to get a suite with a couple of bedrooms. I thought maybe we should stay the night. It's late and we are all tired, let alone dirty. Small cafe next door, so we can eat. Doesn't matter to me which order." For a moment, Kane looked his fifty-nine years, like in just a few short hours it had caught up with him. He glanced at Tyrone. "Where are the ladies?"

"Restroom." Tyrone was blunt and to the point. He was only on this mission because he was ordered to be, and for no other reason.

"Tyrone, you wait here and bring them over to the hotel. Room is registered under Kane. Sam, you and I will go check out the suite. I just booked it, didn't look at it!" Kane turned to face the hotel again, while pulling the band back out of his hair. It fell onto his shoulders, hanging there. He bent down and grabbed his backpack. He didn't need to carry Sarah's now. He had what he wanted from hers.

"Think that dispenses any thoughts you may have had about Kane being cheap, Tyrone," Sam said as a parting gesture, a smug smile on his face, and took off after Kane.

As they were leaving, the ladies returned.

"Where's Kane going? Do we follow him?" asked Corey, half glancing at Tyrone.

"You'd follow him anywhere…" he stopped.

"Tyrone, stop it right there! We are not married to each other! Why don't you look after Sarah? She needs you more than I do." Corey picked her backpack up and stormed off in the direction of the hotel, hurrying to catch up with her new boss, and narrowly missed a cyclist as he went by.

"Really fancies him, doesn't she?" asked Sarah twisting the knife in Tyrone. She pulled on her hair, twirling it with her fingers.

"Yeah…" and Tyrone stared after her.

"He's using her." Sarah thought she was making a smart comment.

"Yeah, babe, he is. Just like he is using you! He's playing you against each other just to pass the fucking time till he finds his wife, and then it'll be like you never existed. Heard about Australian men before. That's what they do. All sport! And you…you are using him and me just to get what you want. It's something. Not sure, but you want something from him. I'll figure it out. I may not like Kane, but I do respect him and he isn't dumb. He'll figure it, too, if he hasn't already," and Tyrone slung his and Sarah's backpack on his shoulders and followed the others, dodging a couple of cars that happened to be in the way on the street.

Sarah followed Tyrone. Maybe, he wasn't as dumb as she thought he was and that could be a problem.

Inside the hotel lobby, Kane waited for Corey. The desk clerk that had spoken English to him minutes before was now missing, and a very foreboding Arabic gentleman now stood there. Kane was trying to convey they wanted food brought in. Suddenly, he was very tired and the thought of sitting next door in a noisy restaurant lost its appeal. He wanted to shower, eat and sleep, in that order.

"Corey, where the fuck are you…."

She came bolting through the sliding glass door and stood next to him.

"Ask him about food, from next door; from anywhere. Just get it and whatever passes for alcohol out here. Water, lots of water and juices," and he left her standing with Sam, while he climbed the stairs to the second floor room.

On the stairs, he passed people that stared at him like they had never seen a man with long hair before; especially long blond hair. If they thought he looked out of place, he thought they would think it funnier to find a Chinese man with long blond hair. He guessed that this wasn't the most expensive part of town, but probably the place most likely to get mugged in.

He turned the key in the lock, opened the door and stepped into the room. It was huge. He didn't know what he imagined, but not this. Two four-seater plaid couches sat in the middle of the floor, another one by the window, and he could see two doors at the far end of the room. Guessing those to be the bedrooms, he moved towards them, passing small oak tables on his way. He wondered just how much money would disappear from his credit card when his bill came in, not that it mattered.

Opening the one door, he found the room housed a giant bed that would sleep three if needs be. It wasn't the finest bed linen on it, but it was adequate. He decided the girls should take that bed. He checked out the bathroom. Seemed fine, aside from the couple of cockroaches he saw scurry away behind the oversized bath. Looked clean enough and right now that's what mattered. Plenty of towels, face clothes and soap. Now, that did look appealing.

He dragged his mind away from the shower and returned to the main room to check out the other bedroom. This one was much smaller, more like a box with a bed and closet in it. Once again, off the room, was the bathroom. Kane dumped his bag on the far side of the now claimed bed, and walked into the bathroom. There was the shower calling his name. This time he listened. He wasn't waiting for anyone else to arrive. Stripping off his clothes, he dropped them on the floor anywhere they happened to fall. Pulling the shower curtain back, he stepped in, turned the water on as hot as it would go and dunked his head under the nozzle.

As water ran down his body, he squirted liquid soap onto him-self and grabbed the sponge to rub it into his body. The warmth and relaxation from the steam was good, and he tossed his soaking wet hair back over his head. He closed his eyes as water tumbled down him and poured down the drain washing away the dirt and grime from the trip. Deciding that he should save enough hot water for the others, he reached down and turned off the tap. So engrossed in the shower, Kane didn't hear the bathroom door open, and someone step inside the room.

Corey hadn't noticed the backpack on the bed when she walked through the room and into the bathroom. She thought it was the maid finishing off the service and her military experience had taught her to check everything out.

Both she and Sam had left the front desk together after ordering food and making sure the others knew where they were. Sam had then stopped to check out schedules for renting a car. Corey had kept on going.

As she stepped into the bathroom, Kane pulled the shower cur-tain back at the very same second, and he wasn't quick enough to grab the towel that hung on the rail.

Kane had never been a shy man and he wasn't now. He wasn't ashamed of his body; in fact, in general, he was very proud of it.

Corey started at the top of Kane, his long hair dripping water, and her eyes moved down his ripped chest. She tried not to look any lower, and failed.

Kane's muscles flexed and he was well aware of the situation that they were now in. "Mind handing me a towel?" He decided he should do something as one part of him was beginning to be extremely hap-py at seeing Corey.

"Er...no...I mean, yes," she stammered. "I mean..." Her brain was flustered.

"I know what you mean." Kane was amused. "I'll get it." He stepped out of the shower and onto the tiled floor, and reached for the towel. Wrapping it round his waist, he turned to look at Corey. She was red, and it showed over her light black skin. Her eyes had never left his body.

"What, you have never seen a white guy before?" and Kane laughed. "Not much different to a black guy."

"That's for damn sure…I mean…well, you know what I mean." Corey was embarrassed.

"Thanks for the compliment! Are you blushing, young lady?" he peered down into her face, and put his fingers under her chin. "You are!"

Kane didn't know why, but he bent his head and kissed her lips, his hand sliding from her chin round the back of her head. He had imagined her hair to be courser than it was, as the silk black strands caught round his fingers.

Corey responded to Kane without even thinking what she was doing. His kiss was deep, lingering and offered promise that was obvious to her he could fulfill. She reached up and touched his shoulders with her fingers, gently resting them there, almost unsure of herself and what she thought might happen next.

Kane knew there was chemistry. He never thought he would follow through. His mind was screaming this was wrong, but his body was telling him to go for it. He let his hands wander her back to the base of her sweatshirt. He fingered the band on it, and then with one expert movement he lifted the shirt straight up and over her, making her hair slick back on her head.

Corey held her breath, and replaced her hands back on his shoulders.

Underneath her shirt she wore a pretty pink lace bra. It took Kane all of five seconds to see it and undo it.

Corey stepped back and let the bra drop to the floor. She undid her own pants and stepped out of them, all the time her eyes fixed on his face.

Kane took the green light and moved ahead. He slid his arms around her waist; one that he realized was tinier than he first thought it would be. Her skin was smooth under his older, tougher hands. His fingers searched the top of her matching pink lace panties, and carefully he slid his hand down inside them, grasping her strong buttock in his grasp.

Corey gasped. She had been with many black men, and Kane was the first white man that she had ever had sex with. His expertise was better than she had ever known before. She raised her head high and moved forward to kiss him.

He met her halfway and as there lips met, she felt a surge through her she thought she would never forget. Her arms slid round his back and she held him in her grasp. She closed her eyes and let the moment take her wherever she needed to go.

Kane clung to her, his thirst needing to be quenched. Gently, he guided her back to the wall of the bathroom, and held her there.

His kisses became more intense as his hands slid the panties from her body and her breasts rested on his chest. When the towel fell from his body, neither of them knew. It didn't matter, only that it had gone from his body and was not in the way of what they both wanted to happen. He bent his head and his mouth rested on her now erect nipple. Her hands reached for his hair, and she pulled him as tightly as she could into her breast. Her head rested back on the wall, and she moaned softly and his mouth carried on down her body to the soft and moist place that waited impatiently for him.

As quickly as he had reached the patch of hair, his mouth nestling into her lips, he raised straight back up and lifted Corey up, her legs straddling round his body. He held her there, her body pressed onto the tiled wall. Kane had never needed any guidance and he didn't now. As he entered her body, Corey moaned much louder than he thought she would, and Kane kissed her hard to stop the others from hearing her cry out.

Sweat ran down her body and she clung to Kane with her legs, while her hands reached into his hair, and she clung almost in an animalistic fashion to him. All Corey knew was that she wanted it to last for ever, and so did Kane.

Chapter 20

"Kane," Corey whispered.

Kane opened his eyes. He blinked hard.

"Kane, you ok?" asked Corey. "I heard you from the other room. I knocked, but you didn't hear me. I had to come in to see if you were ok?"

Kane looked around him. He was standing wrapped in a towel leaning on the bathroom wall. He wasn't sure how long he had been like that. He laughed. "It was all a fucking dream!"

"What was?" Corey asked, appearing just a tad embarrassed that she had found him like that, not that she minded seeing more of him. And, in fact, she wished she had found him in the shower. She silently scolded herself for having such thoughts and turned her eyes away from him.

"You and I were...well, never mind! I thought you were in here... god, I must be tired or something..." Kane's voice trailed off, and he sat down on the chair next to the shower. "Be a good girl and go get me some clean clothes from my backpack," and he leaned his head back on the wall, his hair dropping back onto his shoulders. How on earth could he have dreamed that? Maybe if he had been back on the heroin...but he wasn't. Maybe, some sort of delayed reaction? He didn't think so. Possibly something he had taken on the plane? Now, that could be it! He shook his head. Was he hallucinating? He stood up and looked in the mirror. Pushing his hair back and pulling a band on it to keep it in place, he half turned and saw the marks on the top of his back. He looked again at his shoulder and the very

163

recent scratches made by finger nails. He froze! It wasn't a dream, but why had Corey lied? He removed his watch from the ledge under the mirror. It was half an hour later than when he went into the shower. Where were the others? Wouldn't they have missed the two of them? Corey interrupted his thoughts as she came bustling back through the bathroom door.

"I found these, Kane," and she handed him clean jeans, T-shirt and even underwear, all black and all tight fitting.

"Thanks! You find everything ok?" he asked her, his tone a little less friendly than when she left, and the question could very well be taken two ways.

It was then Kane realized she had changed clothes. They were not the same ones she was wearing on the bus. Beside the sweatshirt disappearing, she was in tight blue jeans and a yellow cutaway top, a far cry from what she had been wearing. Kane didn't have to guess what was underneath, he knew. He looked hard at her. Why was she lying and why in god's name had he had sex with her? What had made him do it?

Corey gasped. As she looked back at Kane, she could see the scratches on his shoulder reflected through the mirror. Had he seen them? She had a feeling he had. His attitude had become frosty since she returned to the room.

"Something wrong, Corey?" he asked, as he purposely half turned away and let the towel drop to the floor.

Corey had placed the clothes on the side of the bath. "No, should there be?" she replied, trying not to seem uninterested in looking at his body.

Kane discarded the underwear, and pulled on his jeans. He zipped them up and buttoned the top. He turned to face Corey. "Just wondered if you wanted to tell me anything. Do you?"

"Not that I can think of," she replied, trying to hide the shock on her face of seeing the fingernail marks on his back.

Kane pulled the T-shirt over his head. A thought occurred to him. She must have seen the scar on his side. In the positions they were in and the bright lights of the bathroom, she could not fail to. Now was not the time to find out.

"Where is everyone else?" asked Kane as he started barefoot out of the bathroom, followed closely by Corey. He carried on walking through the cubicle-shaped bedroom and into the lounge just as the main door opened and Sam and Tyrone appeared carrying bags of food

"Met Tyrone here, carrying this lot. Sarah is behind us with drinks…speaking of the devil!" Sam said a little exasperated. "Slow down, Sarah. We are all hungry," and Sam made haste the table in the middle of the floor to set his load down before Sarah had hogged the whole table for herself.

"Café next door said it would take awhile to get here, well, I think that's what they said! Couldn't understand all of it. In fact, couldn't understand any of it, so I hope you got what we ordered," mumbled Sarah, as she peered into her bag of goodies.

Tyrone set his food bags down, too, and at long last was able to drop the packs from his back. As he did, he glanced up at Corey. He hadn't seen her dressed like that in a long while. He looked from her to Kane, who still had wet hair, and was very obvious where he had been, and now Tyrone wasn't so sure where they both had come from. If he and Sam had been a few minutes quicker getting back up the stairs, he would have known. Tyrone looked at Corey and caught a stare before she lowered her gaze and looked towards Kane. Tyrone could not miss the implication. She may as well have opened her mouth and confirmed it for him; yet, when he looked to Kane there was no sign of anything different to half an hour ago outside in the street.

"I hope you got a lot of solid food and not that crap on sticks like I saw you guys with at the airport!" As Kane rummaged through the bags, it was obvious he was looking for something other than food, as he had bypassed the main bag, and gone for the liquid refreshments. He found what he was looking for, and pulled the bottle of white wine from the bag. "Anyone got something to open this with…." he was pulling at the gold foil round the top. "Oops, don't need it! It screws!" and as Kane said it, he looked up and straight at Corey.

She met his stare full on and, even with her coloring, she was beetroot red.

Sam saw it, too. He glanced at Sarah, who seemed too busy finding her meal to notice. Surely to god Kane hadn't done that! He looked at his father. Kane gave nothing away as he continued to turn the top on the wine. He didn't wait to get a glass, just tipped the bottle up and took a giant swig of the molten gold.

"Don't you want what we got you?" asked Sarah, fishing in the bag for a meal she thought he would like.

"Think Kane already had what he wanted!" Tyrone mumbled under his breath, his dislike for Kane deepening by the minute and anger growing inside him. Suddenly, he had lost any respect he had for the man.

"You say something, Tyrone? Something bothering you? You want a drink? Maybe you should try it sometime. You might like it," and Kane deliberately offered him the bottle of wine.

Sam thought maybe he wasn't referring to the wine at all.

"I had planned on it, but it seems you got there first, *sir*!" Tyrone's temper was rising and he was having a hard time not saying exactly what he was thinking. Now, was not the time for a confrontation of any kind, especially with Kane's son standing by watching every move. "Yeah, I'll take some," and Tyrone reached for the bottle from Kane. He put the bottle to his lips and swigged a good quarter of the bottle before handing it back towards his boss. He turned his hand at the last moment and offered it to Corey. "You want some? Or aren't you thirsty?"

Sarah and Sam looked at each other and then to Kane and Tyrone.

"I wouldn't mind some," put in Sarah.

"Bet you wouldn't!" Tyrone was more than sarcastic.

"Okay, Tyrone! Spill! What's in your craw, mate?" Now, Kane was becoming pissed off. Obviously, Tyrone knew something. What better way than to find out once and for all.

Tyrone opened his mouth to speak and closed it. Corey was staring at him like she could kill him. "Just tired, that's all. Been a long trip, and the worst is yet to come. You heard anymore from your wife, sir?"

Kane had to acknowledge the man had balls and could use them. Why in god's name had that happened in the bathroom? He needed to talk to his son, whom he noted had been unusually quiet the whole time.

"Not again, no," replied Kane. "Maybe I should try calling the number on my cell. I gave it one shot and no one picked up. Sam, you wanna come with me while the others shower? Grab your food and let's step out on the balcony." Kane set the bottle down and stretched his hand out to Sarah for his food, grabbing it from her. "We'll be right back. Just gonna try again," and he headed for the door that he figured led outside to the balcony.

Sam followed, taking a handful of some weird smelling black beans and bread, with him.

Kane closed the door behind them so that they could not be overheard and stepped away from the door, closer to a wrought-iron railing that surrounded the much larger than usual balcony. It housed a table and chairs, plus a rather odd looking, colored umbrella that was probably there for the tourists.

Sam looked at his father, clenching his fist round the bread, with crumbs dropping through his fingers like a sieve. "You fucked her didn't you? Before we got back! God damn, Kane, why? I thought you loved Kelly!"

Kane's face was blank. For once he didn't know what to say, because he didn't know what he had done. He still could not remember what happened. "I do love Kelly."

"But you just screwed Corey, didn't you? You did, right? I saw you both before Tyrone did. You came out of the same bedroom." Sam stared at Kane.

Kane turned to face his son. "Yes."

"Why?!" Sam was furious with his father, and his veins stood out on his neck.

"I don't know. I don't even remember it. I just know it happened. Corey knows how. And she is pretending it didn't happen." Kane's confusion came to the surface, and he thumped the table in sheer frustration. "I don't have a fucking clue how it happened! One minute I was in the shower, the next I was standing outside the shower with just a towel wrapped round me. Or what I thought was the next minute."

"That's the truth?" asked Sam, a little more restrained.

"Yes." Kane set his food on the patio table, pulled his T-shirt up from his back, and moved his hair out of the way. He turned his shoulder to his son. "Did I have those the other day at the house?"

"No." Sam stated, just a little embarrassed. His father, with Kelly, was one thing; his father with a twenty-something-year-old girl was another.

Kane saw the embarrassment. "Sorry, but you asked. I don't know how it happened, but I guess I haven't lost my touch!" and Kane laughed for a second and then the funny side of the comment disappeared. He pulled his T-shirt back down his body.

"Tyrone is really angry, and I can't say I blame him. You apparently just had sex with the woman he thinks is his girlfriend. Why would Corey do that? What has she to gain, except maybe control? It would have made more sense if it had been Sarah." He paused. "Sarah does have a hold on you, doesn't she?"

Kane felt the need to share. He also knew he couldn't. It would make Sam a marked man.

"What makes you think that? Just because she fancies me, too..." and Kane tried to make a joke of it, and he saw the look on his son's face. "Yes, she does. I can't tell you. I can't put your life in danger, too. You know too much already. Anymore and ...well. You know enough. Like I told you before, just get Kelly out. I can take care of myself..."

"Yeah, I can see that..." interrupted Sam, "and by the way, where is Hunter? You do know that, don't you?"

"Kinda. He isn't far away. I had to get someone on the outside looking in. Angel in the outfield." Kane looked out over the railing.

"So now we know we can't trust Corey. What about Tyrone? And, god almighty, who would trust Sarah..."

The door opened on cue. "Someone talking about me? Why, Sam, would that be you?" She flashed her eyes at Sam, then her eyes diverted straight to Kane. "Did you tell him?"

"No, I didn't fucking tell him. But you just did! What's it gonna accomplish, Sarah. We made a deal, remember? Me for Ryan," and Kane's steely blue eyes glared at her, warning her to shut up.

Sam looked from his father to Sarah. He knew they were not telling the truth, and he also knew it was no good pursuing this line of questioning. Kane wasn't budging, and he certainly wasn't saying anymore in front of Sarah. Maybe later, he would try again.

"Well, if you two children are gonna stand out here all night, I am going to get some sleep," and Kane picked up his food and opened the balcony door.

"Thought you were making a call, Kane?" questioned Sarah, drawing him back into the conversation.

"I did, and now I bid you goodnight," and Kane disappeared inside the room, closing the door behind him.

"He told you, didn't he, Sam?" bullied Sarah. "I know he did! He wouldn't not tell his son. He tells you everything, just like he tells Kelly…" and she stopped in her tracks.

"And how would you know that? You couldn't know that, unless you know her…You do, don't you? You've met her! That's how you know where they are over here, and why you are leading us there!" Sam was on a roll. He could see the lights in her eyes. "You met up with Kane in Japan, didn't you? That's how you know so much about him!" Sam was angry. "You slept with him, too?" And he grabbed hold of her wrists.

"What the hell are you doing? Let go of me! You're hurting me!" her voice got louder, and then, suddenly, dropped in register. "Let me go, Sam Branson, or I will yell rape! You hear me?"

"Is that what you did when you seduced my father in Japan? Is it? Is that what you have over him?" Sam was having a hard time dealing with this.

Sarah started to laugh. Her head flew back, causing her hair to hang loosely over her shoulders. "Is that what he told you? My god, I wish he had raped me. I should be so lucky! You don't know, do you? Your father is quite a man! He turned me down! We did meet in Japan. I was sent to watch him, to learn from him, you might say. Only things happened. And now he owes me big time." Her mood changed like magic. "I own your father. I can make him do whatever I want him to do. He wants Kelly back so badly it's literally killing him. He gets Kelly, and kills my father. Oh, yes, Ryan Holden is my father…. and we get Kane."

"Who is *we*, Sarah. How do you control him? With heroin? Is that it?" His hands slid up her arms and he shook her.

"If it was only that easy! He beat the heroin. Hunter saw to that. You've seen the scar on his chest…what did he tell you? He was stabbed? Yes, he was. But a doctor stitched him up. You might want to reopen it sometime and see what else you find in there." Sarah laughed again and then she turned her eyes to Sam, big blue eyes that turned sad as she blinked. "I wanted to be Kelly. I wanted to be her so badly. She has everything that I don't have, and she has a man that will give his life for her…and you know what…I can't do what I am supposed to do, Sam. I can't do it, and they will kill me, too," and Sarah collapsed in Sam's arms and cried.

Chapter 21

"Who is this *we* you are referring *to*, Sarah? I'm not going to let you go till you tell me! So you may as well get it over with." Sam's tone didn't change. He knew he had to find out once and for all who wanted his father out of the way. "Stop crying! That won't work on me. I'm Kane's son, remember?"

She stopped crying mainly due to the fact that Sam was staring into her face and he gave the impression he was going to kill her if she didn't. She peered up into his eyes, but still clinging to his arms with her shaking hands. She could feel his muscles flexing through the shirt he wore. "How can I forget you are his son? He told me all about you in Japan. Kane is so very proud of you. You and Star…"

"He told you about Star? How close were you guys?" Sam was really puzzled now.

"Close, but I didn't sleep with him. I swear. Oh, I asked him a couple of times. I tried to seduce him," she smiled as she remembered. "Even drunk, he wouldn't. Said he loved Kelly too much for that." She started to edge out of the grasp that he had on her, and Sam relaxed his grip.

As Sarah sat down in the chair, it creaked a little. "He is something, your dad. One time we sat up the whole night while he told me about Kelly. I asked him to tell me. I think deep down I wanted Kane to be my father, or at least I didn't want Ryan Holden to be."

"That's almost incestuous…" and Sam grimaced, and sat down on the chair across from her.

"I know," Sarah put in. "I guess I was searching for something, still am…you do know don't you? You must have guessed…" Her eyes questioned his face.

"That you and Kelly are somehow related? Yes, I figured that out. The others on the trip wouldn't know. You two are too much alike not to be. You're cousins or something?"

"Closer. We have the same m…" Sarah didn't finish the sentence.

"Thought you two were tired?" Kane's voice boomed, as he re-opened the door to the balcony, interrupting Sarah as she spoke. "Sarah, need to talk to you right now…inside!"

She looked up at him. "What?"

"Inside, now!" Kane was more than angry, and reached down for Sarah's arm, bruising the flesh as he did.

"Kane, we were just talking…" Sam added, looking very perturbed that Kane was treating a woman like that.

"Yeah, I know…I heard through the door…hopefully the others didn't! Like I said, Sarah, inside, now! Go through into the small bedroom and don't talk to anyone on the way."

"Kane, I don't think…." Sam was trying to verbally defend the girl.

"That's right, you don't think. I do that for us. Maybe, of late, I have been remiss in not doing so much of it, but that stops right now. Miss Holden will be spending the night in my room. At least that way she can't be running off at the mouth, can she?" he turned away from Sam and diverted his whole attention to Sarah. "Go, now!"

Sarah almost jumped out of the chair. "I wasn't doing…."

"Maybe not…see you in the bedroom, Miss Holden. It was what you wanted wasn't it?" And Kane stopped speaking. He waited till she shut the door. "Sam, what ever she told you it's not true. She does have a hold over me, but not what you think. I didn't sleep with her. I'm wanted…"

"I know that. She told me." Sam didn't wait for Kane to explain. "She also told me you talked about me and Star…and Kelly. And before you rudely interrupted us she was about to tell me who she really is. But you know, don't you? This whole thing with her is a charade; pretending not to know her, when all the time you did. They have the same mother, don't they? Her and Kelly, and you are terrified that as you couldn't keep your hands off one sister you may just stray to the other? I mean, you just screwed Corey, and that didn't faze you...I don't believe you can't remember...any man would remember having sex with Corey. For God's sake, Kane, own up to it!"

Kane was shocked by his son's outburst and it showed on his face. This was Sam; the one he thought was on his side. Now, he wasn't so sure. He glared at Sam, and turned away from him, disappointed, and stepped inside the doorway and back into the room.

Sam slumped down in his chair. He almost had Sarah, and Kane ruined it. Why had he stopped him? He looked up at the stars. Sam hadn't noticed till then how dark it was. He looked out at the city lights. Some where out there was his mother-in-law, a woman that he had once saved from death. A woman that his father was going to give his life for and some one that right now he figured was counting the hours till she would see Kane again. For a second his thoughts got the better of him, only disturbed by someone inside the room shouting his name. He jumped up from the chair and rushed inside, leaving the balcony door wide open.

The sight that greeted him was something out of a movie. Kane had Tyrone pinned to the wall, and Corey and Sarah were trying to pull them apart.

"What the fuck is going on here? Kane...Kane!" Sam rushed across the room and with all the strength he could muster pulled his father from the death grip he had on Tyrone. He held him by the shoulders as Kane struggled to get free. "I don't know what is going on, though I can imagine, but this isn't the time or the place."

"Your father knows what it's about! Ask him. He may be a commander, but he sure doesn't have any morals!" Tyrone was now free and was trying to take a swing at Kane.

"Stop it! Both of you!" yelled Sam. "You want to bring attention to this unit?"

"Fuck you, Tyrone." Kane was right back in Tyrone's face. "Sarah is spending the night in my room and that's it. And, if you, or Corey, don't like it, fucking tough shit, *mate!*"

Now, Sam knew. Corey must have seen Sarah going to Kane's room and she was pissed just enough to make suggestions to Tyrone about Sarah.

"Kane, why don't you and the girls take the big bedroom? Tyrone and I will take the little one; after all, we are only taking a few hours sleep." 'Oh, my god!' thought Sam…'Did I really suggest that? The two girls…and him?'

Kane relaxed a little in Sam's grasp. He nodded a 'yes', and Sam let him go. Tyrone and Kane glared at each other.

"Another time, *mate!*" and Kane stormed off into the big bed-room.

"I don't know what started this little incident, Tyrone, but I don't think I would push it right now if you want to stay alive. Kane is still your commander, and it might be wise on your part to remember that." He turned his attentions to Sarah. "Go get his backpack and yours, and go talk to him as Kane requested. Corey, a word."

Sarah ran into the bedroom and grabbed Kane's bag from the bed and then disappeared into the other room, grabbing her pink backpack as she went.

"Now, Corey, you and I need to have a talk. If you want Tyrone here that's up to you. I would think, though, you might want him to wait outside on the balcony. Up to you!" and Sam sat down on the couch and waited patiently for a reply. He leaned on the backrest which seemed hard even to a tough man like Sam.

Corey slid her hand onto Tyrone's arm. "He should stay," and Corey dropped her eyes so that Tyrone could not see her face and looked straight at Sam.

"Okay, as you wish." There was only one way to do this and that was outright. "You had sex with Kane, didn't you?"

"I beg your pardon? I did not!" Corey replied, just a little too fast, trying to look totally shocked.

"What the fuck are you talkin' about, Sam? Corey and Kane? When ?" Tyrone pulled slightly away from Corey.

"You mean that's not what you were about to fight over?" asked Sam very innocently, knowing full-well it wasn't.

"No, man! I was watching Sarah going to his room…" Tyrone paused like his brain was kicking into gear. "You just sent her to him…" he paused again and shifted his stance.

Sam stood up so that he was face to face with them.

"Did you or didn't you, Corey?" Sam asked again, his Asian eyes becoming very apparent.

"Did Kane tell you that?" Corey asked him, dreading the reply. She had felt Tyrone move slightly away from her.

"Kane didn't tell me anything, because he can't remember. But you can. You know, that's why you got Tyrone here to pick a fight with Kane." Sam was pushing her.

"I didn't do that, and I sure as hell didn't have sex with Kane. I heard someone in the bathroom and went in to see who it was. That's it! I object to your line of questioning, Agent Branson. I am on your side. Anyway, he can't prove it," and she pouted her lips hoping for sympathy from both Tyrone and Sam.

"Actually, he can. But that's not the point, is it? Why are you lying and why can't he remember it? That worries me the most, that he has no memory of it, just fingernail marks on his back!" Sam went for the kill.

Corey was crimson. So, Kane did know, as well as Sam; and now, apparently, so did Tyrone.

Tyrone moved away immediately from Corey. "And you joked about him wanting into your pants. You little tart!" he yelled at her.

Corey pleaded with him. "Tyrone...he forced me to have sex. That's why he has marks on his back...." She was desperate now.

"Corey, stop right there." Tyrone raised his hands to her. "Now, I know you are lying! I would really doubt that Commander Branson has ever had to rape a woman to get sex in his entire life. I may not have the respect I should have for him, but that's one accusation I doubt would stand." He looked into her face, a kind of sadness surrounding him. "Why, Corey? Why did you do it, and why can't Kane remember? Answer Sam! Answer him, damn it!" he grabbed hold of her shoulders and forced her to look at his face. "Sam is speaking the truth isn't he?"

Corey paused. Her first and last mistake. "What!? Why are you both staring at me? I didn't do anything, Kane did it..." and as she spoke, her eyes left the guys and her gaze shifted to the other doorway where Kane stood. He was dressed in jeans and nothing else. Only a breath behind him stood a smiling Sarah Holden. Now was her chance. "She made me do it. It was her idea!"

"What the fuck is going on out here? It sounds like a war zone. Made you do what, Corey?" As he spoke, Kane reached round his back with his arm and pulled Sarah into the picture.

Sarah stood there just dressed in a cotton nightshirt that left nothing to the imagination. Tyrone stared at her. Sam had to blink twice to make sure he wasn't looking at Kelly. Her long hair cascaded down her shoulders and the butterfly on her breast could clearly be seen. Painted pink toes dug into the carpet. If Sam had not known it wasn't Kelly standing with Kane, he would have believed it was. Sarah smiled a very warm and sensuous smile. She pulled the nightshirt up around her neck realizing that Sam was staring at her breast.

Kane let go of her arm and rested his arm on her shoulder. "I repeat, Corey, what did Sarah make you do?"

Corey looked at them, but especially at Sarah. Whatever she said now, Sarah was not going to back her. That had been a mistake to blurt out what she had. She had been told to take the blame and she hadn't. And she knew now that she would pay. Sarah had Corey exactly where she wanted her, as she seemed also to have Kane.

"Maybe Corey should sleep out on the couch. Better still I will. You girls can take the room. Sam and I will sleep here. Tyrone you take the small room. And as no one seems to be owning up to anything in here, let's get to sleep." Kane turned slightly to move round to the side of the couch, and Tyrone could quite clearly see the marks on him.

He wasn't sure at that point if he hated Kane or Corey the most. He looked at Sarah, who was still standing in the doorway like she had lost first prize. She was staring at Corey as though she could kill her, and Tyrone feared she just might.

"Kane, you and Sam take the little room. I will stay in here just in case there will be any trouble from the ladies!" Tyrone was a lot calmer now.

It was then that Kane interjected. "Trouble, why would there be any trouble? Sarah, tell them, darling." He took his chance. "No? Okay, So I will. Sarah and I have been having an affair ever since we met in Japan. I was coming home to tell Kelly I wanted a divorce, and that I plan on leaving with Sarah after this is all over. Have to follow through and get the ladies out of here, and then get back home. Right, Sarah?" As he spoke, his arm went round her shoulders and he pulled her more than close to him. The nightshirt slipped and his hand touched her bare flesh.

Kane knew by this act that he was alienating everyone in the room except, Sarah.

Probably Sam would lose any respect for him that he had, and certainly the Americans would turn on him. It didn't matter now. All he had to do was go the extra mile and get Kelly and Reese Wade out. It was the only way he could think of to stop Corey from getting hurt. He knew that Sarah had known Corey had had sex with him. Slowly, he was starting to remember things. When Sarah came in with the food, she wasn't concerned that he and Corey had appeared together in the direction of the bedroom, and he had seen the look that Sarah had just given Corey.

Now, Kane was afraid for Corey's life. He had heard the last few strains of the conversation between his son and Sarah on the balcony, and he knew Sarah was lying. She was playing Sam for a fool.

"Sarah, let's go…" and his arm never let its grip go on her. "See you all in the morning," and Kane frog marched her out of the room, into the bedroom and slammed the door.

Sam stood by the small square table that he thought looked kind of out of place in the room. Corey slumped down on the couch and Tyrone sat down next to her.

No one spoke. The news was shocking, but somehow Sam didn't believe it, just like he didn't believe Sarah on the balcony. He realized Sarah had neatly not told him who the *we* was. But obviously his father knew. He also knew that Kane was protecting Corey, even though they had had sex, and Corey was lying, or maybe Corey didn't remember too much of it either and was as confused as Kane was.

"Corey, you take the room. Tyrone and I will stay out here."

She nodded, and stood up from the couch. "Goodnight," she whispered and took off for the room.

Before Sam could speak, Tyrone pitched in. "She doesn't remember it either, does she? She knows she's had sex with him, and he knows he has with her, but neither can remember how they got there, and exactly what happened. She's not lying and neither is he, right? Someone or something got to them before we got up the stairs. If it's happened once, how do we know it's not gonna happen again? And Sarah Holden, what the fuck is that about? Commander Branson is protecting us all, isn't he? The enemy is already in our midst, aren't they?"

"Yes, Tyrone, they are," said Sam, totally amazed that Tyrone had worked it out that fast. "And she's in the bedroom with Kane right now!" Sam looked at the bedroom door. He wanted to burst in there and stop whatever Kane was doing, and he knew he couldn't. His father was a grown man making his own destiny, what ever it took to do it, and to save the ones he cared for the most.

Chapter 22

"Why in god's name did you tell them that, Kane? We didn't have any affair!" Sarah turned on Kane as soon as they he shut the bedroom door. She all but jumped on the bed and sat staring at him.

"No, we didn't, Sarah, but it wasn't for lack of trying on your part, was it? Even after I told you about Kelly and the kids you pushed it! And why did I tell them that?" Kane pointed vehemently to the room they had come from. "To stop you destroying anyone else's life! I told you I would come with you when this is over. You had my word! What the fuck else do you want?" He paused. "Don't answer that! I can guess. And while we are we talking about sex…"

"Didn't know we were…" she pouted her freshly glossed lips at him.

"Yes, you did…so, what did you do to Corey and me? You gave us something, or someone did. I don't think she remembers either."

"Was she good?" her eyes twinkled in expectation of his answer.

"What!? How dare you! None of your fucking business. One thing is certain; it isn't gonna happen again, because I won't be alone with her. And after tonight, I am not going to be alone with you, either."

"You don't know that. You can't predict anything." Her fingers played with the end of the quilt.

"I can sure as hell try. Tomorrow we get the car and travel to Samarra and, hopefully, arrive in one piece. And Sarah…nothing, and I mean nothing, must happen to Corey or to my son."

"Oh, yeah, your son…he tried to kiss me on the balcony," Sarah stated, not even looking up at Kane.

"Sure he did." The whole time Kane was talking he was looking through his backpack. "Sam isn't like me. He wouldn't do that, and, anyway, I heard the conversation. Why do you think I stopped it?" He found what he was looking for, and stuffed something into his jeans pocket. As he did, he remembered the gun was in the other bathroom, where he had left it, when taking the shower. Maybe it was safer there than it would have been in his room.

"Get into bed!" he demanded of her.

"I like that in a man…brute force!" she lied.

"Yeah, I bet you do. Move!" While he spoke, Kane almost pushed her from the bed and took pillows, making a dividing line down the middle of the bed.

"You think that's gonna keep me from getting onto your side?" Sarah asked, standing on the worn carpet staring at Kane, her night-shirt slipping just a little further down her neck.

"No, but mace will," and he pulled the spray from his pocket.

"You wouldn't use that on me?"

"Try me!" Kane really meant it.

"Is that an invitation?" she quipped, pursing her lips at him.

"Get to bed, now!" and Kane pulled the covers further back on the side he aimed to sleep on. He kept his jeans on, suddenly remembering he didn't have any underwear on. Lots of things were coming back to him in small and meaningful pieces. Obviously, whatever they had given he and Corey didn't have any permanent effects. He wondered if Corey would remember. He actually hoped not. He had never betrayed Kelly till that night and it was not intentional, but he had betrayed her and Kelly must never know. Flashes of the bathroom came to him and he could see Corey's body in his mind. He must not think about it, especially right now.

He lay down on the crumpled sheets, wondering if they had been changed since the last occupant. He thought probably not. He laid the mace on the bedside table and turned away from Sarah as she climbed into bed.

"Well, I can at least say we slept together," and Sarah laughed in a cynical way. "Kane…"

"What?!"

"Was she good?"

After the long day, Kane was drifting into the unconscious. "Yeah, she was…very," and he slipped into fitful dreams.

In the other bedroom, Corey lay on the bed still fully clothed. Tears trickled down her face. She wiped them away with her fingertips. She remembered Kane picking her up and her legs round him and then it was gone again. She thumped her fist on the bed. She wanted to remember. She wanted to know what having sex with Kane was like. She cried now, a little louder. As she did the door to the bedroom opened and Tyrone stepped inside the room. She could see him in the half light of the open door.

"I just need to use the restroom, babe…Corey you okay?" He was genuinely concerned for her.

"No…" she couldn't say anymore. "I did have sex with him… parts of it are coming back."

Tyrone rushed to her side and sat down on the bed. "Hey, come on. Don't cry. If it's any comfort, I think the commander feels bad about it, too. What I can't figure out is what anyone hoped to gain from it, unless they are trying to prove control over you both." He propped her warm body against him, and he envied Kane. "Do you remember anyone giving you anything right before hand? I know you and Sarah left for the ladies room before Kane got this hotel…."

"Oh, my god," she interrupted him. "She gave me a can of soda that she said she had in her backpack, yet we were all dying of thirst on the bus…and didn't Kane look in her backpack at that time?"

"Yeah, he did…so where did she get it and how did it get to him? Do you remember him drinking any of it?" he questioned her.

"No…I don't know…. all I remember was going into the bathroom and he was in the shower…no coming out of the shower… maybe I had it with me…Oh, god, did I drug him somehow?" She looked towards the bathroom door. "See if it's still in there…"

"Isn't going to be, babe. Sarah came back for the backpacks, remember? Any evidence will be gone." Tyrone paused. "Maybe I should stay in here with you tonight?"

"I'll be fine. You and Sam are right outside the door. Just leave it open a few inches. I'm fine, really. How can anyone get to me? It's Kane you should be worrying about. Isn't he with *her*?" Corey asked, afraid of the answer.

"Yeah, he is. Maybe he should have left the door open, too. I'll go take a listen, make sure everything is okay. You sure you don't want me to stay with you?" he noted her nervousness. "I'm not gonna touch you, babe!"

"I know that, Tyrone. I just want to run things through my mind a little, clear my head. I'll be fine." She climbed off the bed and slid out of her jeans, dropping them onto the top of her backpack. All she had on now was pretty black lace underwear and the cut-away T-shirt, showing him most of her body. She seemed to have lost any dignity she had. Climbing back onto the bed, she plumped up the pillows and lay down. "I'm fine, just tired. You go back to Sam, and go check on Kane. If you guys need the bathroom, just come through here," and slowly she, too, drifted to sleep.

Tyrone watched her a moment longer. Confident she was asleep, he used the bathroom, came back by her bed, and back out to the where Sam sat, and perched himself on the arm of the couch.

"She okay?" asked Sam still munching on some food that was left.

"Says she is. Also says she is remembering things about the escapade in the bathroom. Says she remembers Sarah giving her a can of soda on the way back from the ladies room. You think that it was drugged? Maybe something like Ketamine or some other date rape drug? Could Sarah have access to that kind of thing?" Tyrone looked towards Kane's door, and noticed it wasn't shut all the way. "You been in there?"

"No. I guess Kane didn't close it the whole way." Sam paused. "I wondered about the angle of drugs, too. But why? Or maybe it was just meant for Corey. Maybe someone else was supposed to get to her and Kane was in the wrong place at the right time. He must have ingested some of it though. Unfortunately, it doesn't stay in the system too long. So we couldn't get them tested, not that that could happen out here anywhere." Sam stopped speaking. He was thinking. "I never found out what happened at the end of the flight either, you know, when he came down the stairs like superman. Don't know who gave him that drug either. I thought at first it was our new found military friend. Now, I am not so sure." Sam stared at the door. "I can't believe I sent them both in that room. She could kill him in his sleep, especially if…" and Sam dropped the rest of the food into the now piling bag of trash.

Tyrone looked at Sam. "If what? You know more than you are sharing, right? I gotta ask this, Sam? Is Kane injured or something?"

"How the hell did you know that?" Sam was shocked and it showed on his face.

"I saw him flinch a couple of times while we were traveling on the plane. Something to do with his side, right?" Tyrone seemed almost proud he had guessed.

"Right." Sam figured it was no use hiding it. "Kane was stabbed while in Japan. As everyone else knows, including Corey I would think, I don't see why you shouldn't. You seem to be figuring everything else out. My father is getting too far up in years to be acting like a twenty-year-old."

"I think you underestimate your father. I have a feeling that Corey didn't think he was too old earlier tonight!" and Tyrone frowned as he spoke. "He got further in the last few days than I have in months! Drugged or not!" Tyrone kept glancing at the door.

"You in love with her, Tyrone?" Seemed the night for truths.

"I guess I am, or I wouldn't be this jealous or angry, would I?" At last Tyrone had admitted it to himself.

"No, my friend, you wouldn't! Think we should get some sleep. We have a long trip tomorrow. I wonder just how Kelly is holding up?" mussed Sam. He had been thinking a lot about her in the last hour or so.

"He really loves her, doesn't he?"

"More than life. More than life!" and Sam lay down on the comfy couch and was asleep in seconds.

"Good. Thank god for small mercies, because I have a feeling the saga of Kane and Corey isn't over yet." Tyrone lay down on the other couch and covered himself with a moth-eaten looking blanket.

Neither of them remembered that the door to the balcony was still open, and it creaked as Corey opened it wider. All she wanted was some fresh air. The window in her room wouldn't open, so she crept passed the guys in the early hours of the morning and onto the balcony. She stood there just clad in T-shirt and panties with a light blanket wrapped around her. She shivered in the cool morning air. Glancing at her watch, she could just make out that it was only four a.m. Corey moved to the railing and looked over the side. It wasn't that high, not really, and she leaned against the dusty rail. Sleep had been spasmodic and now she wished she had taken Tyrone up on the offer of company. But it wasn't Tyrone she wanted, it was Kane. She needed to talk to him, tell him she remembered all of it now, and tell him she was sorry she had brought the drink in from Sarah. Later on that morning, she would tell them what happened. The bathroom episode was all her fault.

Sarah had got the drink when she she went to the ladies. It hadn't come from her backpack at all. Somehow, before Corey took the drink from the can, Sarah had put something in it, or someone had handed it to Sarah already drugged. Corey hadn't drunk enough to hurt her too much, just to make her forget what she was doing and who with. When she had heard someone in the bathroom, she went in to see and it was there she met Kane, and she offered him the drink.

"My god…I seduced him! I brought my fantasy to reality. God, if ever he remembers the whole thing…"

"I do…and it's okay," whispered Kane. "It really is."

Corey turned to see a jean-clad Kane standing there. She looked at him in the lights from the city and she knew now that she had fallen for him. "Kane, I'm sorry. I didn't do it on purpose. But somehow, I don't regret one second…." she never finished the sentence.

From the city street gunfire rang out. Several rounds from an automatic rifle ricocheted off the wall that held up the railing. The last bullet hit her in the back. She slumped forward and Kane caught her in his arms.

"Corey…nooooooooo." Kane screamed at her. Reflections of his past caught up to him. Once again someone he cared about was dying in his arms.

The noise of gunfire woke them all, and the assortment of the unit tumbled out onto the balcony.

"Corey! Don't die! You cant, I won't let you!" He shook her almost violently trying to shake life into her. His hair dropped down over her, hiding her face as she lay dying.

She hung loosely in his arms as he cradled her body to him, blood dripping down her back and through his fingers onto the patio. Her eyes slowly closed and the last thing she saw was the man she was falling in love with. "Kane, I love y…" and Corey closed her eyes and she was gone.

"My god, no. Corey!" yelled Kane, and he held her as close to him as he could.

Tyrone and Sam's first instinct was to draw their weapons and go to the railing. In the early morning light they could see several men running away. It was too far to take a shot with pistols. Tyrone turned as if to move towards Corey.

Sam grabbed his arm and shook his head. "Leave them a second," he whispered.

Tyrone stopped in his tracks and stared at the sight in front of him. His girlfriend was dead and she lay in the commander's arms. It was obvious to both Sam and Tyrone that Kane had some kind of feelings for her.

Kane turned his head up to the sky, pushed the hair from his face, and made her a promise. "I will kill the son-of-a bitch that did this to you. You have my word, Corey!" and Kane stood up with her in his arms liked she weighed nothing. Her hair fell backwards and her arms hung by her side, her legs flopped over his hand, just hanging there.

It was at this point that Sarah appeared at the door having had to get from the bedroom to the balcony taking longer than the others.

"Oh, my god…is she dead?" and Sarah clutched her hand to her mouth. She looked shocked at the sight in front of her.

"Get out of my sight, Sarah Holden! Don't come near me again! This should have been you, not her!" and Kane passed Sarah on the way through the door.

"Kane, you don't mean that?" Sam yelled to his father.

"The hell I don't! Like I told you, Sarah," he glared at her. "Nothing must happen to Corey or Sam, and it just did!"

Chapter 23

Kane carried Corey into the small bedroom, and put her carefully on the bed. Tyrone stepped in the door behind him and turned the overhead light full on. Kane looked back to the door.

"Tyrone, I'm sorry. I..." Kane could not finish his statement. He pulled a sheet across her as blood seeped onto the linen and made a crimson stain. He leaned towards her and gently brushed her face one last time with his fingers. Kane half turned to Tyrone. "You know, don't you? You know about the bathroom?"

"Yes. She told me that she remembered everything. It wasn't your fault, commander. Corey, well Corey was very impressionable, and you came along like a knight on a white charger." He paused. "That wasn't supposed to sound like that," he whispered.

"I know what you mean." Kane turned further to face the soldier. "As she died, she told me she loved you." Kane's eyes never faltered. He didn't blink and he didn't look away.

"Thank you, commander." Tyrone knew that's not what she had said, but in his eyes the commander had just regained respect.

Kane looked down at his hands. They were covered in blood. "I need to go wash..." and he headed for the bathroom.

As he scrubbed his hands clean, Kane looked up into the mirror. Once again his team was dying, just like before on Lantau Island, all those years ago. But this time he had his son on his side. He reached for his gun that was still sitting on the ledge in full view. Strange... why hadn't anyone moved it? He stuffed it down the back of his jeans. Suddenly, without any warning, a pain shot through his side. With dripping wet hands, he grabbed hold of the sink to stop himself from falling, as he yelled in pain.

Tyrone was with him in a second. "Kane, you okay?"

"Get Sam!" and he managed to sit down on the closed toilet seat. He could hardly breathe. Lifting Corey, and carrying her like he had, had moved something inside him, or so he thought.

"Kane, what happened?" Sam burst in the door ahead of Tyrone.

"Pain…it's easing up a little," and Kane started to breathe easier. He leaned back on the tank and straightened up from the position he was previously in. "I'm okay. It's eased up. Let's go back into the room…" and Kane stood up, almost biting his lip to stop the obvious pain that he was still in.

As he passed by Corey, pangs of remorse shot through him. She should not be dead. If anyone should be, it should be him, and he wondered just how far away that moment would be. He shuddered at the thought and kept on going.

Just as they all re-entered the room, there was a loud banging on the hotel room door.

"Police…open the door…" They banged again.

"Are they real? Could be a trick, Kane," asked Sam, moving very hesitantly to the door.

"Open it…but keep your guns right by you." Kane pulled his gun from his jeans and clutched it by his side. His other hand held onto the back of the couch and he steadied himself. He wasn't sure what to expect when the door opened, but he was ready no matter what. "Sarah, get behind me! Now!" He realized she was very obviously shaken by the happenings. Not what he expected.

She moved in behind him and just touched him very gently on his back to acknowledge she was there. He responded with a nod of his head.

Sam opened the door with his gun clutched to his chest. He was still dressed from the night before, and, after showering, had put on clean sweats, and a black T-shirt. Tyrone, on the other hand had still to shower, and was dressed in the same clothes from the trip.

In front of them stood military police and with them was Captain Kirk. Not what Kane expected.

"Kane, thank god! Is everyone alright?" Kirk burst into the room trying to count heads.

Kane stared at him. "No, everyone is not all right! And why didn't you announce who you were? Corey is dead. One of your own kind!" and Kane turned pointing at the bedroom. "She's in there…go see. So much for the protection you were supposed to supply!" Kane was furious with Kirk, and he had also let something out that till now was secret between the two of them.

Tyrone caught it first. "Captain? Is that true? Is that why the air force is here?"

"Yes, son. There is more danger than we first thought. Your commander here is to get the women back. We are here to get Ryan Holden." He didn't spare Sarah; in fact, he said it rather intentionally to annoy her.

Sarah had been quiet till now. "Captain, if you think I am going to tell my father you are here, you are wrong. I want him dead. I hate him!"

"And why would that be, Sarah…do you even know why? You want me to tell them?" Kirk replied, looking seriously at Sarah.

"No!" She suddenly stepped up her annoyance. "It's not their business! Just that I want him dead!" Suddenly, she was screaming at him. She moved from behind Kane and stood in the room still clad in the skimpy nightshirt.

Kane grabbed the blanket off the couch and threw it to her. "Wrap that round you!" and inclined his head at the three policemen that had accompanied Kirk through the door.

"Thought you never wanted to see me again, commander?!" she yelled at him, and then she turned back to Kirk, dropping the blanket purposely to the floor in defiance of Kane. "He blames me for Corey's death, he does!"

Kane stared at Sarah like she was a maniac. "Sarah, shut up, now! You hear me? What is your problem? We all know you hate Ryan. We all hate Ryan. What makes you so fucking special?"

"Because he was drunk one night, and he raped me! You happy now? You all happy that you know? Captain Kirk here already knew.

That's why I am so perfect to lead you to him. That's why I was sent to watch you, Kane, to seduce you, and to take you back with me." She was telling all, and Kane had to shut her up.

"Sarah, stop it. Please! Don't say anymore." If she let it out now about him being stabbed and why, and what he had done back in Japan, they were all dead, and he would never make it to Kelly.

Sarah was hysterical. Whether it was the situation in hand or the one that had just occurred, Kane wasn't sure. But something had really gotten to her.

"Sarah, shut up. Don't say anymore. They don't know all the facts. What do you think you are doing? Sarah…!" There seemed no way to stop her. Kane raised his hand and hit her across the face.

"Kane!" yelled Sam. "Dad! Stop it!" and he jumped forward to stop Kane from hitting her again, grabbing him by the arm.

"I hardly touched her, and I'm not gonna hit her again. Take your hands off me, Sam. I don't hit women, not twice anyway!" Kane was serious.

Sam knew there wasn't that much force behind the smack to Sarah's face, but even so she was female. He also knew that Sarah was spilling the beans right in front of everyone.

Sarah was shaking. She clenched her fists by her side, almost daring him to hit her again. "Why don't you go for it, Kane? You just got one woman killed, why not another!? Speaking of which, how is your wife?"

It was then Kane lost it. He raised the gun in his other hand and aimed it straight at her forehead. His eyes were fierce and he didn't hesitate in his actions. Slowly, he squeezed his finger back on the trigger.

"He's gonna kill me! For Christ sake, someone stop him…Sam… Tyrone, please. Do something," she was hysterical, her eyes wide and fearful of Kane.

"I'd do the same thing, lady!" Tyrone said, as he didn't even move to stop Kane. "He's had enough of you, just like all of us have!"

"You're not gonna stop him?" she yelled at Tyrone.

"Fuck no. He would be doing us a favor and his wife! And, he didn't kill Corey, you did…oh, not directly, but you upset her so much," and he stopped mainly because Kirk had moved forward as if to stop this incident from going any further.

"Kane, lower the gun." Kirk was trying to talk him down, little knowing that Kane pointing a pistol at her was just a scare tactic for Sarah.

Kane had no intentions of pulling the trigger. Not now anyway, and he slowly let his arm drop back by his side. "Next time, you may not be so lucky," and Kane stuffed the gun down the back of his jeans and walked away into the bedroom.

A tired looking Kirk followed Kane, and they closed the door into Corey's room.

"Did you see that?" she screamed at anyone who cared to listen. "He was gonna kill me? Sam, Tyrone…he was!"

"No, he wasn't! Don't be so dramatic. He wanted to shut you up. You've been a pain ever since you joined us! We would have done better on our own. Not sure why you are here anyway. That crap you told me on the patio was just that, crap!" Sam did not pause for breath till now. He was as disgusted at her as his father was, and in his father's position he may have done the same thing. He turned towards the door and wondered what exactly was going on in the room.

Tyrone was wondering the same as Sam. He felt he should have been in there with them, but he wasn't invited.

By now it was light outside, and the sun was starting to seep through the open balcony door and the adjacent windows. Another day in this hell hole of life.

The policemen did nothing more than stand by the door. Both Tyrone and Sam really wondered why they were there. They glanced at each other and Sam was about to speak when the bedroom door opened.

Kirk spoke to the military police and two of them stepped inside the bedroom. They emerged not two minutes later with Corey's body wrapped in the cover from the bed.

"Can I see her, before she goes?" whispered Tyrone to Kane. "Please…" and he didn't say anything else.

Kane reached his arm to the police carrying her. They stopped and Kane pulled back the covering on her face.

Corey's eyes were closed and she looked just like she was asleep. Tyrone's fingers made it to her hair and he touched it gently, bending his face to see her better. "I love you," he whispered, knowing Kane could hear him and knowing that it wasn't him she had fallen for.

Kane turned away. He at least owed Tyrone some respect and he owed Corey more. If he had moved a little closer to the rail the bullet would have struck him, not her, and he figured that at that point the gunman didn't care who they hit. What he wasn't sure was, was the gunfire random or planned, and that was what he and Kirk had been discussing in the bedroom. He also told Kirk what had happened the previous hours before hand. Kane wasn't proud of the fact when disclosing the details, he also didn't mince words.

Now Kane moved right away and headed for the door, opening it as he motioned to Kirk to join him.

"They will strike anytime now. We do not have a translator. Not right here with us anyway. Sam arranged for a car and we'll be on our way by nine a.m. Shouldn't take us long to get to Samarra." Kane glanced back into the room. "Make sure her family understands and send any bills to me. I want the best for her. I should have told Tucker I didn't want her along and meant it. Sarah was right. I did kill her," and Kane stepped out of the way and let the police by.

Kane closed the door behind them and stepped back into reality. "Now, Sarah, you will get dressed, and you will sit on that couch and you won't move unless I tell you to. You may have a hold over me, Ms. Holden, and I will be coming back with you after this is over, but," and Kane's attitude changed, "you get in my way one more fucking time, you tell any more lies, you do one thing wrong, *darling*, and I will put a bullet in you. Do you understand me? Am I making myself very clear to you? And then I will put a bullet in myself. Do I make myself abundantly clear to everyone?"

"Yes, sir," replied Sam.

Tyrone nodded.

"Ms. Holden?" Kane wanted this over and done, now.

Sarah stared at him and she knew by the look in his eyes, he meant every word. She also knew he would stop at nothing now to get his wife out of there, even if it meant his own death. That alone made him dangerous. She nodded yes.

"I didn't hear you, Miss Holden. What did you say? You need to speak up, darling."

"You bastard! You son-of-a-bitch. Go to hell!" Sarah screamed at him, her body moving towards him as she spoke. "I will do as I please, you hear me, as I please and none of you will stop me!"

"Oh, yes, we will. One of us, anyway. I have nothing to lose. They do." And Kane pointed to the other two men in the room. "Miss Holden, you seem to have forgotten why I am coming back with you. Could that be true?"

"I haven't forgotten and they don't know. I could tell them, couldn't I? I could tell them what you did in Japan. I could tell Sam the real truth about his father." She laughed almost out of control, her hair hanging about her, and her face contorted with hate. "So maybe I will tell them…"

"Go right ahead, now. I just didn't want you telling them while Kirk was with us."

"Okay, I will. Right now! Your father, Sam, killed my fiancé. He was the aid to the Japanese ambassador. He was an American, just like you, Tyrone. Kane killed him in cold blood and now he is a wanted man. The Americans made a deal with him…."

"Stop, Sarah! He wasn't your fiancé, and he was a dangerous man. You omit to tell them that he stabbed me. Not content with that, he left the piece of fan blade he used inside me, and then they stitched me up, giving me heroin for the pain. And you forgot to tell them that he was a corrupt man that deserved to die, and that he was also going to kill the Japanese ambassador. Amazing what you can leave out when you want to, Miss Holden. And Sarah and I did not have an affair. Oh, she tried hard enough! That's how much she thought of her *fiancé.*" Kane stopped to look at the reaction of his son and Tyrone. He continued. "You also forgot to tell them that I am a wanted man both in the USA and Japan. Wanted for murder. Isn't that right, Miss Holden? If I am wanted for murder, what the fuck is there to stop me being wanted again? For killing you!"

Chapter 24

"Get going, Sarah. Go get dressed and come back here." Kane followed her to the door and then closed it behind her.

"You're serious, right? This isn't one of your jokes? I was kinda hoping it was." Sam fell silent as Kane shook his head no, it wasn't a joke. "Why didn't you tell me back in Oz. You could have trusted me." As Sam spoke he sat down on the arm of the couch. "And her, what about her?" Sam looked towards the bedroom. "She can't make you go back with her. She doesn't have any authority out here or in Australia."

"Unfortunately, she does. Australian agent she might be, working for the Americans she also is. But there is something that she doesn't know, and it might come as a shock to her. The Japanese government pardoned me. So she can't take me back there. The only place that now wants me is America, and that's only because she fabricated the story. Truth is, Miss Holden wants me to go with her, and I agreed so that we could get Reese Wade out. And, obviously, Kelly. Sarah will take us to her father for the reason she stated earlier. In that she is telling the truth. She does hate her father."

"Does Kirk know all this?" asked Tyrone.

"Most of it. He is also watching our Miss Holden here. He doesn't trust her. Thinks she is working for someone else. Seems that someone told Ryan where Reese and her husband were, and now the Americans think it might be her. I can't figure out how she knew though. I didn't even know where Reese was and we have occasionally kept in touch over the years. Still a piece of the jigsaw is missing. It had something to do with Corey, and Corey can't tell us now. Very convenient. Corey was…" Kane stopped speaking.

"Kane, what did Corey really say when she died…" It was hard for Tyrone to ask, but he had decided he needed to know. "It was you, wasn't it, that she was falling for…There is a reason I ask, not just for me, but something Sarah had said earlier yesterday."

Kane looked from Tyrone to Sam. He didn't want to say. He walked towards the balcony door, pulled his cigarettes and lighter from his back pocket and lit up the cigarette. He inhaled deeply and blew the smoke out through his nose. Smoke floated out into the morning air, and Kane looked out at the now bright sunshine. Just another day. He turned to face the inquisitors.

"Yes. And if you want the truth, I am not so sure I would have resisted her…" The sentence escaped from his mouth before he had thought about what he had said. "I'm sorry, that was tactless…I don't know why I said it."

"But it's the truth, commander. And, it fits with what Sarah said. She knew it. She said that Corey fancied you, but so does she. Sarah is jealous. One word of warning, Kane, you need to watch out for your wife. I wouldn't put Sarah past…"

"Killing Kelly? Neither would I. Only one thing might stop that," interjected Kane.

"They are sisters aren't they? Same mother, different fathers." Sam wanted to know everything now.

"Yes, they are. Which makes things more complicated. Sarah knows she has a sister, but I am not sure if Kelly knows. The meeting will be interesting." Kane snuffed the cigarette butt out between his fingers.

"So if Kelly and Sarah are stepsisters, that makes you and Ryan Holden related. Kinda weird. The girls are a year or so apart and Sarah's father and her sister's husband are the same age."

"And the point you are making would be?" asked Kane, getting just a little short tempered.

"He's Kelly's uncle, right?" asked Tyrone.

"I guess so. Never thought of it like that. Son-of-a-bitch, he is." Kane turned back to look out of the balcony door. So much had happened since yesterday and so much more was going to happen. He looked down at the blood on the floor. He still could not get over that a couple of hours ago Corey had been alive, and so full of life. Now, she and last night were just a memory. The whole thing had come back to him, all of it.

He sensed someone was behind him. He spun around to face Sam.

"I should get the car and we should be going."

"Right, we should. Sam, I wasn't trying to hurt Tyrone…"

"He knows that. He knew that there was something between you and Corey. Dad," and Sam took a deep breath. "Would you have followed through with Corey?"

Kane never answered.

"I'll go get the car." Sam left him and went back to talk to Tyrone.

Finally, Kane entered the room and his eyes were greeted with a very subdued Sarah sitting on the couch, clutching her backpack and purse. She was dressed from head to toe in black, and had a scarf wrapped round her light colored hair.

"Back in five," and Tyrone disappeared to the shower. Water could be heard through the open door of the big bedroom, and then hurried sorting noises as he went through a backpack for clean clothes.

Kane sat down on the couch opposite Sarah. He was staring a hole through her, while the ceiling fan overhead was creating a noise that Kane had not heard last night. It made him look up at it, and then his eyes dropped to look at her. She had a smirk on her face.

"All yours, commander. Your backpack is still on the bed," said Tyrone, as he hurried back into the room.

Kane thought Tyrone was taking Corey's death very calmly. "Be right back," and Kane disappeared into the bedroom. He was gone about ten minutes tops, and came back ready to leave, dressed all in black, hair tied back, and round his head he wore a black bandana.

At that moment the suite door opened and Sam came into the room, dropping the keys on the table. "Everyone ready to go? Car is gassed up and I bought some water and snacks just in case."

"Case of what?" asked Sarah sarcastically, as she played with the purse strings.

"Case you get thirsty again, Miss Holden!" replied Kane, still agitated at her. "We would all like to feel safe!"

"Cute!" and she stood up, swung her purse up onto her shoulder and picked up her backpack from the floor. She marched to the door and stood next to Sam. She glanced back at Kane, almost daring him to make an issue of it.

"Let's go. We have wasted too much time..." and Kane paused, almost regretful at saying the words. He looked back at the bedroom and for one second his thoughts were back in the bathroom.

They all noticed.

Kane led the way down the stairs and stopped at the desk. He looked around for the translator. She wasn't there. Of course, she wasn't there. She was dead.

Kane did the best he could with the aid of his son and Tyrone. Between them they made sure the bill was for only what it was supposed to be.

Sam jumped in the car and Kane climbed in beside him. Sarah and Tyrone seated themselves in the back of the rented car, which seemed to be more than cramped when filled with four people and backpacks.

"All I could get! Seems everyone round here rents cars, probably cause their own get blown up so much!" Sam tried to make a joke of it, but he had a feeling driving seventy miles in this car was not going to be fun.

"Do you think they will get the guys that shot up the balcony? I saw them. I know who it was!" Kane was thinking out loud.

"Did you tell Kirk?" asked Tyrone. Leaning over the seat to talk to Kane.

"Yes, I told him. He thinks they are terrorists. Just bad timing!"

"But you believe what?" continued Tyrone.

"They are not. They were sent or led here." Kane looked up into the vanity mirror and his eyes focused on Sarah. "Someone wanted her dead, and they got their wish. Kirk knows how to reach me should he find out."

"You think it was Corey and not you they were after?" asked Tyrone.

"Makes sense doesn't it? Took out our interpreter, an American force operator, indispensable to us, but not to them. They knew who they were after. They don't want me, not yet. You guys better watch your back, especially you, Tyrone." Kane fell silent, and stared out the window and watched the traffic as Sam sped through the town.

Sam looked in his driving mirror and raised his eyebrows at Tyrone. He was having a hard job following his father's logic.

The car was warm and Kane dozed, as did the other two. Sam seemed to be the only one who was cognizant, and possibly the only one with a clear conscience.

Kane's head fell onto the glass and he awoke with a start. "Where are we?"

"About half way there. I was going to wake you. There seems to be a line of traffic up ahead. Cars slowed down a half mile back. I thought I could hear gunfire, too. Something is going on, look..." Sam pointed through the dirty windscreen.

Kane sat up in the seat. He, too, could hear gunfire in the distance, and up front the cars were certainly backing up. Kane noticed that some drivers were walking away from the line of cars, and were busy looking up the road.

Suddenly, without any warning, a chopper seemed to come from nowhere like some giant silver bird of prey, and appeared right over their heads, its blades making a loud whirring sound blowing brush and sand everywhere.

The other two in the back awoke instantly, and pressed faces to the windows on the car to see what was going down.

"Keep your heads down. The chopper isn't friendly. It's sporting fire power. They are looking for someone...could possibly be us! That's probably what the line is for, too!

Fuck! How the hell do they know all our movements? Time for the false papers." Kane reached in his backpack and pulled a wad of stuff out that Tucker had given him.

"Here. Everyone has a false passport and ID. Stick your real ones somewhere that cannot be found. If not on you, then under your seat. We can always use these to get out of the country, or our good friend Captain Kirk can fly us out if needs be. Someone will take care of you...." Kane changed his own wording. "Tyrone, switch places with me. I just noticed that Ms. Holden here is listed as *my wife*. Great!

Couldn't be better," he added sarcastically. Kane waited a few moments till the chopper made a pass over them, and then he opened the creaky car door, swapped places with Tyrone and sat down on the ragged leather seating in the back of the car. He glanced at Sarah more out of habit than anything else.

All the occupants of the car were dressed in black. Sarah could hide her hair under the scarf. She had pulled it tightly up on her head and the fair coloring could hardly be seen, whereas his and Sam's were very obviously blond. Nothing either of them could do but ride it out.

The line of cars slowed down to a crawl.

"Fucking great! Obviously, they are looking for someone. I thought maybe by the gunfire sounds that they had found them. I guess not." As Kane spoke, the chopper circled again. "Go pick on someone else," he muttered.

The cars still crawled along.

"Armed police on the left!" Sam saw them first. "They are going along the line. You're right. Someone did tip them off."

Kane looked at Sarah.

"Well, it wasn't me, if that's what you are thinking. I don't want to be bloody well shot by terrorist forces either!" Sarah was indignant.

"Who said they were terrorists, Mrs...." Kane couldn't remember his new name and looked at the ID. "Bonner."

"Bonner? Where did that come from?" Sarah asked, looking back at her papers. "And why did I have to be your wife? Why not Sam's?"

Suddenly, Tyrone turned in his seat, his eyes sharp and angry looking. "You know, lady, why don't you shut up! At least you are alive and not dead like *my wife*. Corey was supposed to be mine!" and Tyrone tuned back to look out the window at the advancing john hordes.

Kane smiled to himself. So, Tyrone really did care. He had wondered when Tyrone had said '*I love you*' to Corey within Kane's earshot, if it was just for his benefit. Now, Kane knew Tyrone was sincere. His thoughts were disturbed by someone banging on the windows.

"Iftah albab...!" and a gun-toting man, wrapped in a black toweled headdress, pummeled again on the glass with his fist.

This time Sam didn't hesitate and rolled the window down as fast as he could.

The first thing that came through the window was the rifle barrel, followed by verbal abuse that no one could understand. They did, however, understand the laugh and mocking gesture he made about the woman in the back seat.

Sarah leaned towards Kane, who automatically put his arm around her shoulders. This gained even more gestures and the Arab called to his friend to come and look. The other soldier sauntered over from where he had been standing. He had seemingly been keeping an eye on the car from a distance. All anyone could see of this man were his eyes, and two hands holding a rifle.

The two soldiers conversed with each other for several seconds, as they seemed to be deciding if they would just look at papers, or make the party get out of the car. Suddenly, the second man opened the door to the back of the vehicle.

"Kharig!"

Neither of them moved. "Kharig," he repeated and motioned with his hand to make Sarah and Kane climb out and stand by the car. Sarah scrambled out first, leaving her purse and backpack on the seat. Kane followed her almost defiantly, and he, too, left his backpack behind, with his gun.

The gun-toting man mumbled something in Arabic and, even to him, it was quite obvious they could not understand. "Papers!"

Sarah handed hers over immediately. She was actually terrified, fear written all over her face. He grabbed them from her and looked for the picture and name.

"Sarah Bonner. You are Australian housewife? This your husband?" As he spoke, he leaned forward, very close to Sarah's face.

"Yes," she replied timidly.

"Why you here?" and he got even closer to her and touched her hair with his fingers.

"Back off, mate!" Kane stepped forward and tried to get between Sarah and the soldier.

"You, keep out! You old man!"

"Really! You want to see how old my fist is?" snapped Kane.

"Kane, no. It's okay. I'm fine. He will kill you, and I don't want that..." she stopped mainly because the soldier seemed to understand every word she was saying.

Kane caught it, too.

At the sign of trouble, the second Arab stepped into the picture and stuck his gun- barrel into Kane's chest, and held it there. Kane raised his hands so that they didn't think he was provoking the situation, but he knew they were just itching to pull triggers on white foreigners.

"Papers!"

Kane motioned he would need to put his hand down to get them from his jeans pocket. Slowly, he reached around, pulled them from his back pocket, and handed them to soldier number two.

"You Kane Bonner...you architect. Why you go to Samarra? Look at mosque...why bring young wife? Who are others with you? Helpers?"

"If you can figure all that out, why ask me?" Kane retorted.

"You have arrogance. You need lesson!" and soldier number two shoved Kane hard in the chest with the rifle, winding him.

As Kane tried to get his breath, the towel-headed gentleman hit him with the rifle-butt on the side of his face. It bruised immediately. This time, Kane would not take it and turned on the Arab. As he doubled his fist ready to hit him, Sarah screamed, and Sam was about to get out of the car and join in the fray.

Another man showed himself from the line in front of them. He appeared to be an officer, or at least someone with a higher rank. He yelled to the offending man, and the Arab dropped his gun slightly.

Kane touched his face. He didn't think anything was broken, but it was bleeding and it hurt like hell.

The other man approached Kane, and kept staring at him. Kane blinked his eyes, mainly to clear his sight, but also because something seemed familiar about the person in front of him. Kane looked at the eyes, and then he knew him. Thank god he had shown up when he had or all of them may have ended up dead.

Chapter 25

"Are you hurt," the third man asked, as he motioned for Kane to move several feet away from the car.

"Course I'm bloody hurt. What do you think? Your guy just hit me with his rifle, so course I'm hurt. Can't you see that?" Kane's cheek was still bleeding. Kane's eyes creased at the man.

The man pulled a handkerchief from his pocket. "They should not have done that. I'm sorry. I should have come down the line sooner. We stopped the cars too soon. You ok, Kane?" he whispered.

"Yeah, I am. Just need some water to wash the blood off. I'll survive. Is everyone watching?" Kane just thought about that.

"Fraid so. Couldn't do much about it. Where is Corey? I don't see her," he looked around Kane to the car. As he did a piece of long black hair surfaced. He pushed it back.

"Didn't Kirk tell you? That surprises me. Figured he would get a message to you of all people." Kane paused. "Did you find out where Kelly and Reese are?"

"Yes and no…found out where they *were*. Ryan has moved them. Someone is still tipping them off. It's not me and it's not you. You trust your son?"

"Completely! So that leaves the other two in the car and Kirk."

"Wondered about that…I gotta go. Can't blow my cover now. Commander, be careful."

Kane nodded.

The man yelled commands in Arabic to his subordinates, and they handed Sarah back both sets of papers. Moving to the car, Kane glared at the gun-toting character that had hit him. He clenched his

203

fist by his side and then thought better of it. Making sure Sarah was safely in the car, Kane went round the other side, opened the door and climbed in.

Sarah was shaking. "Are you okay?" she asked Kane, and grabbed a bottle of water, opened it, and handed it to Kane.

Kane tipped water onto tissues and soaked his face with it. As he touched his bone, he realized there was more damage than he thought.

Tyrone turned around. "Geez, Kane. That's gotta hurt. Here," and Tyrone took the tissues and wiped blood from Kane's face. "Left side of your face looks like a battle ground! You wanna look in the mirror?"

"No, don't think so. If it looks as bad as it feels, I would rather not see." He clutched the tissues to his face.

Sam was watching it all in silence. He had seen Kane clench his fist. Normally, he would have killed the man for doing what he just got away with. Sam could also see the pain his father was in and the front he was putting up.

Kane leaned back on the upholstery, as Sam put his foot down on the accelerator and the car picked up speed.

"They moved the women." Kane muttered. "Fucking hell, they moved them!" and Kane thumped the side of the car so hard that Sarah jumped in her seat.

"How do you know that?" She asked hesitantly.

"Just know." Kane realized he hadn't told them who he was talking to outside, and for some reason neither Sarah nor Tyrone had guessed. He figured by Sam's silence, that he had.

Sam glanced up into the mirror and caught his father's stare. He mimed the word *Hunter.*

Kane nodded yes.

They cleared the offending traffic, passing a couple of cars held at the road block. Now they knew why they had been held up. Whoever the soldiers had been looking for, they had found. Three bodies hung from the one car, explaining the gunfire, each one seemed to be shot to death, blood dripping from them to the dusty earth.

"I'm gonna be sick," muttered Sarah.

"No, you're not! Swallow hard. Breathe," insisted Kane. "Pretend you're pregnant! Breathe!"

She looked at Kane like he was insane.

"Do it!" he yelled at her. Then again, pain hit him in the face. "God damn, son-of-a-bitch!" The bone was chipped and he knew it, and he clutched the side of his face with the tissues. "Anyone got anything for pain with them?"

"Yes, I do," and Sarah started for her purse.

"Don't want any from you," and he caught her arm before she had a chance to produce anything ever again, like she had given him on the plane, from her bag. The look on his face was not friendly, almost warning her.

"I have pain killers. Standard issue," offered Tyrone, and handed some over the seat to Kane.

Kane gulped them down with a bottle of water, without even checking what they were, leaned back on the seat and closed his eyes. Why had Holden moved the women and where to? He needed to speak to Tucker and even more to Kirk, and right now he couldn't do either.

As if someone heard him, his cell, now carried in his back pocket for easy access, rang. He reached for it. "So what the fuck is the excuse this time? I heard they moved them…" he paused to listen to the explanation from the phone line. "Well, you are supposed to know. Isn't that what the military have you for, *sir*?" Another pause and it was now apparent Kane was getting agitated. He wasn't in control and he didn't like that. "Well, I would think he knows we are coming, shit how much working out does that take, especially as someone amongst us is feeding him information. How? How the fuck do I know? You are the one supposedly in charge here. Oh, I am? News to me!" and he slammed the phone shut.

No one spoke. Tyrone thought about it, but decided against it. Overhead the chopper circled, its silver blades glinting in the sun, and flew low to the ground right behind them. Kane turned to look. He knew who was in it, supposedly his back up, or so they had just said, and then the chopper was gone back to the skies.

Tyrone also turned to look where the noise was coming from. "Isn't that one of ours…"

"One of yours, yep…not mine, mate!" Kane changed the subject, anxious now to get to Samarra and to find where his wife was. He knew time was running out. What he really wanted to know was who was tipping them off. No one but him had a phone. There were phones in the hotel. Phones by bathrooms; phones all over the place. Could be Sarah or Tyrone. Or, someone was wired. Sarah certainly wasn't wired in the bedroom in that nightshirt! But someone was, today. Kane didn't even question Sam. Maybe he should. He doubted it. Not his own flesh and blood. "How far?" Kane asked Sam.

"Another twenty miles we hit the outskirts of Samarra. Only you know where after that. Right? You do know?" asked Sam, glancing in the mirror again.

"Sam, if you are gonna keep lookin' in the mirror, why don't I sit by you, better still, I'll drive! Pull over and stop the car!"

Sam indicated and pulled the car to the side of the road. Kane jumped out and went round to Sam's door. Bending his head inside, "Tyrone, you go in the back. Keep your gun ready, just in case. Switch with Sarah. Would rather not have her right behind me," and Kane waited for Sam to get out of the car. As they passed each other, the two exchanged a look, their eyes meeting, father and son. And the son knew the father was questioning his loyalty.

Kane waited till they were all resituated in the car and then, making sure the road was clear, took off at the usual Branson speed of zero to eighty. As he drove, he glanced at Sam. He wanted so much to believe it wasn't him. As if in slow motion, Sam returned the look. And Kane knew it was not his son.

"Slow down, Kane. You're going to kill us all!" yelled Sarah, as she clung to the seatback.

"He might do that, but not in the car! He once drove in the British Grand prix and won!" interjected Sam.

"How did you know that? I never told you?" asked Kane, rather surprised that Sam knew.

"Kelly told me…" Sam stopped, and stared through the front window. "She also told me you are crazy, and that I believe." He laughed. "I have a fucking crazy father! But like I said, he isn't going to kill us."

"Kelly told you that…" and Kane thumped the steering wheel. "When we get to the mosque we wait. Someone will meet us there. Give us more firepower. We only have a gun each, the spare one and so much ammunition. We need much more. Ryan has half an army waiting for us and more than a lot of firepower. He also has the element of knowing we are coming on his side. He'll be ready, but so will we."

"Someone? Who is someone? Kirk and his men? Or?" asked Sam.

"That's all you need to know for now. Someone. Take a nap. I'm fine. Need you all fresh and alert."

"Alert? When you drive like this? How can we be anything but alert, and how the hell can we take a nap?" asked Sarah, still hanging onto the seat.

"Relax, Mrs. Bonner! I am not gonna kill you…yet!"

He sped on up the road, totally ignoring the rest of his unit and their complaints. He had one thing on his mind now and that was to get to Kelly. Kirk had told him more than Kane had told the others. They had moved the women like Hunter had said. One of them was also dying. What the sources didn't know was which one. One of Kirk's own men was a plant in Ryan Holden's small, but very effective army, and had relayed it back to Kirk at some length. Kirk had also given Kane some fresh info that had made him think he knew which one was the traitor in his group. All Kane had to do was prove it.

Kane looked through his driving mirror. It was misty. He cleaned it with his hand and turned the angle slightly so he could see the people in the back. Both were asleep.

"Sam, you asleep?" asked his father.

"No, just thinking," replied Sam, still lost in thought.

"When did you start working for the Americans?" Kane ploughed straight in.

"What?" Sam looked staggered.

"You heard me! When?" Kane was his usual belligerent self.

"I'm not, Kane. They are," inclining his head to the back seat. "You know that. What brought about those accusations?"

"Someone in this car is passing on info one way or another. Either by phone or one of us is wired. The only thing I know is that it's not me." Kane was confident.

"How do we know it's not you? Maybe it is..." Sam stated very calmly.

Swerving violently, Kane almost crashed the car. "How the fuck can it be me?"

"Because Sarah said we should open up the surgery and see what we would find inside you," he whispered, as the two in the back seat woke up.

"Are you serious? She said that? When?" Kane asked.

"On the balcony, at the hotel, before...well...before Corey..."

"Are you sure...." he stopped speaking, realizing the other two were wide awake.

"What's going on, Kane?" asked Sarah looking more than puzzled.

Kane brought the car to a screeching halt, and jumped out. He opened the back door.

"Out! Now!" he yelled at her.

"What is wrong with you?" she was screaming back at him, struggling to climb out before he jerked her out of the seat.

"The crap about the fan blade still being in me...is it true? Or, is there something else in there, like you told Sam...is there? Am I some sort of homing device? Is that it and it's me that has been feeding the information and locations back all the time? Is it?" Kane grabbed her by the shoulders and shook her.

Tyrone jumped out, as did Sam, to try to stop him, but Kane would not be stopped.

"Yes," she screamed. "It is you!" and Sarah started to laugh uncontrollably, pulling violently in his grasp. She broke free, backed away from him and pulled the gun from her jeans, and aimed it straight at Kane's chest.

Chapter 26

Sarah didn't falter. She clutched the gun between both hands and didn't waver even a fraction of an inch.

"You were stabbed by a ceiling fan. That was true, but you blacked out right after you killed the would-be assassin. You were right in your assumptions there, too. He wasn't really my fiancé. It was all a sham. The only part that was true, I was sent to learn from you. You are good, really good! But I digress, commander. After you blacked out they took you into another room, while the Japanese ambassador was recovering from the incident. As you were out, and the doctor was there, they pulled the fan blade out, attached a homing devise to it and put it back. Then they just stitched you up. Why do you think it hurts so much when it moves around in your chest? I bet it's like having a heart attack?" and Sarah's laugh was maniacal and her eyes wild.

Sarah started again. "You are leading everyone to their death, Commander Branson. My father is waiting for you, and so is my sister!" She paused and looked at Kane's facial expression. "I can see you are shocked. You are wondering if Kelly knows she has a sister? I can assure you she does. You see, I came back here with her from Australia. Didn't you ever wonder why I left Japan days before you did? The night she disappeared from Sydney with the dark-haired man, I was there also, waiting in the car for her. She never even put up a fight. All she wanted to know was where you were. Funny, really. I told her we were sisters, same mother. Told her I was with you in Japan. Also told her that you and I had an affair. Wasn't hard to convince her. I could actually tell her a lot about you, as I was in the room when they operated on you."

Kane was trying to take all this in. He wanted to take his chance, lean forward, grab the gun and then break her neck. But he had a feeling there was more. There had to be a reason she was spilling this just a few miles from Samarra. "She wouldn't believe that I had an affair with someone like you!" snarled Kane.

Sarah continued, still holding her position, her arms outstretched, the gun still aimed at Kane. "No? You had sex with Corey, didn't you?"

This was enough for Tyrone and he stepped forward as if to grab Sarah.

"Take one more step and I will kill the commander right in front of you!" she hissed.

"Go ahead, Sarah. Kill me! You don't have the guts to do it," Kane was trying to provoke her. She couldn't shoot them all.

Tyrone backed off.

"Finish it, Sarah! What else is there. Is Tucker in on this too?" yelled Kane.

"Course he is. This was his idea, he and his pals back in the USA. They want my father, just like I do, and they set the whole thing up just to get you to come right here and kill him. Oops, did I say I want my father, too…slip of the tongue there. I am helping my father. Always have been. I led Reese Wade into the trap that caught her. I baited her husband. Was easy to get Reese. Seems every women you meet, *sir*, falls in love with you, including me." Sarah stopped again. She hadn't meant to say that out loud, only think it. "I pretty much told Reese you wanted to see her again to discuss her husband being a witness. When she knew it was you, she came readily. Silly bitch!" She changed tactics, feeling that maybe the commander wasn't buying all this.

"And Corey. Same thing. Tyrone, here, was smitten with Corey. Once again the great Kane Branson was the dominant male. But Corey was different, wasn't she, commander? You had some kind of feelings for her. Wonder how Kelly would feel about that, if she knew? And Corey had started to work things out about me. She was on the balcony wasn't she? Was she waiting to talk to you? The drug I gave her wore off quicker than I intended it to. Was supposed to last for hours, but when you drank some of it you both ended up drugged and split the dosage. Unfortunately, you both remembered what happened. Sad! It was very convenient those gunman opened fire when they did." Sarah's eyes gleamed knowing her plan was working.

That was enough for Tyrone. This time he leaped at her, grabbing for the gun. Sarah pulled the trigger and it missed Kane by a milometer.

But it gave Kane enough time to pull his own gun. Tyrone pushed Sarah towards the ground and as she tried to stabilize herself and fire again at anyone in her path, Kane aimed his gun at her head and fired a single shot right between her eyes.

As if in slow motion, Sarah Holden fell back into the parched earth, her body crumbling as she did. He legs buckled underneath her and her arms flopped beside her, allowing her dead hand to drop the gun.

Kane's nightmare of the last few weeks had come true. He had just killed Sarah Kelly Holden, the sister of his wife and the image of Kelly. He felt sick, and turned away as if to throw up, still clenching his gun to his side.

Sam bent down by the girl, and for no reason but to be sure, felt for a pulse. She was dead, as he knew she was. He picked her up off the ground and lay her on the grass next to the car, having no idea at this time what they were going to do with her body. He gently closed her eyes and watched the blood trickle down her face. He knew that Kane had no choice. The way she was waving the gun around, she could have hit any one of them. Still, he knew his father was bitterly regretting having to kill her. She was, after all, family.

Kane stared at the earth. He had just killed a woman. A first. Reese Wade's staged death didn't count.

It was Tyrone that spoke first. "You didn't have a choice, sir. She would have killed either you or me. Sarah was bitter and twisted… and she killed Corey." Tyrone moved to the car, opened the door and sat inside, leaned down in the upholstery and silent tears flowed from his eyes. At last, the grief he felt for Corey could be released.

Kane turned to his son. "Sam, I…" For once in his life, Kane was lost.

"Like Tyrone said, she would have killed anyone of us without even thinking about it. She was crazy, Kane. Some of the things she said didn't even make sense, except…"

"Except what?" Kane mumbled, while stuffing his gun back down in his jeans.

"Except the part about the 'bug'. It is in you which means they know every move we make. Wherever we go, they go. So what do we do now?"

"Split up. You and Tyrone go to Samarra. I'll get there, but not with you. They won't know we are travelling in two groups. A bug doesn't count! I'll find Hunter again and come in with him. Or…" Kane paused.

"Or, what…you're going to do what I think you are, aren't you? You're not going to open up the wound and remove it? Please, god, tell me you're not." Sam was horrified, and yet he could read it on Kane's face. "Come on, Kane. You're my father and it will kill you." Sam didn't believe he was hearing this from a sane man.

"Maybe, maybe not. Didn't kill me to put it in there, did it? Why should it kill me to take it out?"

"And just how are you going to remove it? I don't see any hospitals round here." Sam's eyes squinted even further at Kane. "God, no! You're not going to take it out with a knife, are you? Kane, don't be crazy!"

"I'm not, no…" and Kane walked over to Sarah's body. He pulled his cell from his jean's pocket, turned away from Sam and made a call.

By now, people in cars on those roads were used to seeing shootings, admittedly by Arabs but not blond haired men. Even so, they didn't seem to be paying much attention to the fact. Couple of folks from cars that had slowed down, craned heads to get a better look, but no one really cared. No military or police came either, and that seemed a little strange.

In the car, Tyrone composed himself. He wished he had pulled the trigger and not Kane. He felt no sympathy for Sarah, but did feel some for Kane, and realized that perhaps Kane needed some help right now. Tyrone climbed back out of the car and ventured over to Sam.

"Is Kane okay? I mean, I know he is not okay, but…"

"I know what you mean, Tyrone. I guess he is as okay as one can be when you have just wasted your sister-in-law. He made a call, I think to either Hunter or Kirk. Says he is going to split us up and go with Hunter into Samarra. What I don't understand is why she told us now, right near the destination, almost like she was warning us. But that can't be, can it?"

"I don't think so. What does Kane think? Did you ask him?" Tyrone wouldn't let it go.

"No, not yet." Sam didn't want to disturb his father's thoughts right now.

"You said Hunter. The same Hunter? I thought we abandoned him way back…we didn't, did we?" Tyrone thought about it. "Mr. Military police down the road…was that Hunter? It was, wasn't it? Thought there was something familiar about him. Maybe we should go talk to Kane, before we split up," and Tyrone walked towards his boss. "Commander, why did this happen now so close to our destination?"

Kane pulled his cigarettes and lighter from his back pocket and lit one up. He took a long draw and inhaled deeply, letting the smoke find its way down his nose and out into the air. "I think maybe in her own way, Sarah was trying to warn us. For all her accusations, Sarah hated herself. I knew how she felt about me in Japan. She made it all too clear. Good job my morals were in tact." 'Geez! How tactless can you be, Kane?' he thought. "Tyrone, I am sorry about Corey. I would never have done what I did. Tucker sent her to distract me, didn't he? He could have sent two men. Worked better than even Tucker thought. I think that with all the confusion and the drugs, I was more inclined to notice her." Kane was getting in deeper and he knew it. "Shit…" he took another drag on the cigarette.

"I know what you mean, sir." Tyrone glanced down at Sarah. "You did what you had to do, Kane. Never easy killing a woman, but Sarah was leading us all into a trap. Sam says we are splitting up. Is that right?"

"Yes. It's safer. The bugs in me…for now. You guys will be much better off without me. Sam," Kane called him over to join them. He didn't continue till Sam was in his rightful place by his side. "There is something else that Kirk told me. One of the women is dying! I just don't know which one it is, so now time is of the essence," and Kane snuffed the cigarette out between his fingers.

"Dying? Dying how? Sick, raped, tortured? What, Kane?"

Kane grabbed Tyrone by the shirt. "If I fucking knew, would I be standing here talking to you about it? I need to get there and get Kelly out, and, of course, Reese, but I have a feeling it's Kelly. If Ryan finds out I just killed his daughter, then Kelly will be dead."

Sam hadn't thought of that till that second. Kane had just killed one of their bargaining tools. Kane was the other. As they were weighing up the options, the chopper appeared once more overhead.

"Ours?" asked Tyrone.

"Yep," replied Kane. "For Sarah. She can't go to her father."

Kane didn't glance behind him, but seated himself in the driving seat of the car. Sam sat beside him and Tyrone climbed in the back. Now they were three. Once more they took off up the road. Kane was trying to figure out how all this killing had happened. Wasn't only supposed to be him that died? At least now no one had a hold over him. He was free to come and go as he pleased. That at least was relief. Tucker wouldn't force him back to America. It wasn't worth it.

Five miles up the road, Kane got a call. He didn't answer it. He didn't have to. He knew it was Hunter. He stopped the car on the side of the road. "It's all yours. Sam, take the car onto Samarra and meet your contacts by the mosque. They will find you. Just park somewhere and wait. Make sure you are armed and ready just in case. And Sam, always remember…I love you. Tyrone," and Kane grabbed his backpack, opened the door and stepped out of the car.

Kane shot round the front of the old car and never looked back. An Iraqi jeep pulled up alongside of him, engine revving, and Kane jumped into the far seat. The Iraqi- looking driver glanced into the car and Hunter's features could just be made out. Tyrone and Sam watched the jeep turn right and disappear in a cloud of dust. Kane was once again doing things the only way he knew how…his own way.

Chapter 27

"Guess we are on our own. Better do what Kane said and keep going." Sam climbed into the driver's seat and Tyrone joined him in the front. "Once before, Kane told me to go it on my own, and I made it then and we'll make it now. Funny, Kelly was involved that time, too." Sam accelerated from zero to eighty.

Tyrone clutched anything he could find to hold on to. "You drive like your damn father, too! God damn it, slow down! What do you mean Kelly was involved, too?"

"Kelly was with him in Hong Kong. She was pregnant at the time. Lost the baby there, too. She goes everywhere with him…that's what this is about. He left her behind. If he hadn't, she would be safe at home in Sydney, and my father would not be exchanging his life for hers out here. God damn it!" and Sam thumped his hands down on the steering wheel, and if possible picked up even more speed.

Tyrone could feel the tension in the car. Sam was more than worried about his father. He was also worried about his step-mother. Tyrone hadn't really thought about that, Kelly being his step-mother. But then he had never met Kelly, only her piece-of-shit sister. He wondered where Kane was going.

Kane's jeep sped up the side streets of Samarra. Hunter drove as if his life depended on it. To a certain degree it did. "In the back. Some rags to wrap round your head. You are too damned obvious, commander. Spot you a mile away. Might want to cover your arms, too. Black military jacket on the seat." Hunter glanced at Kane. "Rest of you is okay."

Kane pulled the stuff over the top of the seat. The dust blew round him, but didn't hinder him sporting his new look. He peered in the mirror. Still, his tanned face looked pale for an Iraqi citizen. "You got anything to make me darker-skinned?"

"Yeah, but it's at the safe house. This is just to get you through the streets."

Kane nodded. "By the way, when we get there I need to find someone who can remove a bug from my chest."

"Just flick it off, or kill it!' Hunter was confused by this line of conversation.

"Not that kind of 'bug'. It's inside me! A homing device!"

"What? How? You mean it's you who has been sending signals? Dear god! Thought you were just stabbed, not carrying a damn 'bug'. When did you find out about this useful piece of information?"

"Just before I killed Sarah," declared Kane, almost ashamed.

"You did what?! You are joking, right?" And Hunter had a job to control both the car and his surprise.

"I wish to hell I was. She tried to kill me, well, all of us." Kane paused. "You know that dream you were not supposed to know I was having?"

"Yes," replied Hunter, a tad quieter.

"Well, it came true, but with Sarah. Shot her in just the same way." Kane stopped speaking. Reality had set in.

Hunter could see a problem. They only had one bargaining tool and that was Kane. Ryan Holden had two. He thought for a moment. Maybe this team did still have two. Kane had a son…Sam Branson.

"Where do you think they are now?" asked Tyrone, rolling the old fashioned handle on the door to let the window down.

"Are you going to ask me that every five minutes?"

"No. I was just curious. We have to be close to the centre of Samarra now. Look, on your right, the Mosque. Aren't we supposed to park here and wait for whomever we are supposed to meet? That's what Kane said wasn't it? He said they would find us. How are they going to know us, without Kane along?"

Sam thought Tyrone was just a little anxious about knowing where Kane was. Why did it bother him so much? "You know, I am here. I can fight, maybe not as well as Kane…"

"I'm sorry…it's just that Kane is …" Tyrone stopped, mainly because there were people everywhere seemingly staring at them and it was hard to concentrate on two things at once. "You think it's always like this here? I think it's you they are staring at, Sam."

Sam gave up. Obviously, Tyrone was going to keep this up for a while, so he may as well get used to it. Tyrone was handling things his way, and right now he seemed nervous. But he had a point. Sam had forgotten that blond hair on a man was not the thing out here. He stopped the car and pulled something from his backpack. A black knit hat was better than nothing and he forced it down tightly on his head, covering all the blond hair. And how were people going to find them?

Stuffing his backpack under the seat, Sam climbed out of the car and leaned his back against it. From his pocket he pulled out cigarettes and a lighter. Sam slid one out of the pack and then put it to his lips. He lit it up, took several drags from it, and turned to look at Tyrone, who was still sitting in the car. In fact, he hadn't moved an inch. Sam banged on the window. Still nothing. He dropped the cigarette to the ground and opened the car door. What he saw shocked him.

Kane had a feeling something was wrong. Kane's feelings were usually right. "Exactly who are meeting Sam and Tyrone?"

"Couple of scouts that can help them out. They know roughly where one of the women is. Possibly the women are split up. Would make a lot more sense to make our job even harder. Wasn't easy to find these things out. Like you saw first hand these guys here play for real. As long as I kept my mouth shut and listened it was okay. One of the guys in Ryan's unit is also on our payroll. Course, that means nothing anymore. Half of your unit is corrupt. But seems you took care of that little situation." Hunter glanced at Kane wondering if Kane was even listening. "Commander? Are you listening?"

"Sure. Course I am." Kane was, but his mind was elsewhere and it concerned his son.

"We need to go find Sam!"

"What? I thought you wanted to split up from them? Isn't that the point of me picking you up, almost blowing my own cover, and didn't you just say you want to get rid of the bug. They are tracking you and me right now, not Sam and Tyrone."

"Hunter, shut the fuck up! I am trying to concentrate. Turn around or whatever, and go find the mosque. It can't be that hard to spot. Great big bloody tower." He paused. "Stop the jeep!'

"What?"

"Stop the fucking jeep! You got a knife on you? Sure you do. All *Arab's*, make believe or otherwise, have a knife. Give!"

Hunter pulled over and stopped in some back alley. Washing hung from clothes lines and hungry dogs seemed only interested in finding food on the cobbled streets of Samarra.

"Give," and Kane stuck his hand out to Hunter.

Reluctantly, Hunter pulled the blade from its sheath, and handed it to Kane. He pulled the T-shirt out of the belt of his pants. "You got some more of these rags?" Without waiting for his answer, he continued. "If you don't, pull one of my long sleeved shirts from the backpack and make a bandage."

Kane pulled his lighter out of his pocket and flicked it open, holding it under the blade. It soon became red hot and sterilized.

"Kane, think twice about what you are doing. It's gonna hurt like hell. You already have a smashed face and now this. What are you? A glutton for punishment?"

"Something like that. You gonna help me or just sit and fuck-ing watch? The bug has to be near the surface, right? Or it wouldn't transmit if it was in too deep. So all I have to do is slit the scar open a little and pull it out."

"That's all?! You make it sound like slicing bread. Geez, Kane. You are insane!"

"Maybe. Half hour ago I took a bunch of pain killers Tyrone gave me…should still work. Okay…let's do it."

Kane felt for the scar and looked up at Hunter. He smiled, and then split the scar with the red hot blade. Kane growled in pain as his skin parted and blood oozed out first in a trickle then a more steady flow. But Kane was right; the bug was just under the surface. He could feel it with his fingers but not grasp it.

"Take your fingers and pull it out! Or would you like me to bleed to death in front of you?" he stated to Hunter.

Hunter leaned across Kane and did as he was asked. He pulled on the piece of plastic and the bug moved with him, unhinging itself from Kane's flesh. It didn't appear to be attached to the shaft of the blade like Sarah had said.

"You got it, I hope…cause this fucking hurts!" Kane was speaking very low, the pain overwhelming him.

"Yes," replied Hunter, as he stifled a churning feeling in the pit of his stomach, like he was going to throw up.

Kane leaned back in the seat, feeling like he was going to black out. "Wrap it round me like a bandage. Pull it tight. The bleeding will stop. Not like it was deep. Just a flesh wound." Kane was fighting for control over his body and his staccato speech showed that to the other man. Never-the-less, Kane wished he had a needle and thread with him. It would not have been the first time he had stitched himself up.

Hunter ripped the sleeves off the shirt and bound them tightly around Kane's chest. Kane's breathing eased a little and he sat more upright.

"You okay?" Hunter was genuinely concerned. He didn't want to lose Kane.

"Yeah, fine." He pulled his T-shirt back over the mess he had just made. "You got water? Need to wash the blood off…" Some blood he could never wash off.

"Right here." Hunter marveled at Kane. He had just cut himself open, and now he was washing away the evidence.

"Want your knife back? Second thoughts, I'll keep it. Might come in handy for Ryan Holden. Need something to cut his black heart out," and, as he laughed, the pain brought him back to reality. "Just give me a second and then we'll get going."

Hunter cleaned his hands on the rag. "What you want me to do with this thing? It's probably still working." He fingered the small object like it was gold dust.

"See that chicken right there? Just place it on its feathers, make it stick. Then let's go!"

Hunter returned to the jeep after having made a very unknown chicken more than important. He looked at Kane, who appeared on the surface to be very composed and in control. Hunter did know that he could not have done what the commander had. It took guts and Kane had those.

"Let's get going. Wasted enough time here. May be too later already," Kane murmured.

"What's maybe too late? You're not making sense, Kane!" Hunter pulled away from the side of the street and pulled into faster flowing traffic

"Just drive to the mosque where you told them to park. They won't be hard to find," replied Kane. He shifted in the seat to get into a more comfortable position. "Hunter, the night Kelly left Sydney, where were you?"

"What?"

"Why don't we change your name to *what*? It's all you have said in the last ten minutes. I said…where were you that night?"

"At the station, why?" Hunter didn't hesitate.

"Report said that Kelly left with someone who looked like you." Kane never faltered either. He just had to make sure of his travelling companion. Australian agent definitely, but also one who was working with the Americans.

"And you are thinking it was me?" He stopped. He knew Kane had his suspicions of why he was put there at the house in Sydney. Kane was a very clever man and not one you could fool easily. "I am not working with Tucker, if that's what you are thinking. Yes, he was initially the one who set up the meetings through me with you, but that's it. Have I been working with Kirk? Yes, I have. Kirk is on our side. He doesn't trust Tucker either, just like you don't. But then Kirk already told you that, didn't he?"

Kane didn't answer. His thoughts returned to his son. "Find them Hunter. Find my son!"

Sam leaned in the car. What greeted him was far more than he bargained for. Tyrone was motionless.

"Tyrone, what's wrong, mate?" Sam tapped him on the shoulder, and Tyrone fell forward in the car, almost hitting his head on the window.

"Oh, my god! NO!" Sam rushed around the other side of the car. Tyrone's window was down and as he looked at the American's head, there was a bullet wound straight to the temple. Sam had never heard a thing. Obviously done with a silencer by someone passing by. Sam didn't panic. He was trained better than that. He rounded the car back to his side. Sam looked up and saw someone in front of the car and he breathed a sigh of relief.

"Thank god! I hoped you would come back."

Chapter 28

"He's dead. Shot straight through the temple. Was it you?" asked Sam.

"Yes. My gun has a silencer on it." Kirk slid the weapon down the back of his pants.

"Anyone see you? Where are my father and Hunter?"

"Managed to direct them round the other side of the temple. It's gonna be you and me, son. You do know Tyrone was going to kill you? Your father killed Corey in Tyrone's eyes, despite what Tyrone said. An eye for an eye. After Kane suggested the unit split up, he felt something was going to happen. Kane remembered Tyrone had made some comments earlier about Corey was to be his wife when you used the forged papers. When Kane called me in the chopper, to get Sarah, he asked me to do some checking. Seems our Corey was married once…to Tyrone's brother! Tyrone wanted to move in after his brother was killed out here in Iraq. He thought this would be a great time, only, apparently, Kane got in the way. The bullets on the balcony were meant for your father, not Corey. I had been watching from the sidelines, when we saw the men running away. That's how I managed to be at the hotel door so fast."

"And Hunter? What is going to happen to him?" Sam asked Kirk.

"We need him for now. He's the only one of us that can pass for an Arab. You and Kane certainly can't."

"Is Kane okay? Please tell me he didn't do what I think he did?" His face grimaced at the thought.

"Fraid he did. He has been in contact with me most of the time now. One hell of a man your father! Not sure I could have taken that thing out." Kirk shivered at the prospect of removing a bug from his

223

own chest. "Let's get out of here before your *supposed* contacts arrive. I'll ride in the back. Just prop Tyrone up for now. We'll get him back to base. Tucker only knows that Corey is dead, and that's how it has to stay for now."

"Are you sure he had plans to kill me? I mean you killed him…" There was a doubt in Sam's mind. It was a little bit too neatly packaged. "Had Tyrone ever met Kelly?"

"Yes, I am sure he had to die, and no, Tyrone hadn't met Kelly. None of us had." Kirk was very quick to answer.

That wasn't what Sam had asked. How he wished he could talk to Kane.

Kane's jeep pulled around the corner just as Sam and Kirk pulled out from the parking place and into the flow of traffic.

"Follow them, at a distance. There are three of them in the car. I can make out Sam, Tyrone, and I think Kirk is in the back. Why would Kirk have joined them? He was supposed to supply air power only. Just stay back or they will spot us. Doesn't matter if Sam does, but not sure I want the other two to know it's us." Kane paused. He could feel something wet under his T-shirt. He didn't want to look, knowing already what it was. He was bleeding and he knew it, but he had to finish the job. They were almost there. He would find Kelly, get her and Reese Wade out and his job was done. Kane was tired. Suddenly, he felt his age. Only a few days away from his kids and he missed them, especially Star. He wanted to hold her in his arms and keep her close. He shook his head. His mind was wandering and he knew it. It was hard to focus on the matter in hand.

Hunter noticed something was wrong. "You okay there, Kane? Your chest alright?"

"Fine. I'm fine. Just follow them. Something is very wrong." Kane knew by instinct that things in the car were not as they should be. He clutched his chest tighter. Hopefully, the bleeding would slow down a little. He needed to be in good shape before he got to Kelly, and Ryan Holden. He was desperate to kill Holden, one way or another.

The giant ornate mosque disappeared into the background as both cars picked up speed. Hunter kept his distance from Sam, as Kane had instructed, so it would be hard to discern who actually was behind Sam. Kane didn't look like Kane from a distance. With the black rags wrapped completely round his head, and a jet black jacket covering the top of his body, he could hardly be recognized. A darker skin tone would have been better, but there was no time to do that.

Sam turned at the next exit out of the town and onto a dirt road. Tailing them now was a lot more difficult. One or two cars turned as well, seemingly in front of them. Kane realized that the car with Sam and Tyrone was being followed.

"Drop back! Now! We aren't the only ones following them."

"I see that! How the hell? You had the bug in you. How can they be following Sam..." Hunter didn't get to finish, as he slowed down and pulled back, letting another car pass him.

"It's Kirk they are following. In that car right behind them, is either military or they are Ryan Holden's men! My guess? Ryan Holden's men. I don't think your Captain Kirk is as honest as he says. Do you?"

"No," admitted Hunter. "He's been giving me instructions where to meet and where the ladies are the whole time, knowing I would feed them to you. I wonder if they were ever split up from each other? When I told you the women were separate, Kirk's inside man told me that piece of information. Now, I wonder if there was an inside man..." he paused. "Kane, does something look funny in the car to you?" Hunter was peering over the dirty windshield of his own jeep.

"Yes. Tyrone has not moved an inch. Yet, they turned corners and both Sam and Kirk have moved with the car. I think the Sergeant is dead! Fucking hell! Another one. And, if he is dead, I believe that the gentleman in the back of the car is responsible for it. Has to be him. Sam is in more danger than he knows. Stop the jeep!"

"Now? We might lose them!" exclaimed a very anxious Hunter.

"Move over, jump out and get in the back. Whichever, but move. I'm driving. You get down in the back seat. Have your gun at the ready, just in case. Gonna get closer. If Kirk recognizes me, shoot the bastard. Kirk is one huge traitor. Makes me wonder if Tucker is a traitor, too." Kane slid across the seat as he talked. "God damn, how do you see out of this side of the window? Passenger side is bad enough." He rubbed his arm across the dirt. Didn't improve it any. Kane realized it was on the outside more than the inside. "Shit! You in?"

"Yep, drive!"

Kane gripped the wheel and accelerated at high-speed. Hunter scrunched down in the back as far as he could, with his gun hand ready, just in case. He pulled Kane's backpack closer to him to act as a shield, and cover any signs that there was someone in the back of the car.

Kane passed the car in front of him, then hung a couple of cars back, hoping he was not now in the middle of the entourage following Sam. One good thing. Without the bug, Kirk nor Tucker or Ryan Holden could determine Kane's location.

Advantage Kane.

Sam could not stop thinking about his father. He had the distinct feeling he was in the near vicinity. He had no clue where they were going, except that Kirk was the one giving directions. How did Kirk know how to go all of a sudden? Obvious! Kirk was working for Holden and probably, by now, Sarah Holden's body was with her father. Kirk had killed Corey and then Tyrone. They were expendable, as now he and Hunter would be. Sam wondered how much money a traitor cost now days. Maybe he should ask him.

"Captain, how long have you been working for Ryan Holden?" He looked straight ahead as he spoke.

"Don't be so stupid! I am an in the American Airforce. Why would I work for someone like him?" Kirk was taken off guard.

"Money, power…several things, really. When?" As Sam spoke, he happened to glance in the driving mirror. He realized that the same cars were still very much in evidence behind him. Then, as he looked through his side mirror, he noticed a car he hadn't seen behind him before. It was a jeep that seemed to be passing the other cars one by one, but still hanging back a car length. As far as he could tell, it looked Iraqi. There was something in the way the man was driving it. Fast and furious. Sam would know his father's driving anywhere, even if Kane was smothered in black rags. Sam smiled.

"I am not working for Ryan Holden! Only with Tucker."

"If you say so, Captain," but Sam knew better. Kirk was working with Ryan Holden. His mind was racing. Hadn't his father said that in the report, Kelly left with a dark-skinned man? But he had an accent, the witness said. Maybe the witness was wrong.

Sam kept driving the car at the same speed as before. He didn't want to do anything else to spook Kirk. Never-the-less, he kept his eyes on the rear view mirror.

"Kane, do you have to drive like this? He is gonna spot you!" asked Hunter.

"Sam will. I want him to. But Kirk won't. He doesn't know me well enough, nor the way I drive. Thinking about that, he does, doesn't he?" Kane slowed to a better speed, but didn't let Sam's car out of his site.

Suddenly, Sam's car took another side road, followed by the tailing car. Now it really was tough.

"Shit! I can't follow on this open dirt road. Fucking hell! They would see us." He pulled the jeep over to the side and pretended to be looking at the tires. Only the two cars turned.

Sam realized that the jeep had stopped. Now he really was alone, except for Kirk and one very dead soldier.

Hunter sat up in the back of the jeep. "What are we gonna do?" He jumped out of the jeep and stood next to Kane. "I have a map of the area here. Must be another road that goes to the same location. Just wish we knew exactly where they are heading, and only the folks in that car know that. Or do they? Sam must be driving blind…maybe if we look at the map it might just help us. There can't be that many places in this area that could house a small army." Hunter pulled the map from under the jeep seats and spread it out on the dusty hood of the car. He pinned it down with his hands.

Kane poured over it. He put his hand on one end of the map. Immediately, he made red finger marks on it.

"You're bleeding. Why didn't you say something, Kane? Let's take a look…"

"Stop fussing…Or I'll think you really are gay!" Kane tried to make a joke of it.

"Lift your shirt up, and let me see how bad it is…oh, and I am!" Hunter never faltered in his commitment and continued to help Kane.

Kane couldn't speak. So the reasons he had given everyone about Hunter leaving were true without Kane even knowing it. "Pardon me? What did you say?"

"Why do you think I went along with the plan? I am. You're ok, commander. Corey figured it out. You're not my type!" Hunter pulled the shirt high enough to see the blood seeping through the rags that Kane had wrapped around his chest. As he touched them, Kane winced in pain. "Hurt?"

"Course it fucking hurts, especially with you pressing on it! Just wrap more bandages round me and let's look at this map and find out where the hell we are going."

Hunter pulled rags from the car and bound Kane's chest as tightly as he dared. "Sorry if this is too tight, but you said you need to be able to take out Ryan Holden. If he sees you bleeding, that isn't going to happen. We need to make this look like part of what you are wearing. Here..." and Hunter wrapped the whole thing round Kane, standing back a little to admire his work.

"Are you really?" was all Kane could muster.

"Yes. I thought you knew. Does it make a difference? Do I look different in your eyes now? Does it make me a less valuable agent?" Hunter looked hurt.

Kane looked Hunter square in the eyes and rested his hand on his shoulder. "No, mate. It doesn't! You are one of the best!" Kane paused to collect his thoughts. "Let's take one look at the map and get going." Kane pulled on the map that had curled itself into one long piece of paper and was lying on the windshield.

"I think we are about here." He followed the road with his fingers to a small village about five miles away. "There is another road that seems to wind around here and double back. Take us longer but, hopefully if that's where they are going, we should be able to reach there, and if there is no road, we'll make one. Get in! We have some fast driving to do. Let's do it!"

Kane started the jeep up and Hunter jumped into the passenger seat. Branson's speed excelled to ninety in nothing flat. Burning rubber could be detected in Kane's wake. Hunter hung on to the side of car, just in case! They blasted up the road and took the next right. All Kane could think was that his son was driving straight into a trap... one into which his wife had already fallen.

"Stop the car, Sam. Pull over by the next house you see. Yeah, that's it, the rundown one on the side of the street." Kirk's voice was a little muffled.

Sam slowed down. He glanced in the mirror and could see Kirk fiddling with something that looked remarkably like a gun. The gun became a reality as Kirk looked up and pointed it over the seat and into Sam's shoulder. "Pull over and stop."

Sam had no choice. "So not working for Holden, huh? I bet if I walk in that house, he's just ready and waiting for me, right?" Sam half turned in his seat to look at the man behind him.

"I said I wasn't working for Ryan Holden. I didn't say I wasn't working with Holden!" he smirked.

"You didn't, did you? Slip of words on my part. How silly of me. You think he is going to let you work *with* him? That I doubt, my friend. Ryan Holden works with no one, or didn't he tell you that?"

"Well, I guess you can ask him yourself, Agent Branson. If you look at the door to the house, he's waiting for you." Kirk gestured with the gun towards the direction of the house.

Sam turned to look out of the car window and there in front of him stood a tall, well built man. His once black hair, now turning grey, hung loosely about his shoulders. He wore a shoulder holster that sported two guns. His hands sat on his hips and his body flexed strength. Holden's very suntanned face was full of anger, anger at losing his daughter, and his cruel-looking mouth barked orders to his men.

"Get that mother-fucking son-of-a-bitch out of that car, and bring him here. There is someone I want him to meet!" Ryan's voice boomed out in the thin, dry air and as Holden's men approached the car, Sam Branson felt his doom.

Chapter 29

With a gun pointed at his back, Sam opened the car door and stepped onto dry, sandy soil. The only way to stay alive was to bluff his way through this situation and play Ryan Holden at his own game. He took a few steps closer to him, escorted by Holden's gun-toting Iraqi soldiers. Being pushed in the back with rifles made him hurry, just a little.

"You must be Ryan Holden. Sam Branson, Kane's son!" He didn't offer a handshake or anything else.

"I know who the fuck you are! Full of arrogance like your father! Gonna knock some of that shit out of you before the day is out, just like I knocked it out of him!" Holden seemed pleased with his statement.

"Not what I heard. Heard he kicked the shit out of you once or twice, especially over Peta." Sam didn't back down.

Holden froze where he stood, his men almost falling into him. Anger spread across his face. "He told you about that? I'd almost forgotten about that piece of insignificant trash!"

But Sam could see it had rattled his cage and Ryan Holden wasn't used to being rattled.

"She was a nobody. They all were back then. Even Sarah's mother was trash." What it had done was force his mind back in time and it also reminded him of Kane. "Has he changed much?" Ryan was curious.

Sam knew the 'he' referred to his father. "Actually, *he* has. He is even more arrogant than he was when you knew him, and he is twice as lethal! I'm sure you are going to find out very soon!" Sam was holding his own. His father would be very proud of him. Kane! Where was he? Was he magically going to appear like a genie from

231

a bottle? Sam didn't think so. Holden's deep and foreboding voice brought him back to reality.

"I look forward to seeing him again, but before I do, there are some folk I want you to meet." Holden yelled something in Arabic and his men seized Sam by the arms, and not very gentle either.

The whole time the introductions were taking place, Kirk was thinking of Sam's statement about working for Holden. He thought it may be more accurate than he wanted it to be, because as of yet he hadn't seen any money, and did seem only to be taking orders from Holden. Kirk glanced back at the car and Tyrone. He had killed him on Holden's orders. Now he was having regrets. Tyrone had never done him any harm. He was just in the way.

"Mr. Branson, please join me and meet someone you know!" and Sam was forced into the shanty of a house, whether he wanted to go or not.

His eyes adjusted very quickly to the darker atmosphere of the room. He could see several men seated round a fireplace, where a couple of dingy looking dogs scrapped for food. When an emaciated dog got too close, one of the bigger-looking men lashed out with his boot, making the others laugh, as the poor hound limped away in pain.

Sam wanted to yell out. If that's how they treated dogs, god help the women.

"This way, Branson. Up the stairs!" Holden urged his men to push Sam, making him fall a couple of times on the rickety stairs.

Sam tried not to be intimidated by anything he was made to do or what he saw. He tried to see more of what was around him, but the darkness made it difficult. The whole place was filthy and stank of urine. As he reached the top of the stairs, he thought he could hear a woman crying. He knew it wasn't Kelly. Kelly would not cry.

Sam started to speak, when suddenly Holden pushed in front of him and unlocked a bedroom door. Shafts of light hit his eyes and in the glare he could make out a figure, almost in the fetal position. Sam stared in horror. Before him on stark bare boards lay Kelly.

She wore just a sack cloth dress covering the trunk of her body and nothing else. Her long, blond hair was caked in blood and her body bruised from head to toe.

"Dear god! What have you done to her?" Sam raced to her and kneeled down beside her. "Kelly. Kelly!" and he felt her pulse to see if she was even alive. It was there, just! "Kelly," he tried again. "It's Sam, Kelly," and she moved very slightly.

"Sam," she whispered and tried to raise her head.

It was then Sam saw her face clearly. It was something he would never forget. Holden had taken a branding iron and branded her cheek with the letter K.

Sam turned his head to Holden. "You fucking bastard. Why did you do this to her? Did you rape her? Did you? Because, god help you if you did. Hell is coming in the shape of a man and he will cut your black heart out! Do you hear me," screamed Sam. "My father will gut you for this! What did she ever do to you? What?!" he yelled.

"Nothing! But he did! Her loving husband, Kane Branson. Now she carries his initial forever! Now she knows who did this to her… Kane!" and Holden let out a laugh like he was the devil himself.

Kane shuddered at the wheel.

"Kane? What is it? Kane? Are you okay?"

For a second Kane wasn't in the driver's seat. "It's Sam and Kelly. Mainly Kelly. We have to get there. It's me Ryan Holden wants, and now he has two members of my family."

"You don't know he has S…I guess you do know, don't you?" Hunter looked down at the map. "Another couple of miles and we should be at something marked here on the map. Some tiny village… Oh, shit the road stops…"

Kane came to a screeching halt…he had just discovered that for himself. "What the fuck? It just stops! Can't do that, must go somewhere." Kane looked all around him. In the distance he could see buildings. In between was a stream and fields that long ago had housed animals. Now, they housed dust bowls, decay and mortar shells. "We walk!"

"What? You can't walk!" Hunter looked at Kane as if he had gone nuts.

"I'll fucking crawl there if I have to. Just take what we need. Guns, ammo, your rifle, papers, water. Let's go!" Kane grabbed what he needed and was gone. He didn't care about his clothes. He wasn't going to need them where he was going.

Hunter grabbed anything he could in the time Kane allowed him and followed his boss, something he would always be doing.

The distance didn't look too far across the fields to the village, but it was and it took longer than Kane thought. Night was descending fast, and the failing light impeded them in unknown territory. All that kept Kane going now was reaching his family. In the distance, they could see some lights getting closer by the second. Kane knew by instinct and experience that's where they were.

Sam cradled Kelly to him on the floor. Holden left them there, locked in the not-so ivory tower, with only a dozen candles for lighting. Sam could still hear crying in the next room, but for now, Kelly was his priority. Sam found his cigarette lighter and lit them all.

"Sam, is it really you?" she whispered in the half-light. "Kane... don't let him come here. Holden will kill him..."

"Shush, Kelly. Kane will get us out. It will be fine. Shush, Kelly." He rocked her in his arms, as he sat on the piss-stained floor, and she lay in his lap.

"No. Don't let him come. Please. Let him remember me as I was before..." and she buried her head in his chest.

"Before what..." Sam was frightened to ask.

"He raped me, Sam..." and Kelly cried big tears that flowed down her face onto Sam's hands. "Several times, he..." Kelly could not continue.

Now, Sam knew Kane would rip Holden's heart out. Kane needed to come now and get them out, and at this minute Sam had no clue how his father would do it. He didn't bank on the support he would get.

Downstairs, in the grime and filth, Kirk talked to Holden.

"So you are going to let the girls go when you have Kane?" Kirk asked casually. He and Holden sat in the main room drinking whiskey from the same bottle, passing it between each other with a rare familiarity.

"Are you fucking insane? They would lead the whole United Nations here. Course not. Never was the plan." Ryan laughed this deep, crude laugh, and continued. "Once Kane is in, you will go out and let the government know we want a ransom, and then tell them the girls can go free. That one bitch upstairs will let her husband testify. She can't ever go free! Use your brains." Holden undid the seal on another bottle of whiskey and handed it to Kirk.

"Why didn't you just ask for the ransom in the first place? They would have paid up. Enough for us all." Kirk seemed to be on a fishing trip, asking questions of Holden. He took another swig of whiskey. It went down bitter.

"Because I wanted Kane. He will come, you know? Hell, yes, he will come. This is the end of the road for Commander Branson. This was the only way to get him, to take what he treasured most. His son is a bonus. Hated him all these years, and when I knew they had picked him for this job, it was a dream come true. Everything fell into place. Having you on our side was even better. And Sarah. Like you, she would do anything for money. Like father, like daughter. Thanks for bringing her back, by the way." Holden wasn't even grieving for her. "Good thing she was in Japan when Kane was attacked. Never could have got that bug in him any other way. Seems Kane is still in Samarra, according to the bug. Strange, thought he would be closer by now."

Kirk wanted to change the subject. He was getting in way too deep, and if he kept drinking, might give away something he shouldn't.

"Why don't I go now and be ready to ask for the ransom or do you have communications in here? I have a phone in my car…could go get it…"

So preoccupied with his success, Holden didn't realize that Kirk was making a break for it. He didn't want to be involved in killing both Americans and Australians. That was never part of the plan. He wanted out and now. Sam had been right. He was working *for* Holden and not *with*. Kirk had begun to know Kane well and by now he would be close, and Kane would also have figured out that Kirk was military gone bad. And that Tucker was not. Kane had to have fire power and Tucker could supply that and then some. Kirk needed to talk to Sam.

"Mind if I go see the girl? No good if she is dead. Kane won't come in for a dead person." Kirk knew he was pushing it with Holden.

"Sure, go ahead. And then, yeah, go get your phone and get ready to make the call. You know who to? Been here so long I can't think who," and Holden laughed and then his demeanor changed like someone flipped a switch. "Say, you were right, Sarah does look like Kelly. Didn't notice it so much till they were next to each other. Kelly is...correction was...prettier though."

Kirk stood up to leave. Holden looked up.

"Before you go up there, you packing?" Holden stopped drinking just long enough to get the words out.

"Course not. Gun's in the car. Just want to make sure she's alive, that's all," and a very nervous Kirk climbed up the stairs.

Holden yelled to one of his men and Kirk found he had an escort. At the top of the stairs, the escort unlocked the door and Kirk stepped into the candle-lit room.

Sam looked up at Kirk. "Come to gloat? Get the fuck out of this room! We don't need you here!"

"Sam, I didn't know he was gonna kill you all...I thought he was in it for the money, like I was." He pleaded and bent down by Kelly, moved one of the candles closer, and looked at her face. "Mrs. Branson? My god, did he do that? He was just supposed to hold them... Jesus Christ! He's insane! Is she going to make it?"

"No thanks to you, you bastard. Don't touch her!" and Sam pulled Kelly closer to his body. "I suppose you told Holden that Kane took the bug out?"

"No, I didn't. This wasn't the plan. Kane is real close. I know it. Listen, if I help you now, would you help me? They will court-martial me. I'll be a dead man!" Kirk leered at Sam. Reality had set in. Indeed, he would be a dead man one way or another.

"Good, then justice will happen, won't it? Maybe you should have thought of that before you got involved. How the hell did Holden get to you anyway?"

"Sarah. Met her in a club in Japan. I was there, too. She was looking for an ally. She found me. I had some gambling debts that needed to be paid. It was Sarah and I that took Kelly from Sydney. I was the dark-skinned man they saw leaving with Kelly that night at the base. It was so easy. She would do anything for Kane." He stared at Kelly and shook his head, and sat on the damp floor next to the pair. "We convinced her Kane was out here. She came readily then. I swear I didn't know what he was doing to do to her here. It was me who was lying to you all the time, not Tucker. He tried to stay in touch with Kane, but I blocked that. He was the only one on the up and up, except for Corey. Poor girl had no idea that Sarah doped her drink, the one she took back to Kane." He stopped, just in case Kelly was listening, not wanting to cause her anymore pain by mentioning her husband and Corey in the same breath. "Poor kid. If only she hadn't figured it out. She had to be killed, don't you see? And Tyrone. He was in the wrong place at the wrong time. He should have been in the jeep with Kane. Hunter should have been with you. Could have dealt with him without killing him."

"You're insane! And what's Hunter got to do with this? Is he working with you, too? Not Hunter, too!"

"No, he's not, though Kane probably thinks he is by now. Laid enough ground work along the way to implicate him. Hunter is just what he says he is. Totally loyal to Kane, and negotiating with Tucker. He got Kane off heroin didn't he?"

It was at that moment, upon hearing her husband's name that Kelly came back into the conversation. "Kane…is he here? Kane doesn't do drugs…not Kane…I need him…" and she cried in Sam's arms, clinging with her frail arms to Sam. "Will he come, Sam, will he?"

"He'll come, Kelly. He will kill the bastard for you. Kelly? I can hear someone crying. Is it Reese? Is she next door here?" Sam spoke gently to Kelly, all the time holding her tightly in his arms trying to reassure her. A step-mother ten years younger than him.

"Yes, she's in there. She's not as strong as me." She turned her head slightly so she could see Kirk and spoke in a low voice. "My husband doesn't do drugs. I did…Kane wouldn't, right, Sam?"

Sam couldn't answer. It didn't seem as if Kelly really noticed.

"I'm tired, Sam. Is it okay if I sleep a little till Kane comes for me?" She looked back at her son-in-law. "Just a little bit. Want to look pretty for Kane when he gets here."

Sam wanted to kill Ryan Holden himself. He also wanted to clean Kelly, wash her, something, and anything, just to help her. He held one of the candles up into the darkness. He could see a bucket in the corner. He fancied he wouldn't find water in it, judging by the smell in the room.

"You want to help Kelly? Find some fresh water and something to put round her. Her clothes must be somewhere in this stinking hovel. Better still, see if you can get into the next room and check on Reese. Make sure she is alive. The crying stopped some time back. You're the man of the moment with Holden. He will let you do anything, as long as he thinks you are still working *for* him."

"With him…"

"Whatever! Just do it! Especially if you want me to put in a word for you. You can manage that can't you?" asked Sam sarcastically.

"Yes. Then I have to go outside and get the phone so we can call for the ransom for the girls…"

"You stupid bastard. He's not going to let you do that. He plans to kill everyone here, including you. We all know too much." Sam was gaining ground.

"No, he won't…he wants money…he said so!"

"And you believe him? You are dumber than I thought…where is the phone anyway?" asked Sam. Now, hopefully, he had convinced Kirk he was also going to die.

"Back seat of the car. Left it there with my gun. Maybe I should go for that first. The phone, I mean." Kirk was nervous and it showed, sweat pouring down his face.

Sam knew the man next to him was insane. All he was thinking of doing was saving himself. "Yeah, *mate*, maybe you should go for the phone. Make the call."

Unknown to either of them, someone else was using the phone right now. Someone who had crawled the last half a mile on his stomach past outlying sentries, regardless of how much pain he was in. Someone who had recognized the creaky old car parked outside the rundown house, with lights on in different rooms, and while searching the car, had found the phone. And someone who had just used the coded phone line straight to Tucker in Australia, and had just secured air power to help him get the ladies out of Iraq.

Chapter 30

Reese Wade sat in total darkness in the small bedroom. All she had to go by was the full moon shining through the window. She at least had a mattress to lie on and a water bucket by her bedside, and she still had her clothes on, tattered as they may be.

She could hear noises in the next room and voices that were not familiar to her. Sounded like two men, and Reese could not hear Kelly screaming now as she had done the last few days. She listened at the wall. The voices had mystified her. Quiet and gentle.

"Kelly. Kelly. Are you there? Kelly, please answer me. Don't leave me, Kelly. Don't die!" Her voice became more urgent as she spoke. "Kelly...."

"Reese...are you okay in there? It's Sam Branson, Kane's son. Reese, can you hear me?"

"Kane doesn't have a son, not an adult son! It's a trick...Kelly! Kelly!" Reese tried again. "Leave her alone! She's been through enough."

"Reese, I am Kane's son. I can prove it. You were in love with my father years ago in Australia. You helped him get Kelly out of the compound...is that enough?"

"Only three people knew that...I believe you. Is she ok? How did you get here? Where is Kane? Kane is coming, right?"

"Yes, he's coming. Kelly is not good. She's slipping in and out of consciousness. I need water for her and some clothes. Reese, did Holden rape you, too?" he hesitated in asking.

"Yes," she whispered, "but not like he hounded Kelly...Sam...at the bottom of the wall, there is a hole right by the floor...can you see it?"

"Hold on," and he rested Kelly down on the floor. Picking up one of the candles he carried it carefully to the wall where Reese's voice was coming from. He looked along the side and came across almost a foot gap in the wall. Gently he pushed on it and a little more gave way. It was just plasterboard, not a real wall of brick and cement. "Reese..." and Sam stuck his hand through the now larger growing hole. "Pull some of the wall from your side. It's easy to break it. Try it. You might be able to squeeze though it. Try, Reese. Would be better if we were all together."

Reese broke a little more, going gently, and quietly, trying not to make any more noise than possible. Finally she had cleared enough space to crawl through. There was nothing in the room she needed. Holden had long ago taken anything personal, including her passport.

"Sam...I am coming through. It won't collapse on me will it?"

"I have my hands under it, just in case. Come on, Reese, now. You can do it!"

She had nothing to lose as she squeezed herself under the makeshift wall and into the world of Sam and Kelly Branson.

Kirk had asked to be let out of the room only moments before Reese spoke. He'd gone down the stairs and was venturing outside, complete with an escort.

Hunter saw the door of the house open first and light shine out. "Kane!"

Kane saw it and backed away from the car and into the surrounding bushes, along with Hunter.

"Did the call go through?" asked Hunter, hoping to god it had. He had watched Kane try several times from his own cell and failed each time. It was blocked.

"Yes. I got Tucker. Help is on the way. Kirk had called him and said we were dead. They were about to call off all help because there had been no radio contact for the last two days." Kane glanced back to the car. "Speaking of which, isn't that the son-of-a bitch now?" and Kane rose up, pulling out the knife that Hunter had lent him from his belt.

"Kane, no! They would miss him instantly! Just wait. You will get your chance." But Hunter had other ideas. He wanted Kirk for his own reasons. "When is Tucker sending us backup? Did he say how long?"

"About an hour out of Samarra." He looked up at the house. "Hang on, Kelly. I'm coming, baby."

Kelly propped herself up on her arm and tried to see what was going on. In the candle-light she thought she saw a person crawling through the wall. "Sam...what's happening?"

"It's ok, Kelly. It's Reese. Shush, Kel...I'll be right with you," and Sam turned his attentions to Reese, and helped pull her through the wall.

It was a tight squeeze, but she made it with help from Sam. Her long black hair was covered in dust, and the plasterboard clung to the back of her T-shirt. She crawled into the middle of the room, and it was there she caught site of Kelly. She tried to restrain herself from exclaiming out loud and failed.

"Kelly...oh, my god!" and she reached out to hold her.

Sam was trying to tell her not to say anything about how she looked, but he wasn't quick enough.

"Your face! What he did he do to your face?" Reese was openly shocked as she looked at the once beautiful Kelly, now disfigured for life.

"What's on my face? Sam, what is on my face?" Kelly reached up and touched her cheek. She fingered the K. "Oh, my god." Kelly shook, and then she looked down at her legs. Bruises covered her thighs, big black whelp marks and blood caked in them. It was as though Kelly had seen them for the very first time. "He cannot see me like this. He cannot." She tried to brush them from her body. The more she brushed and they didn't go away, the angrier she became. "I can't let Kane see me. He wants me to look pretty, my hair to shine, always to be ready for him. I am none of those things. I would be better off dead!"

"Kelly, Kane doesn't care what you look like right now. He just wants you back. He wants to hold you, make love to you, be with you..."

"No," and she pulled away from Sam. "You're lying. He will hate me! I should have fought harder. Should never have let Holden rape me...oh, god," and she buried her face in her hands and wept.

Sam didn't know what to do at that precise moment. He obviously could not help her. Only Kane could do that and Kane wasn't there. Sam figured she was loosing her mind. He looked at Reese, who just sat staring at the window, realizing once more that she had failed Kane, the man she had loved for nearly ten years.

Why didn't Kane come for them? Why was he letting them all suffer? As Sam's mind was contemplating his next move, he heard the key turn in the lock.

"We can't wait for Tucker's men. We have to go in now. I am loosing Kelly. She is leaving me! I have to go get her, or die trying. You wait. When the choppers get close, you know what to do! Be careful, Hunter," and Kane was gone in the clearing and around the side of the house.

"God damn him!" and Hunter took off round the other side of the house.

It was Kane's good fortune that the sentry on that side was having a smoke. Kane pulled out his knife, grabbed the Arab from behind, and slit the man's throat. He released the body and dropped it to the ground, as Kane wiped the blood on his pant's leg.

He slid round the building to the back and leaned flat on the wall. All he had to do was get in there and find them, and get them out before Tucker's men arrived. Dressed as he was, they wouldn't notice him, not if his face was darker. At the back porch was an oil drum. He tipped it slightly and black molten gold streaked onto his hands. It was all he needed. Dangerous, but needed. He smeared it over as much of his face as he could, and the rest on the back of his hands. Now he had a chance, as long as he didn't open his mouth. What Kane had omitted to tell Hunter was that Kane had told Tucker to open fire and destroy everything. He had told him they were already out!

When the key turned in the lock, Sam didn't know whom to expect to walk through the door. Reese scuttled back into the corner of the room with the cockroaches and tried to hide. She failed.

"What do we have here? How the fuck did you get into the room? Guess it doesn't matter much now. You..." and he pointed to Sam. "Pick up my niece and bring her down the stairs." He mumbled something to his soldier, who picked a now-screaming Reese bodily up from the floor.

"Reese, don't fight them. It will be okay..." Sam yelled, while trying to pick up Kelly, and talk to Reese all at the same time.

"The fuck it will. I waited for hell and he didn't arrive." Holden laughed, loud and long, standing there with his hands on his hips, confident and arrogant, backed by his men. "The bug tells me he went the wrong way. He couldn't even get that right! And, now, I have both his wife and his son, and, if I am not mistaken, his mistress."

Reese squirmed in the soldier's arms. "I was never his mistress. Never! He only had eyes for Kelly."

"Yeah, like he is gonna have now, right? I should have cleaned her up a little before he comes to get her and before I kill him. Stand her up!"

"What?" asked Sam.

"Stand the bitch up. That's it, so I can see her better. Kinda grubby now, isn't she?" Holden yelled again to one of his men, and they disappeared. "Sent him outside for some water. Then we can wash her. Her clothes are here somewhere."

They waited. Holden got angrier. The man did not return. Dead men don't usually walk, and this one lay very dead with his throat cut.

Hunter had gone the other way round the house, and made sure that no one would interrupt Kane and what he intended to do. He had also watched Kane and knew that the bleeding was taking its toll. Only grit and determination kept him going. That…and seeing Kelly. As he skulked in the shadows, Hunter made sure Kane did not see him helping out. As Kane entered the backdoor of the hovel, there was no one to stop him. Inside was a different story. It was full of men.

'Pity they don't just wipe the lot out now. Drop a fucking bomb on them.' Kane mumbled as he moved on through the room to the fireplace. He was on his own. Someone offered him a drink from the whiskey bottle. He took it, and laughed and drank like the others. Seems Ryan Holden's men were just a little over-confident today.

It was then Kane heard a voice he hoped he would never hear again. It boomed down the stairs.

"Where the fuck is that idiot with the water? Can't have her looking like this when *he* arrives can we?"

The words chilled Kane to the very bone. He knew it was Ryan Holden, and Kane knew they were talking about Kelly. His hand gripped around the bottle of whiskey so hard that it shattered with his strength. Blood seeped through his fingers as cut glass dug deeply into his hand. He moved with some of the other men to the bottom of the stairs, and there he saw her in the dimly lit reflections of the upstairs candle-glow. If he could have taken his gun out there and then and shot Holden, he would have. Anger raged in him like he had never known. He couldn't think straight. Kane looked again and behind her stood his son and another woman. For a second he didn't recognize Reese Wade. She had changed, and not really for the better. She looked like she aged twenty years instead of ten, and was thin and gaunt in the face. He looked away and back to Kelly standing there, Sam holding her up, knowing if he let her go she would fall a million miles into oblivion.

"Obviously the fool isn't coming back, so let's go down the stairs to the water!" bellowed Holden. "Pick her up and carry her, *Mister* Branson. Bitch can't walk on her own!"

Sam lifted her into his arms and Kelly hung there, seemingly life-less. He took each step carefully. A fall would kill her. He reached the bottom and stood with Arab soldiers all around him, laughing, jeer-ing, and grabbing at her hair. This time Kelly pulled away, burying herself in Sam's chest.

"Take her outside. There's water there. You," and he pointed at Reese, "help wash her. And I am right beside you. So don't get cute!"

The party moved towards the door. It was then that Sam looked up and around the room, and it was then he saw his father's blue eyes standing out amongst the native brown. Sam saw the hate in them and he saw rage such as he had never seen before.

Soldiers followed the group outside, amid them was Kane. The water barrel sat just a few feet from where the oil barrel leaned against the wall. Sam let Kelly down gently on the parched earth and held her upright. Her eyes were open and she stared around her, no lon-ger afraid of her destiny. Holden moved towards Kelly, touched her shoulders, and then ripped the sackcloth dress straight off her back.

"You bastard. Haven't you degraded her enough?" and Reese pulled her own long T-shirt over head, revealing a black lace bra un-derneath, and handed it to Sam.

Sam grabbed it with one hand and pulled it over Kelly's head hiding her body from the gawking men. Under the moonlight of the

Iraqi night, Kelly stood tall. She awaited her fate feeling that now she was going to die. She looked at Sam.

"Tell Kane…tell him I love him. I always have…tell him…" she tried to make her voice strong.

Kane moved forward and in behind Ryan.

Kelly knew what none of them did. Holden was going to kill her there and then. He didn't need her anymore. He had Sam.

With one swift gesture, Kane swung his arms up and around Holden's neck and the knife he carried held Ryan by the throat.

"Tell me yourself, Kelly. I am right behind you, baby!" his voice low and husky.

"Kane!" and Kelly, with a look of disbelief in her eyes, gazed at her husband.

"Branson!" hissed Holden. "You won't get away with this. You really don't think you can just walk out of here with them, do you? Just one man?"

"Two," added Hunter, his rifle aimed at Holden's men, "actually three," and he tossed Sam a gun.

"You have another one of those," yelled Reese.

Hunter acknowledged her and threw her the gun.

The blade dug deeply into Ryan's neck, with blood trickling down to his chest.

"Move, you filthy fucking bastard. Just move you gutless wonder. You and I have something to settle." Kane pushed Ryan out from his men. "Now, it's just you and I."

In the distance choppers could be heard like winged horsemen coming to take what was rightfully theirs. Any thoughts of helping Holden escape from Kane's grasp were left behind in the dust as Holden's men fled for their lives, leaving Sam, Kelly and Reese surrounding the arena. The lights from the choppers illuminated the area and now Kane could see Kelly clearly. Only Ryan Holden stood between her and Kane. He didn't care that her face was branded. He didn't care about anything, except she was safe. He didn't care that he himself was dying.

Kane spun Ryan round to face him. After nearly forty years of hating this man, he could avenge Peta's death, and what he had done to his wife.

"Give him a knife..." Kane never took his eyes from Holden's stare.

"What? You can't be serious, Kane," yelled Sam.

"Just do it. I want it to be a fair fight." As he spoke, Kane pulled the rags from his head and the blond hair fell out from underneath it. He rubbed off the oil from his face, and then dropped the rags to the ground, kicking them away.

"When has Holden ever been fair," screamed Hunter, and tossed the knife at Holden's feet.

"Kelly, did he rape you?" Kane's eyes never looked her way as they still focused on Holden

"Yes," she whispered, so softly he almost missed it.

"Kelly," he continued. "I love you, and always will," and with that he charged at Holden with the knife venomously going for the throat.

And the fight to the death had begun.

Conclusion

Lightening cracked from the skies and the parched earth was dry no more. Tears from heaven ran down the faces of the two gladiators in the arena.

One was fighting to stay alive and one for the pride of his wife, a wife that stood and watched Kane fight for her.

Kelly didn't know that Kane was already wounded in the chest. She could see his face clearly now in the glare of the chopper lights. Could see that one side was bloody.

Reese could see him, too. A man she had never stopped loving, even though she had married and moved on with her life. She watched him now, big, powerful and determined. How she hated Ryan Holden and how Reese knew that Kane would not stop till one of them was dead. She glanced at Kelly, a broken woman, knowing she was safe, but also knowing that at any second Kelly may lose what she loved the most; and Sam, Kane's eldest son from a life light years away from this moment in time. To his side stood the man she now knew as Hunter. He was watching Kane in a strange way. Reese wasn't sure what that meant. In slow motion, she looked back at Kane.

Kane wiped the rain from his face. The first blow he dealt Ryan Holden caught him on the shoulder, just as Holden had jumped back from the shining steel. This time Holden lunged at Kane and missed him completely. The whiskey consumed a half hour ago had impaired Holden's judgment and the wound in Kane already had made them equal.

Both men took a step back.

"I have waited for you a long time, *Commander Branson*. Ever since that night you shot Peta. Do they all know you killed her? Someone you were sleeping with? And Sarah? Didn't you just shoot her the same way? One of your own family? Next it will be Kelly you shoot." Ryan Holden's laugh rang out in the pouring rain of Iraq. He tossed his head in arrogance and his hair draped back behind him.

Kane froze. Someone had told Ryan about his dreams, his nightmares. Someone close. Only Sam and Hunter knew...and Kirk! Where was Kirk?

"Shut the fuck up, Ryan! You always did exaggerate the truth. You slept with Peta, too, and you pulled the trigger! As for your daughter, she was gonna kill one of us. That wasn't going to happen, and you may as well have killed Corey."

"Corey...why don't you tell Kelly about Corey? Someone you had sex with on the way here." He touched his neck and the blood trickled down. Ryan Holden thought he was invincible, and stood there confident of immortality, feeling that the blood was just rain running down his neck.

Kane turned his head, the black bandana he had tied there hours ago, still in place around his hair. "Kelly, I..." He could not explain to her, not now. He could see the look on her face, Kelly not knowing what to believe. "Sam, explain to her..." and he turned back to kill Holden.

This time when he lunged, the knife blade stuck in Holden's arm. Kane pushed harder and then, as fast as the knife went in, Kane pulled it out.

Holden growled in pain. "You fucking bastard..." and he went for Kane's chest.

Kane jumped back, but not before the blade cut him. They were evenly matched, one no tougher than the other.

"Hunter told you, didn't he? Did you pay him well? Or was it something else you promised him?" yelled Kane.

Sam turned his gun on Hunter, something he had wanted to do for a long time, and, as he did, Kirk appeared from the trees. He had thought about fleeing, but came back to settle a score with the not so honorable Ryan Holden.

"Yes, Kane, Hunter did tell. But to me, not to Holden. Your boy here is just that, *your* boy. He is devoted to you, and me, well I just played both sides. Sam can vouch for that. Which ever pays the most!"

Now the rain beat harder, so the hovering chopper elevated to escape the downpour, and in the distraction of the moment, Hunter turned and shot Kirk dead to stop him saying more than he should.

Kane breathed hard and knew he must finish it now before the chopper light was gone. He flung himself at Ryan and knocked him to the ground, dirt and rain spraying out around him. Ryan Holden's blood mixed with the wet earth and Kane breathed harder. He pulled the blade lower down on Holden's body and with one slash, slicing through his pants, took away the parts of his body that had raped his Kelly.

Holden didn't scream out. He lay there twisting under Kane. Kane moved the knife one more time and, as he himself rose up, and cried out to his god, he sent the knife to its final resting place in Holden's black heart. Then all was silent.

Sam ran forward to his father and pulled Kane onto his back. Kane didn't move; just lay there, his hair dragging in the dirt.

"Oh, my god, nooooooo!" and Sam dropped to the ground beside Kane, Sam's own gun falling in the rain onto the dirt. He ripped Kane's jacket open expecting to find the one single wound. Instead, he found a running river of blood straight across Kane's chest. "Hunter, help me! He's dying! How in god's name did he finish that?" Holden hadn't missed after all.

"He did it for me," and Kelly ran forward, dropping to her knees on the ground beside her husband. She leaned over Kane, and touched his chest, blood staining her hands. She wiped them down the front of the T-shirt. "Did he sleep with someone on the way here?"

"No. I never saw him do anything like that," replied Hunter truthfully. He hadn't seen it. To tell the truth would be insane and there was enough insanity around this place.

"I didn't think so," she smiled and bent down further to kiss her husband's lips. She felt him respond to her like he had for so many years and through so much passion that they had shared. Sliding her arms under Kane's head, she cradled his wet body to her and held him there, his head resting on the broken wings of the butterfly. His eyes never opened, and the rain beat mercilessly down on them both. "Will you give me a minute alone with him?" Kelly looked up at Sam, her eyes pleading with him, a look Sam would never forget.

"Kelly, we need to help him. You don't know he's dea…" he didn't finish. He nodded his head. It was a mistake he would live to regret.

Sam backed away and pulled Hunter with him. Reese stood with her hands over her mouth to stop the scream that wanted to escape. Sam and Hunter turned away together for just a second.

A single shot rang out, to be heard even through the pouring rain, and what was left of Kane's unit turned almost in disbelief as Sam realized he left his gun on the ground by his father's side.

Kelly fell across Kane. Kane felt her fall, her thin and bruised body covering his, protecting him, with him like she always had been. Inside of him, he felt peace.

Tomorrow, the unit could take them home, back to their children, back to the land they both loved so much. Tomorrow, the sun would shine…tomorrow, was another day!

www.ingramcontent.com/pod-product-compliance
Lightning Source LLC
Chambersburg PA
CBHW072352030726
47505CB00014B/1766